Eye Sleuth

A Yoko Kamimura Mystery

Hazel Dawkins

http://www.murderprose.com

Library of Congress Cataloguing-in-Publication Data:

Dawkins, Hazel R.

Eye Sleuth, a Yoko Kamimura Mystery/Hazel R. Dawkins

This is a work of fiction. Although many of the characters are real practitioners of behavioral optometry or associated in some way with this optometric specialty, some of the characters and most of the events are inventions of the author.

Cover design by Stella Bella
Page design by Dennis Berry
Sketches throughout the book by A. Mitchkoski

ISBN-13: 978-1463773090
ISBN-10: 1463773099
1. Behavioral Optometry; 2. Optometric Vision Therapy; 3. OEP Foundation, California; 4. The College of Optometry, State University of New York; 6. New York City – Gramercy Park, National Arts Club, the Quaker Meeting House on East 20th Street, now the Brotherhood Synagogue; 7. England – Bournemouth, Christchurch Priory, Royal Bath Hotel.

2011 CreateSpace Trade Paperback Edition
Also available as an ebook.

Printed in the United States of America

http://www.murderprose.com

NOTE TO READERS: This symbol: ✉ , on pages 117 and 183, indicates recipes at the back of the book.

To Colin

Acknowledgments

My deep gratitude goes to the many people who have been so generous with their help and expertise.

Dennis Berry, with whom I collaborated on *Eye Wit*, the second Yoko Kamimura mystery, was untiring and valiant with help when it came to resolving issues about this book, *Eye Sleuth*, the first Yoko Kamimura mystery. Whatever the problem or question, he always found answers and shared valuable information with speed and grace. I thank him for his expertise and many kindnesses.

Special appreciation goes to Aggie Mitchkoski, for her willing and expert assistance at many levels, from editorial sleuthing to taking the photograph for the jacket to creating the sketches that open each chapter. Aggie also rescued me from my bewildered wanderings on the Library of Congress web site when I was trying to register the copyright.

Dr. Gus Forkiotis and Dr. Bob Bertolli were very encouraging from the start, although they told me they were worried that I would drastically reduce the number of practitioners because of the murder and mayhem in *Eye Sleuth*.

The eagle eye of Dr. Earl Lizotte, who doesn't usually read mysteries but who was persuaded to do so, caught some technical errors, for which I am most appreciative.

Bob Williams, the Executive Director at the OEP Foundation, was always willing to respond to my queries even though he has a demanding job and travels a great deal. I am grateful for his help and support over the years, ever since the initial publication and various updates of my factual book on behavioral optometry, *The Suddenly Successful Student & Friends*.

My life was made smoother, despite hours of sitting at the computer, by sessions of the brilliant, restorative shiatsu of Maribeth Dawkins.

Some years ago, I took the first draft of *Eye Sleuth* with me when I visited Pam, my brother John's partner, in England. She read it with interest. "Oh," she said when she'd finished. "I think you're on to something." That was encouragement indeed.

Thank you, one and all.

Eye Sleuth

A Yoko Kamimura Mystery

One

Lunch was all I had on my mind when I walked out of the building where I work into the spring sunshine flooding downtown Manhattan. An early lunch to help make up for the breakfast I'd skipped because I overslept…again. The sidewalk was a swift stream of people dodging each other in search of fast food. I headed for Lexington Avenue but stopped abruptly when someone tugged my arm and called my name. Startled, I turned to see a woman I didn't know. She spoke, her voice so low I strained to hear her.

"What? What did you say?"

The stranger spoke again and this time I heard her clearly but before I could say a word, there was an ear-shattering burst of sound and the stranger lost her hold on my arm. Stunned, I watched, unable to move, as the life began to drain from her eyes. Her body fell away from me in a macabre arc. I've lived in New York all my life but I've only heard gun-shots at the movies yet I knew with grim certainty the staccato burst of noise had been bullets blasting the stranger to the ground. The crowd scattered, leaving me staring down. The woman was still, her eyes aimed sightlessly at the sky. Panicked, I looked around wildly. Where had the bullets come from? A crazy boyfriend or a gang war?

I desperately wanted to run and hide, to scream for help, but I was frozen in place, filled with high anxiety. Gulping air, I tried to think but couldn't. My eyes were riveted on the woman lying on the sidewalk. Her glossy black hair haloed her head on the grimy cement and a spatter of blood welled up on her silky white blouse. Sickened, I closed my eyes to blot out the sight but the after-image on my retinas was horrific. Bitter saliva flooded my mouth. The woman had tugged on my arm, had spoken my name, but I didn't know her. All I knew for sure was that she'd warned me of danger and that her heritage was Japanese. Like mine.

The stranger's warning circled in my mind, a maddeningly endless loop. *"Ki o tsukenasai. Kiken-desu."* I knew enough Japanese to understand she'd said, "This is a warning, there's danger."

What did she mean? What was the danger? Why would a stranger come up to me on the street and warn me about danger? Was someone about to gun me down too? I opened my eyes and looked around nervously. People on the other side of the street were standing and staring. Even the traffic had halted. Horns blared and drivers were leaning out of their windows yelling and craning to see what was going on. As suddenly as the gunshots had come, the scene changed. Cars started to drive off slowly and people began walking away. On my side of the street, the space around me and the stranger on the ground was a strangely empty circle, no one wanted to step near where I stood by the woman lying on the ground.

Was my problem that I'd been in the wrong place at the right time? Did the stranger think she knew me? I squeezed my eyes shut again but couldn't blot out the scene from my mind's eye. Cautiously, I opened my eyes. Nothing had changed. A woman lay on the sidewalk on East 24th Street, a dead woman unless I was mistaken. A few morbid souls edged back from the safety of doorways to stare curiously. I definitely lost my cool. I almost lost the breakfast I hadn't eaten.

I'm Yoko Kamimura, third-generation Japanese American born in the U.S., that makes me *Sansei*. The woman sprawled on the sidewalk looked about my parents' age, *Nisei*, the second generation born here. Or was she freshly arrived from Japan? Later, when the police questioned me, it dawned on me that although she'd spoken Japanese, the stranger's accent was more that of someone brought up in the U.S.

I'm an optometrist, not what you normally consider a perilous line of work. If you want to talk about peril, I was living in Manhattan on 9/11. When the Twin Towers were hit, I was over a mile away, but no one in the city escaped the horrendous fallout. That cataclysmic event sent shock waves across the country. Now, years later, time has helped to leaven the searing memories but the terror of it flooded back as I stared at the woman lying motionless on the sidewalk. Then I swear I saw the woman's blouse flutter slightly. Was she breathing? Had she survived? Bending over the body to check for a pulse, I heard a familiar voice.

"Yoko, what happened?"

No pulse. Reluctantly I removed my fingers from the stranger's neck and looked up at the man who'd pushed through the crowd gawking at the woman on the ground. It was Allan Barnes, the IT guy from the office next to mine. Before I could speak, Mike, the head security guard, a tall Jamaican with the buttered vowels of the Islands, came hurrying out of the college.

"Dr. Kamimura, are you all right?" Mike took a long hard look at the body on the sidewalk, stretched a strong arm protectively in front of me and started talking into his intercom. Fending off voyeurs, he guided me into the lobby. My legs moved stiffly, my face was rigid. I was a walking robot. Until a car backfired and I jumped inches in the air, clutching Mike, clenching my jaw to block the scream in my throat. *Damn, what happened to the calm woman of science I think I am?*

"Here, sit. You're safe now," Mike said. *Safe? Really? What about the warning of danger?* I didn't say a word about the double trouble of death and that warning, I couldn't. Mike turned to Allan, who'd followed us in. "Mr. Barnes, did you see what happened?"

"Not really," Allan said.

"She doesn't have a pulse. The woman is dead..." I choked on the words.

"I had Fred call the police," Mike said quietly. "Don't you worry now."

That's it. The police. I can talk to the police about the warning. Relief swept over me.

Mike settled me on one of the chairs behind his central lobby station and waved over a guard, sending him to close the main doors and funnel the lunch crowd emptying out of the elevators to the side exit. Allan hovered, despite Mike's attempts to persuade him to sit down at the other end of the station.

"So did you see who shot her?" Allan asked me.

"No…no, I didn't see anything."

"How weird that someone came up to you and was standing right by you and you wouldn't see anything. Did you know her?"

"No I don't…didn't know her."

"Looked like she was saying something to you just before the shot. Maybe that's a clue to why it happened?"

Finally, when I sat silently, not responding to him, Allan walked over to the other side of the security station, picked up the phone and made a call. Probably to let his boss know what was happening. I couldn't bring myself to call my boss, Dr. Forrest, I couldn't move, just sat.

By the time a police car and an ambulance had roared up to the curb outside, my stomach had stopped heaving but I was still in shock. Discreetly, I wiped the sweat off my face and a façade of stillness settled over me until a nonsense rhyme revved up in my mind. "One fine day in the middle of the night, two dead men got up to fight." Giggles gathered in my gut and my shoulders started to shake. Mike was watching me from the corner of his eye—good security guards have excellent peripheral vision. Poor peripheral vision causes a lot of traffic accidents but Mike had never been in a traffic accident, not even a fender-bender. No way could I crack under Mike's gaze. Even though he was looking directly out at the activity on the street, I knew Mike had me clearly in his peripheral vision.

I banished the jingle. *Settle down, focus.* A woman had been shot in front of me. In broad daylight. Why had she been killed? Was this random violence or deliberate? A drive-by shooting? Then that last question, one I couldn't avoid any longer: Were the shots meant for her or for me? Sweat beaded my face again at the last question. *What the hell was going on?*

4

I'd been warned of danger and the messenger had been killed right in front of me. I started to feel frantic again. *Call yourself a scientist? Act like one. Put emotion aside. Examine the facts objectively.* My mental nagging helped. I forced myself to stop thinking about the murder and what the danger could be. I began to calm down and the cogs in my brain started to mesh. OK. First, try to analyze what happened. Start at the beginning. Who was this woman?

I was certain I didn't know her. Had she ever come to one of the college clinics? Much of my work, first as a student and later as an optometrist, has been at the Infants' Clinic under the guidance of my mentor, Dr. Elliott Forrest, who was now my boss. Challenging though it is to give youngsters vision therapy, it's so rewarding. Whether youngsters are having difficulty reading or are hyperactive, vision therapy makes a huge difference. I've never worked at any of the college's adult clinics. Had this woman brought a youngster to the Infants' Clinic? Of the patients I've treated there, I could recall only two Asian families but they were Chinese not Japanese. Perhaps the stranger had come with a neighbor to the clinic and I'd been intent on child and parent, not noticing the second adult with them?

Mike interrupted my thoughts. "Thought you'd like some water, Dr. Kamimura."

I took the glass carefully because my hand was shaky. The cool liquid was calming as it trickled down my throat. It began to feel safe behind the solid protection of the chest-high counter with the reassuring presence of Mike and Allan close by.

Outside the building, officialdom had swung into full action. Two more police cars were angled in at the curb and a trio of police officers stood in strategic positions, watching passersby and occasionally checking on technicians who were busy with plastic evidence bags. A police photographer snapped picture after picture. He didn't look concerned that the subject of his photos was dead. Why would he? It's probably what he saw all the time in his line of business.

"Excuse me."

It was one of the uniformed men from the street. He must have come in the side door because I hadn't seen him until he was standing right next to me. Normally, my peripheral vision is excellent but it had to be constricted right now, tension does that. Quietly the policeman asked me to go with him to the station house for an interview. I must have looked blank because he added, "Thirteenth Precinct? East Twenty-first Street, between Third and Second Avenues, a few blocks away. Detective Riley will interview you and take a statement."

Now I knew where he meant. I often saw groups of rookies walking to the subway from the station. Sure, an interview. That's what happened if you saw a crime, the police want to talk to you. Good. I wanted to talk to the police. I looked over to where Allan sat and saw another police-man was talking to him. Allan nodded and the two walked out to one of the police cars. Time for me to go, too.

"I'll be back as soon as I can, Mike."

"I'll let Dr. Forrest know when he comes in, Dr. Kamimura," Mike said.

I managed a lukewarm smile of thanks and nodded at Mike as I fol-lowed the policeman who'd spoken to me. When he helped me into the second car, I cringed as I felt his hand on my head, protecting it as I slid onto the back seat. Bizarre, I'd watched that movement on TV and now the hand of the law was on my head.

At the police station, I saw Allan being shown into a room down the hall from where I was being taken. The man who followed me in to the small, sterile space was around my age, early thirties. He was tall and wiry and his wavy brown hair was overdue for a trim. Alert, deep-set brown eyes with ridiculously long lashes. His black sweater hugged wide, bony shoulders and his jeans were neatly pressed. Pressed jeans? Not my idea of how a police detective dressed but what did I know. This guy looked resourceful.

"Dan Riley," he said and we shook hands. He clicked on the tape re-corder and I spelled my name for him and caught myself checking his left hand, doing my own detecting. No wedding ring. No paleness or inden-tation where one might have been recently, though some guys don't wear wedding bands. My flippant thoughts shocked me. Was I in denial? No. I knew I'd witnessed death and I knew I'd had a warning of danger. My errant thoughts had to be my psyche helping my hormones settle, trying to divert me from the overload of stress. Luckily, Riley hadn't a clue what I was thinking. He didn't waste time with chitchat.

"Where do you work?"

"At the College of Optometry, I'm an optometrist."

"That's part of the State University of New York, isn't it?" Riley said. "SUNY, right?"

"Yes."

"Are you full-time at the college?"

"Yes, private practice isn't for me."

"Tell me what you do at SUNY."

"Three mornings a week I work at the clinic where infants and children come for vision therapy. The rest of the time I do research." *Quiet, peaceful research. The work and the atmosphere suit me. Optometry is safe, guns aren't part of the equipment.*

"Your area of research?"

"I'm a behavioral optometrist, it's…."

Riley interrupted me. "Yes, I've heard about behavioral optometry."

That surprised me. Not many people had heard about it.

Riley ignored my look and repeated his question.

"What do you research?"

"I'm working with Dr Anders, he's developing new vision therapy equipment, prototypes. Right now I'm transferring his handwritten notes to the computer." I shook my head, I was giving him information that really wasn't useful. I focused on the important part of the work I was doing. "My priority is to prepare the material for a paper Dr. Anders will give at an international conference, so I'm comparing the prototypes with existing equipment."

Riley nodded, apparently satisfied with my explanation and commented, almost an aside, "You're not a secretary, so you must be editing as you go?"

"To a certain extent," I said, surprised at the man's insight.

Abruptly, the questions shifted to the murder.

"You told the officer at the scene that the woman who was shot was a stranger to you?"

Riley's voice was brusque and his eyes had a penetrating look that made me think of an x-ray.

"The woman came up to me right after I walked out of the building," I explained. "I don't think I've ever seen her before. I didn't recognize her." I swallowed a gulp that threatened to turn into a sob. *Hell's bells, I don't cry in public.* I felt panic rising in me again. I shuddered at the memory of what I'd witnessed.

"Are you all right?" Riley sounded concerned and I could tell from his eyes it was genuine because the x-ray stare was gone. The retina, the lining of the back of the eye, is made of the same tissue as the brain, so unless you're an experienced liar, your eyes give a good indication of what you're thinking.

"Yes," I said, dragging myself back to the here and now. "Look, that woman who was shot, she warned me of danger and I'm worried. Can something be done, you know, to protect me?"

Riley looked at me thoughtfully and shrugged his shoulders.

"What do you think the danger might be?"

"I don't know."

"Then I'm sure you understand there's little we can do."

I stared at the detective. Was that it? He was dismissing my concern just like that? I grudgingly understood what he'd said, though it was no comfort. Riley carried on with his questions as if I hadn't raised the question of danger.

"Do you know a Mary Sakamoto?"

"Is that the name of…" I hesitated, "…the woman who was shot?"

"That's the I.D. found on her. Mary Sakamoto. Upper West Side address."

"No, I don't know that name."

"Do you have any contacts, friends, family, in the Upper West Side?"

"No."

"Exactly what did she say to you? You told the officer who brought you here she spoke in Japanese?"

I was impressed and a little uneasy at how rapidly the comment I'd made on the short ride in the police car had reached this guy.

"Her voice was low," I said, "but it was clear. She said, '*Ki o tsuke-nasai. Kiken-desu.*' That means, 'This is a warning, there's danger.'"

"And you don't know what she was warning you about?"

"I wish I did. It's a terrible feeling, first I'm warned about danger then the woman is shot right in front of me."

My anxiety returned in a rush. Riley didn't look concerned. Did he think I was lying about what the stranger had said to me?

The door opened and a woman came in, nodding an unsmiling hello to Riley and scanning me quickly, a thorough, probing look. She was maybe ten years older than Riley, about his height, heavy in a zaftig way. She had on brown corduroys and an embroidered vest over a pale blue sweater.

"Detective Stevens has entered the interrogation room," Riley said, recording the woman's arrival.

"Sorry, court went long," Stevens said. Her voice was gravel rough, a smoker's voice, though police and firefighters aren't allowed to smoke. Who knows what they do off duty.

Stevens sat down heavily, staring at me impassively. The pleasant smell of cinnamon wafted in my direction. Some believe cinnamon helps you stop smoking but it wasn't enough for Stevens, she needed a prop. She pulled a pencil from a pocket and held it between her fingers, a safe substitute for a cigarette.

"Would you write down the Japanese words and what they mean in English?" Riley asked. He left the tape recorder on but slid a pad and pen across the table to me. Carefully, I wrote the Japanese then the English words, struck again by their significance.

"This is a warning, there's danger," Riley said thoughtfully. "You say you have no idea what she could've been warning you about or why she spoke in Japanese?"

"No, I…." I'd been about to say I didn't speak much Japanese and someone brought up in Japan would know from my school-girl Japanese that I wasn't born there but it didn't seem relevant so I stopped. Riley was quick to question my pause.

"What is it?"

"I don't think it's important but now I think about it, the woman's Japanese had an American flavor to it."

This got me a nasty glare from Stevens.

"You think she's a cook or something?"

I ignored the woman's sniping and explained that flavor in speech, or lack of it, was a fact frequently criticized by language teachers. Dan Riley nodded as if he understood. He went on smoothly, fixing me with that penetrating look.

"Can you think of any reason why you'd be warned of danger?"

"No, I don't have a clue. But it's really worrying."

Riley tilted his head back and looked away, his own variation on an eye roll. Then he looked directly at me.

"To recap, you don't have a private practice so you're not the woman's eye doctor but you're on staff at the college, full time."

"Yes. I told you, I work part-time at one of the clinics but I don't think that woman ever came to the clinic with a child when I was on duty. I don't remember her and I don't know her name."

"Let me be clear about something. She spoke to you in Japanese but you insist you never saw this woman before?" It was Detective Stevens and if her stare was neutral her voice was positively frosty.

"I don't think I ever saw her before." *Good grief, this isn't the good cop-bad cop routine. It's mean cop-mean cop.* Between the two of them, I felt like a suspect, not an innocent witness. "Perhaps she spoke Japanese so no one else would understand what she was saying?" I said, keeping my voice calm.

"So what do you think is the danger you allege you were warned about?" It was Stevens.

Uh oh, there it was. They doubted what I was saying. And why had they circled around and come back to the warning of danger, not dealt with it when I first mentioned it? Trying to shake me up? I took a deep breath, I wasn't so easily rattled. I didn't know if I could convince them I was telling the truth, but they were wrong if they thought I was lying.

"I don't know," I said slowly. "I wish I did. All I know is that a stranger came up to me and warned me of danger. I don't know what to think." *And it's pretty damn scary, even if you two don't think so.*

Stevens pressed a few more times for answers but it was with an abstract, practiced ease. As abruptly as she'd arrived, Stevens labored to her feet and left. *Going for a walk to distract herself from wanting a cigarette?* I felt a twinge of sympathy for the woman, glad I'd never got hooked. I never got beyond token puffs of Pall Malls I liberated from my dad's pack in a futile effort to be accepted by the cool clique at high school.

"Look, I don't know if the woman was mentally ill but she gave me a warning and then she was killed. Are you sure you—the police—can't do something?"

"It's early. We'll talk to her family, her neighbors. Find out where she worked. But right now, there's nothing to go on. We might have more of a handle on it if you could tell me of any reason why you'd be in danger or why someone would say so?"

Riley waited and I couldn't read anything from his body language or the look in his eyes, just neutral, professional attention. Did he think I was a nut case? I shook my head and took comfort in the fact that he hadn't said *alleged* like Stevens.

"No, I told you, I don't have any idea."

"I'm sorry, but there's nothing we can do at this time," Riley's voice was firm. "Could be, it doesn't mean anything." He paused, then said. 'It's important you tell us everything."

"I have."

"Sometimes, after the shock of witnessing a crime, memory isn't crystal clear." He watched me carefully. When I remained silent, he said, "If you remember something later, get in touch with me right away. Deal?"

He made a certain amount of sense, even though I was certain I hadn't blotted out anything. My memory banks were frighteningly filled with the whole scary scene.

"Okay."

Riley didn't miss a beat or pause in his questions but said, "So you're sure you don't know this person. Do you think she was born here or in Japan?"

"I don't know." I sounded irritated and I was. *What a weird question, what the hell did it mean?* "I told you, just as she spoke the shots came. I didn't have time to think about *who* she was or where she was born. All I could think was *why* was she shot—was it a crazy boyfriend or gang war?"

"I see." Riley's voice wasn't as brusque as before but his eyes were sharp, intent. "Tell me, do you think she was someone who'd just arrived from Japan?"

What did that mean? Worrying about immigration when someone's been murdered?

Now I was getting exasperated but I had to cooperate. Diffidently, I explained about intonation and phrasing.

"No matter how hard a third generationer like me tries, there's a qualitative difference in the way someone born in Japan speaks, reads and writes the language compared with someone born outside Japan."

My parents, born in California, had been chagrined to discover this on their one trip to the land of their ancestors. Even so, they'd insisted I go to Japanese language classes until I left high school, although we rarely spoke anything but English at home.

"I speak a little Japanese, read less and never learned to write it." I thought of the teachers who'd struggled to teach me. "It's a complex language."

"So I've heard. We've a detective here who's Japanese American. He says the same thing."

Was that the photographer I'd seen outside the college? Would a photographer be a detective? I didn't ask, I wasn't that curious. What I really wanted to know was why I'd been warned of danger. Was I ever sorry I'd understood what Mary Sakamoto had said to me. Her murder was mind-blowing. Piled on top of that horror, she'd warned me of danger. Why? Homeland Security made sure we heard about it when the danger code was hoisted up a few notches. Terrorism doesn't feel personal. The shooting of Mary Sakamoto did.

Detective Stevens came back into the room. "We've made contact with the victim's employer. She worked at Lord & Taylor's on Fifth Avenue for years, in the designer clothes department. Born in Hawaii, came here in the sixties. Retired last year."

"Ring any bells?" Riley asked.

"I don't see any connections and I've never been to Hawaii." *As for my budget, it runs to thrift stores.*

"What about Lord & Taylor's? Maybe you didn't recognize her out of her regular setting?"

"I live downtown. I don't go uptown very often."

"She wasn't always in sales," Stevens said. "She worked on fashion shows, last-minute adjustments to the clothes. Her manager said she was brilliant. She often sent business Mary's way, clients who were willing to pay for someone to go to their homes to make alterations."

I stared at the woman. This was so way out of my league. Stevens must have read my thoughts.

"Yeah, can't say my wardrobe runs to haute couture," she said.

In the heavy silence that followed, I did my best to consider their point of view. Yes, I'd told them a stranger had warned me of danger and then that person had been shot. Could be they thought I was lying. The possibilities were endless. Had I hired a killer in a fight over a lover? Was it a drug deal gone wrong? Riley interrupted these lurid thoughts by asking about my work again.

" Let's hear more about what you are researching, Dr. Kamimura."

"I told you, I'm gathering data on the prototypes one of our top professors is developing. We need to document how they affect the vision system."

"How your eyes react, right?"

"Not just the eyes, they're part of the vision system…."

Again Riley interrupted, *God, what an infuriating ploy, if that's what it was.*

"Does the work involve drugs in any way?"

There it was, a leading question. Drugs and death. Did Riley think that I was involved in the murder in some way?

"No, not now, not specifically," I explained. "Last year, I spent about ten months evaluating the reactions and side effects some of the most widely prescribed drugs have on the vision system."

"What will you be working on after your current project?"

"It depends on what my boss wants."

Riley looked at me and the pause was lengthy. I braced for more probing but he didn't say anything and finally turned off the mini-recorder. Was that it? I felt relieved the interview had ground to a halt.

Detective Stevens shifted in her chair and asked if I wanted coffee.

"I'm legally bound to warn you," she said, "It's not Starbucks, just from a machine, but it's hot."

That made it official. We were done. My mouth was sandpit dry but I shook my head, refusing the offer. Maybe she had a heart despite her steely glare and sniping. Riley walked me out to the station's main entrance, probably making sure I left the premises. I glanced around but didn't see Allan. Either he'd left already or was still being interviewed. He was quite the talker so that was possible.

"Here's my card, keep in touch," Riley said. "Call if you think of anything else."

"That's it? What about me? Do you think I'm in danger? What if that shot was meant for me? She did say I was in danger."

"You haven't given us any reason to think you're in danger. Perhaps you were mistaken for someone else or the woman was shot at random by some nut. Lot of them out there."

I took the card. Why would I call? I'd told him everything and he'd flatly dismissed my worry. The desk sergeant in the front lobby nodded pleasantly to Riley but the look he turned on me was laser sharp. What is it about the police? Do they learn how to give x-ray looks at the police academy?

I groaned when I looked at my watch. The time I usually allowed myself for lunch was way over but at least my queasy stomach had settled to the point that I could bear to think of eating. The guy I'd seen taking photos outside SUNY came in. He was balancing two large boxes of pizza and the tantalizing smell had me salivating.

"Hungry anyone?" He ignored Riley and nodded to me. Finally, a policeman who didn't examine me with an x-ray stare or look at me as if I was a suspect. The questioning had left me feeling guilty, even though I didn't have any reason to feel that way, I was an innocent bystander, damn it. Riley's voice broke into my confusing thoughts.

"Pizza's always good, doesn't matter if you're hungry," and the detective laughed, his attention on the boxes.

"Bye," I said hurriedly, and Riley barely glanced in my direction.

What a relief to leave the police station and an interrogation that made me feel as if I was under suspicion. I headed for the Blimpie on the corner of Third and Twenty-first and ordered a tuna sandwich to take back to the office. Not the first time I'd eat at my desk.

All afternoon, people dropped by my office. Even my boss, Dr. Forrest, stopped in briefly. He was the only one who didn't quiz me for the gory details about the shooting.

"Yoko, are you all right?

"Yes, still a bit shaky but I'll be fine."

"Let me know if I can help," he murmured. Short, simple, comforting.

The nonstop flow of visitors kept me from thinking clearly about what I'd witnessed so the interruptions weren't that unwelcome. Everyone had an opinion but I kept my mouth shut tight about the warning.

"The shooting had to be random street violence," most people said.

Then there was the fairly common comment, "Nothing to do with you, Yoko."

Eventually, Allan surfaced from his lair next door.

"A gang shooting, Chinese gangs are always in the news," he said confidently when I told him I didn't know the woman who'd been shot.

"She was Japanese," I said peevishly.

Allan was a fixture at SUNY way before I graduated, though he was about my age. He was the college's resident IT genius. Couldn't have been more different from the other IT specialist I'd known, Charlie, my ex. Allan, your classic geek, was adept at unscrambling technical problems but inept at social contact though he didn't know that. He was a true brainiac, an admirable quality. Less admirable was the fact that Allan was always certain he was right, even when proved wrong. He was also irritatingly sure that one day I'd come to my senses and go out with him. He ignores the fact I've told him pointblank he's as appealing to me as mud, even if he's a Mensa man. He's patronizing and patriarchal and his attitude doesn't do a thing for my libido. Need I go on?

"You got there pretty quick. Where were you when the shots were fired?" I asked.

"Crossing the street," Allan said. "At first, I didn't know you were involved, didn't see you till I got up close."

"Trust me, I didn't want to be involved," I muttered. Interesting…hadn't Allan told me this morning that he'd seen that woman talking to me? Maybe he was just confused, mixed up with all the drama. We swapped details on the police questioning. Allan was, of course, certain he'd breezed through his time at the station.

"The two detectives who interviewed me were borderline smart," he said. "How about the detectives you saw, were they street smart?"

"Allan, you're too much." I didn't say that the detectives who interviewed me were fairly obnoxious and their attitude dismissive and irritating. Allan would want to know exactly what happened and who said what and why. No way was I going to tell anyone, particularly Allan, about the warning of danger. I wasn't going to open that nightmare to the world. If the police dismissed it, I'd keep quiet for now.

"I don't think the police have a clue," Allan carried on as if I hadn't spoken. "What do you think?"

"How could they if *I* don't know what was going on?" I said. For a second, I was tempted to tell Allan about the warning of danger. But I buttoned my lip. He was such a gossip and would never stop chewing it over with me and anyone else who had a spare moment.

Allan leaned forward, put his hands on the desk and stared at me. "Yoko," he said, "Don't let it worry you. If you need someone to talk to, I'm right here for you."

For one brief moment, I didn't find Allan such a pain. Until he winked at me and said his shoulder was ready whenever I needed to cry.

"I'll even throw in a drink at the local watering hole."

"Thanks but no thanks," I told him, wondering yet again about the size of his ego, and I pointedly started shifting the papers on my desk. Allan had to have the last word.

"Knock on the wall when you want to call it a day," and he headed for his office, whistling cheerfully.

Close to six, when Allan stopped by to re-issue his invitation, I didn't even lift my head, just shook it and he breezed off. The guy had the hide of a rhinoceros. The college had quieted down in the lull before evening classes and clinics. I shut down my computer for the day, part of my personal attempt to save energy. It was time to make a few notes about the shooting and the warning. I sat and thought about what I'd witnessed. Twinges of panic surfaced. Deep breaths, I told myself, you can't bring Mary Sakamoto back to life. Right now, try to understand what happened.

New York is a big city, crime doesn't take a lunch break, my logical side said.

Sighing, I pulled out a notebook. Perhaps the act of writing down the little I knew would take me past this endless wondering. Just then, someone tapped on the door, even though it was open, and I sighed again when I saw Matt Wahr, the college's business manager. The man positively enjoyed sharing news about budget cuts. Tonight I was definitely not in the mood for a chat about his financial skill. It was a relief when I realized that he, like everyone else, was only interested in the details of Mary Sakamoto's shooting.

I kept my answers short and wound up with the disclaimer I'd perfected earlier.

"That's all I know. I don't have a clue who the poor woman was."

"You lived in Brooklyn with your parents till they moved to Arizona. Perhaps she was someone your family knew? A neighbor?"

I shook my head, amazed at the man's memory for minutiae.

"The police said she lived on the Upper West side, not in Brooklyn. I don't know her. I called Brooklyn when I got back to the college. Mary Sakamoto wasn't someone from the neighborhood. End of story." I didn't explain I'd spoken to my aunt, who was all the family I had since the death of my parents a year ago.

Wahr lingered.

"Matt, I'm getting ready to leave, it's been a long day."

"I understand," and he disappeared quietly.

Determined to try to put something in writing about the shooting, I opened the notebook and scribbled out a list of obvious questions. They were just as troubling when I saw them written down as when they were circling in my brain.

1. *Why did the stranger say there was danger?*
2. *Who shot her?*
3. *Was it random violence or was the shooter aiming for me?*

One why, one who and a number 3 that was downright disturbing. I stared at the list. Up to this moment, I'd avoided trying to think clearly about what the danger might be. Perhaps the warning was meaningless. It certainly didn't mean anything to the police. The phone rang. What now, damn it? I don't give evening classes, those are taught by senior faculty, though sometimes I'm asked to fill in if a lecturer is sick. Reluctantly I picked up. It was my boss, Dr. Forrest.

"Yoko, the police called. They want to come to the college as soon as it can be arranged to interview Mike and the security staff and anyone who may have seen something. They'd like to talk to you again."

Irritation and anxiety flared in equal amounts. Was I really a suspect?

"I'm sure this is not unusual," Dr. Forrest said. "We're in capable hands, I know Detective Riley, the young man who telephoned. He grew up next door to me and his family's still there, though Dan moved into the city some years back."

So that's how Riley knew about behavioral optometry. My boss was famous for his papers and lectures. He had the unique ability to explain behavioral optometry in ways non-optometrists could understand. I knew Dr. Forrest had a private practice out on Long Island, where he lived.

Did that mean Detective Riley ever had vision therapy? Not everyone needs it but for sure he would have known what Dr. Forrest did.

"It's getting late, you're not still working?" my boss asked.

I stared at the sheet of paper with the three questions but didn't mention it. "I'm about to leave," I told him.

I tore up the list and threw it in the trash. No need to keep the paper, the questions were neon in my mind. Right then I made a major decision. I'd take the warning at face value and not wait for the danger Mary Sakamoto warned was headed my way. Detective Riley might not think I was in danger but I had seen Mary Sakamoto's eyes right before she died. She'd looked sincere. I'd try to do some detecting of my own. I wasn't guilty of anything. Science is based on curiosity and I was damn curious—confused, true, but very curious. I'd handle this horrendous situation the way I worked on optometric research, with scientific detachment, one step at a time.

First step, why didn't I contact Mary Sakamoto's daughter? Maybe I'd get some answers. I looked in the phone book. Not one single listing for anyone with the last name of Sakamoto. Damn, did the family have a cell phone, not a regular phone? Perhaps the daughter was married and had a different name. I certainly wasn't going to ask the police for the address. What about Allan? Would he know how to find out someone's address through their cell phone—except I didn't have their cell phone number and maybe the daughter's last name wasn't Sakamoto? No way would I ask Allan for a favor. So much for my first stab at sleuthing.

It was time to call it quits for the day. On the way home, I tried not to think about the nasty fact that someone with a gun might be stalking me. I forced myself to consider the questions I'd written down objectively. If answers didn't come, then I'd change my perspective, consider different points of view. I got a kink in my neck from looking over my shoulder, looking for what I didn't know, wouldn't recognize if it bit me. I stopped for a hot turkey sandwich smothered in gooey gravy at KK, the little Polish restaurant next door to the rickety old building where I live. The food was lead in my gut. I was exhausted. I needed a good night's rest. That's not what I got. I tossed and turned for hours.

I couldn't get Mary Sakamoto's warning out of my thoughts. What the hell had she meant? Danger comes in different sizes and shapes. Had someone stolen my identity? Or could it be a case of mistaken identity?

Was it possible the woman wasn't level-headed? Who knew what trauma she'd been through? After September 11, it had been months before I slept peacefully. That night, when I finally dropped off, my dreams were filled with the terrifying image of Mary Sakamoto's eyes as her life force ebbed from them.

TWO

It was not quite 1 PM when I panted my way through the doors of the National Arts Club at Gramercy Park. The morning clinic had run long, as usual, so I'd hurried, not wanting to be late for lunch with Lanny. It was the day after Mary Sakamoto had been shot to death in front of me and I couldn't wait to vent to Lanny. She was my godmother, a dear friend and the big sister I never had.

"You missed Mrs. Oldenburg by a minute, Dr. Kamimura," Andy at the front desk told me. "She just went upstairs to the office of the Newswomen's Club." He usually calls me Yoko. We'd worked many an evening shift at the club together when I was a college student. Today, Andy was cordially formal because visitors were arriving for the current art exhibit. Lanny, one of the judges for it, had invited me to the opening a month ago but I hadn't been able to make it.

"Thanks, Andy," I said and was about to head for the miniscule elevator behind the main clubroom so I'd meet Lanny if she was on her way down, when Andy jerked his head at me in a signal to come closer.

"Word to the wise." Andy kept his voice low so no one could overhear. "A man I didn't recognize came down from the show at the public art gallery and passed Mrs. Oldenburg as she was talking on her cell phone. I think he overheard what she was saying because he turned right round and followed her up the stairs and started talking to her. His tone was quite angry but I couldn't hear what he said. My impression was she was startled by him."

"D'you think he's an artist whose work was rejected for the show?"

"No, this exhibit is the work of high-school students, he definitely wasn't a high-schooler," Andy said. "I didn't catch sight of his face but I'm certain he's not a member."

"Strange," I said. "Thanks, Andy."

I ran up the wide marble steps to the club rooms puzzling over what Andy'd said. People going in to the public gallery next to the private club area stared curiously as I unhooked the red velvet rope barring the entrance to the members' lounge. As I hotfooted it through the deserted main room to the bar lounge, I calculated it was at least three weeks since I'd seen Lanny, she'd been out of town so much. Perhaps she'd have some insight into yesterday's strange happening. For sure she wouldn't be dismissive of Mary Sakamoto's warning the way the police had been.

The bar lounge was deserted except for a waiter going into the dining room with a tray of drinks. I never cross the bar lounge without pausing for an admiring look at the stained glass ceiling arching over the long sweep of mahogany bar. Crafted by master designer MacDonald of Boston but routinely mistaken for the work of Tiffany, the ceiling's spectacular vaulted dome dated from the 1870s. What I saw when I looked up stopped me cold. The shadows of two people merged in an embrace were clearly outlined behind the glass of the ceiling. Who could be up there? Strange place for romance, if that's what it was. For months, the upstairs balcony that ran around the dome had been off limits because the flooring was in terrible shape, rotted almost through.

The shadows swayed from side to side. It didn't look friendly. Puzzled, I stared up. What was wrong? Then I got it. I was witness to a struggle. Suddenly, one heaved the other over the railing. The only place to fall was onto the dome. *Not through it, please not through it.* I swear I stopped breathing. The body landed with a soft thud on the dome and it shook, a subtle rippling movement. I definitely stopped breathing, just stood and stared, mouth hanging slack, wondering desperately if the glass would hold.

It didn't.

The exquisite stained glass ceiling burst with a roar, a nightmare Niagara Falls. *Whoosh*, a rush of air surrounded me as the dome disintegrated. Three hundred square feet of history rained lazily down, a glistening torrent of lethal shards cascading onto the bar below. The magnificent folly, over a century old, was shattered, much of it reduced to a glittering mound of green glass. I gaped in disbelief. The air grew still and the room was quiet.

Where was the person who'd fallen? I dragged my bug-eyed stare away from the mountain of glass on the bar and looked up at the yawning space where the dome had arched. Incredibly, a substantial part of the dome hung above me still but it was in dangling fragments, tenuously connected by delicate antique leading. Along one edge of the ceiling's remains, a jagged lacework of metal struts somehow supported a woman. It was my dear Lanny. My adrenaline spiked in total anxiety. She moved ever so slightly and slivers of glass tinkled onto the bar. She muttered and her words reached me clearly.

"Damn it."

My adrenaline spiked again, this time in hope. Lanny was coherent enough to swear. If she kept still, we might get her down safely.

"Don't move, Lanny. Help's on the way."

I kept my voice calm, like it's normal to find her hanging precariously from the remains of the club's famous glass dome. A heartbeat later, I realized someone was standing at the railing glaring down. It was the other shadow, the one who'd attacked Lanny. I didn't know the man but I know pure rage when I see it. This was one angry guy. We strained to see each other in the dim light then the stranger quickly stepped back out of sight. The warped floor creaked loudly and the pounding noise of his steps sounded down the length of the gallery. He was running away. Hell's bells! The rotting wood could give at any time and the floor collapse. That didn't worry me. Let the sorry bastard fall through, all the way down to the basement. My concern was for Lanny. It wouldn't take much to shake her loose. A fall onto that mound of glass could be fatal. The footsteps faded and it was quiet.

Someone touched my arm and I jumped nervously. When that happened yesterday, a woman had been shot to death in front of me. I was relieved to see it was Val Sangrassio, the club manager. Close behind him was Aldon James, the club's 16th president. Both stared in disbelief at the glass piled crazily on the bar then their heads swiveled back in unison as they looked up to assess the full damage. Shock replaced disbelief when they saw Lanny in her precarious situation. Val reacted first, pulling out his cell phone and called 911. He signaled to the staff crowding at the dining room doors on the other side of the lounge to warn them to stay where they were, not to cross the bar lounge in case their movements caused vibrations and dislodged Lanny. The wailing of a fire engine came closer and closer and finally it stopped.

"That's the emergency response team from the fire station, they're right outside. I'll bring them up," Val said. He was back almost immediately, followed by four firemen, who swung into swift, efficient action, their only comment a terse, "We got to get her down before there's a full collapse."

Calmly, they positioned two ladders under Lanny. A metal platform was slotted across the rungs near the top of the ladders. One of the firemen, a muscular wedge of a man, went up the rungs with lithe speed, stepping carefully onto the scaffolding and reaching cautiously for Lanny, who lay motionless. She hadn't made a sound since the mutter that told me she was alive.

"Slowly, move slowly," Aldon breathed, pushing his signature horn rims higher on the bridge of his nose. Tensely, we watched as the fireman gently lifted Lanny off the metal struts. Their burden removed, the supports groaned and shifted, releasing a stinging shower of glass slivers but the man didn't flinch.

A subdued cheer went up when he stepped off the ladder and there was a rush to help him put Lanny on one of the sofas in the main clubroom. Blood was smeared down the side of her face but no cuts were visible. Hidden by her hair, I thought, noting that my panic had gone, replaced with impartial focus. My optometric training was taking hold. Not a moment too soon. Clinical work at the college has exposed me to a wide range of trauma, from metal slivers to pencils stuck in eyes. None of it means I'm licensed to practice medicine but optometrists study anatomy as well as pathology, even psychology, all of which is helpful in learning your way around the human system and psyche and extracting debris from eyes.

"The doctor will be here any moment," one of the fireman said.

Before anyone could stop me, I knelt by Lanny and felt the pulse in her throat. It was a rapid thread of movement. Her breathing was shallow. A fifteen-second interruption of blood flow to the brain means you lose consciousness. God forbid the lag increases to four minutes; that spells serious damage to the brain. How many minutes had passed since I'd heard her speak? It was hard to think of real time. Had Lanny hit her head when she fell? If your head is brought to a sudden stop, your brain bounces off the skull and the consequences are severe. Half the cerebral cortex is devoted to visual processing and I was acutely aware how profoundly brain trauma affects visual function. I put my hands over Lanny's. They felt clammy.

"Lanny, it's Yoko," I said softly. "You're going to be all right."

Lanny was still.

"Dr. Peterson," Aldon said, relief in his voice.

Someone with a black bag was standing over me. Behind the doctor were two orderlies with a stretcher. Scrambling to my feet, I moved out of the way but stayed close enough to watch as the doctor lifted Lanny's eyelids, one by one. Bending even nearer, I saw that the pupil of Lanny's eye was dilated. Emotion or pain causes large pupils. This had to be pain, the parasympathetic system was in control. Lanny was in deep shock.

Checking Lanny rapidly but thoroughly, the doctor nodded to the orderlies. They handed her an orthopedic support collar and the doctor expertly fitted it round Lanny's neck. Gently, the orderlies lifted Lanny onto the stretcher.

"Let's get her to the hospital," the doctor said, stripping off rubber gloves and snapping her bag shut. The orderlies were maneuvering the stretcher into the hall when two men came into the lounge. One raised a pudgy hand to stop the orderlies.

"Detectives from the police station," Val murmured behind me.

The doctor and the newcomers exchanged brief words and the orderlies moved off. "Statements from everyone," the older man wheezed, nowhere close to catching his breath from the climb up the club's grand staircase.

"I must go with her, she can't go alone," I insisted, hearing the urgency in my voice and not in the least embarrassed by it. Aldon joined in before the police could object and smoothly explained why I was the best candidate to go to the hospital. I caught phrases here and there. "She's family," and, "Swedish consulate." The older detective nodded permission for me to leave and I rushed after the orderlies. They were slotting the stretcher into place in the ambulance when Val hurried out and steered me to the front of the vehicle.

"You're not allowed in the back but they'll give you a ride to the hospital," he said. "I telephoned the consulate already."

"What? Why?"

"Standing instructions from the Swedish consulate," Val said, "for emergencies."

Made sense. Erik, Lanny's husband, had been deputy consular general there for twenty years. Since his death, Lanny continued to help with the peacekeeping trips the Scandinavian ombudsmen and negotiators made to hot spots around the globe. They'd been busy before 9/11. These days, they were even more active.

"Val, please call them back. Either speak to Lars Oldenburg or get a message to him, say it's urgent," I said as I ran to the ambulance's passenger door. "I know, I know," when Val protested he'd done just that. "Tell Lars it's vital he find out if there's a neurosurgeon on staff at the hospital who knows the work of Dr. Ghajar."

"Dr. Ghajar," Val repeated and hurried back into the club.

I squished myself next to the ambulance crew in the front seat, breathing a sigh of relief that I'd remembered what I'd read about head trauma victims. Anyone in a medical emergency needs an advocate but it was more than that, correct treatment as early as possible is vital for victims of head trauma. After her savage beating in 1996, the correct treatment had saved the life of the woman the newspapers called the Central Park Jogger.

What New Yorker could forget the hideous attack on the jogger, Trish Meili? Not expected to live, reports of her incredible recovery stressed that the miracle was due to a radical new way of treatment developed by a Dr. Ghajar. Despite the documented success of this treatment, it was taking time to percolate through the hierarchy of the medical ranks. I hoped desperately that the hospital had a neurosurgeon who knew about Dr. Ghajar's innovations. I sat staring blankly at the streets as we drove, siren blasting. For years, I'd beefed about the ear-rending sound, now it was comforting.

At the hospital, I was detoured to Admissions to help the woman at the computer fill out Lanny's name, address, age, the minutiae of implacable routine. Val had found Lanny's purse and pushed it into my hand as we left the club so I had all the details.

Eventually, I was allowed into the cubicle where Lanny lay, still unconscious. The neck collar had been removed and she was strapped to a rigid spine support to keep her immobile. I sat holding her hand, speaking to her now and then in what I hoped was a reassuring voice. People who are unconscious can hear what's said to them, I'd read enough first-hand reports testifying to that. I stuffed my anxiety deep in my gut where it surfed uneasily over hunger pangs. It was almost two PM. Barely one terrifying hour since I'd dashed into the club for lunch with Lanny but it felt like a month ago.

Why had my godmother been attacked? What was going on? Was it something to do with the club? It was true the place was in discreet turmoil. Members' unhappy rumblings at the club had skyrocketed way beyond disgruntled some time back and percolated at roiling boil ever since. Matters had been outed nationally with a *New York Times* article. "Records Seized in Investigation at National Arts Club." The *New York Post* wasn't as restrained. "City raids posh Gramercy club over 'tax dodge.'" The coverage by the New York *Observer, Newsday* and the *Daily News* fell somewhere in between the sober *Times* and the strident *Post*. Headlines sizzled, club members seethed. Lanny, I was certain, would not be involved with any of the groups. Where was the connection?

Early one chilly January morning, twenty-four detectives and agents from the New York City Department of Finance arrived at the club with a search warrant. They were on a mission to investigate possible larceny and tax evasion by the club. The club founders had to be twirling in their graves. Mark Twain and Teddy Roosevelt were among the members whose vision had been for a national arts club that would be educational, not juicy media fodder. Articles in the Gramercy weekly newspaper, *Town & Village*, alerted local readers that there might be trouble. "State Slams

Arts Club" ran one heading. Another pointed out that the club's bylaws protected the board and the president from responsibility and legal fees.

One headline aimed straight for the viscera, "Aldon James labeled racist, liar by Harlem Opera director." The bottom line was that the club was allegedly guilty of tax evasion. The newspaper then took the usual step of mailing their articles to the city's finance department for investigation. But Lanny wasn't a tax lawyer or an accountant, so that surely wasn't any reason for her to be embroiled in that particular mess.

Then there was a group of members agitated about the club's financial activities. Aldon James labeled the group of "Concerned Artists" pure dissidents. The group retaliated, claiming their queries about finances had gone unanswered for years. While the charges, counter-charges and investigations were ongoing, people strained to hold on to their tempers and stay civil. Had someone from the Concerned Artists group or any one of the other factions had too much to drink and lost control, attacking Lanny in a rage because he thought she didn't agree with them?

It didn't make any sense. Nothing made sense.

I sat holding Lanny's hand and mulled over the little that I knew about the lawsuits spawned by the club's dissenting members. Was Lanny ever involved in one? She'd never mentioned anything to me. Had she been legally bound to silence? Surely Lanny wouldn't have concealed something like that from me, she knows I'm not a blabbermouth. Perhaps it was nothing to do with the club but fallout from one of her peace-keeping missions. I shivered as I visualized the fury of Lanny's attacker. And I considered one more nasty fact: was this the danger I'd been warned about yesterday?

A nurse hurried in. "People from the consulate are here," she said. "The doctor says they can come in but we'll be taking the patient for a C.A.T. scan soon."

Lars Oldenburg, the Swedish consulate's UN delegate, arrived on the nurse's heels. Erik's brother, he was Lanny's dearest friend. After she'd been widowed, Lanny had made a living will giving Lars durable power of attorney for health care, a sign of their closeness. Impeccably groomed as always, the intensity of his slate blue eyes and the faint flush on his fair skin were the only outward indications of his concern. He had two men in tow. To my immense relief, Lars told me that one was a neurosurgeon on staff who knew about Dr. Ghajar's work. The other was introduced simply as Dag, an attaché from the consulate, a Nordic diplomatic type, useful whether he was at a party or a panic station.

Lars and the neurosurgeon moved over to Lanny. Tears pricked my eyes as Lars bent over Lanny, kissing her cheek gently, stroking her face and murmuring her name. She didn't respond, didn't move, and he straightened up, a stunned look on his face. The neurosurgeon reached for Lanny's chart and conferred quietly with the nurse.

Someone else hurried in and identified himself as the staff doctor and rapidly explained what they knew so far.

"Slight cuts, all in the hairline, above the left temple. Minimal bleeding. Preliminary tests indicate the aftermath of what was possibly a small stroke, perhaps the shock of the fall. It's hard to evaluate the combined effects of the trauma at this stage." He hesitated, reluctant to pile dire news on top of bad. "It could be there's damage to the brain stem. It's a question of time, of wait and see. We'll have a C.A.T. scan and that will give us more information."

Lars absorbed this wordlessly then turned and gave me a hug.

"Thank heaven you're all right, Yoko. You are, aren't you?"

"Yes. Shaky but okay."

I didn't add that I was dreading the complete evaluation. I didn't have to. Lanny was deeply unconscious. If that lasted for more than a few hours it was likely to cause permanent brain damage. Would she be identified as traumatic brain injured, TBI? Even mild TBI has lasting consequences. Every year, over two million in the U.S. are left TBI after sports, industrial and auto accidents, an incomplete estimate because only hospitalized patients are counted. Add a new category I thought angrily: vicious attack.

The doctors turned their attention to Lars. The neurosurgeon, a tall, balding man, didn't sugarcoat his words.

"Now is a critical intervention point, so soon after the accident. We need to monitor pressure on the brain, try to avoid causing any more insult to the body, which would be like a second injury—the first injury, of course, was the accident. It's possible that part of the brain was bruised during the accident."

"What must you do?" asked Lars. His self-control was complete but he was deathly pale, the faint flush on his face gone.

"We monitor brain pressure by putting a tube into the middle of the brain. That gives us a number to tell us how swollen the brain is. Then we try and prevent the brain from swelling more and causing a second injury."

"How do you do that?"

"We'll talk later," the neurosurgeon said firmly. "At the moment, the patient is not breathing adequately so we'll monitor her carefully." As if on cue, I heard Lanny struggle for breath and heard her ragged, short breaths.

"Surely she needs a respirator?" Lars, skilled at diplomacy, couldn't keep the agitation out of his voice.

"No, we would not use a respirator. It can cause the individual to breathe so rapidly that blood pressure drops and not enough blood gets to the brain. The standard response has been to give steroids but these have no effect on head injury in terms of outcome. The drugs cause you to lose so much fluid that eventually blood pressure drops. Then you die."

Lars nodded his understanding of the terse explanation.

Orderlies arrived to take Lanny for the scan. The doctors huddled in intense discussion. Lars only had to look once at Dag, the diplomatic type, and the man immediately fell into place behind Lanny's gurney, following it out of the cubicle. The doctors started to follow and the staff doctor paused to speak to Lars.

"If you want to talk to me or the neurosurgeon, you could wait in the office next to the nurses' station, but it may be some time before we're free." The two doctors left.

Grabbing Lars' arm, I steered him down the hall. He sighed, a shuddering release of tension.

"Yoko, what happened? Val called to tell me Lanny was at the hospital. You two were meeting for lunch? Val said Lanny'd had a terrible fall and was unconscious. When he gave me your message, I called Lanny's family doctor and told him what you'd said. He immediately told me he recommended this neurosurgeon who is, thank god, on staff here."

I shepherded Lars into the doctor's office, glad to find it empty. I told him what I'd seen at the club, how Lanny had been deliberately pushed over the upper gallery. Lars was by turns shocked and angry.

Nothing I told him helped make sense of the attack. Finally, I asked the questions bothering me.

"Could this attack be anything to do with a peace-keeping mission? Or one of the lawsuits about problems at the club?"

"No, she's not involved in any lawsuit," Lars said heavily. "I doubt it's anything to do with peace-keeping trips. Sounds like a spontaneous assault. Today's terrorists would be embarrassed at the lack of sophistication, the lack of planning, lack of arms. It's got the mark of an amateur, an unpremeditated attack. What did the man look like?"

"Thin face. Short dark hair, lots of it. No beard or mustache or glasses. A dark gray jacket, pale blue shirt. Solid dark blue tie. I only saw him from the chest up." I rattled off the sum total of my visual impression and for the first time wondered what Lanny's attacker had seen when he looked down at me. I was wearing a navy blazer, a red blouse and khaki pants. I tend to be casual, the natural look of underpaid college faculty. This was quite dressy for me, in honor of lunch with Lanny. My straight black hair is cut a couple of inches below my ears. Epicanthic eyelids show my Japanese ancestry.

"Would you know him again?"

"I think so." *Unfortunately. Would he know me again? Bleak thought.*

At the back of my mind, I wondered again if this attack was connected to yesterday's warning of danger? Could it really be coincidence, *two* crazy situations when I was around? Before I could say anything, an orderly stuck his head round the door.

"A police detective has asked to see you both as soon as possible."

"I also want to see the police," Lars said.

The police officer in the bland waiting room was a plainclothes detective, one I recognized—Dan Riley. Today he was in baggy chinos with a black Yankees' windbreaker. Very Gap. Very nice. We stared at each other for a surprised moment. My heart thudded uneasily. What would he think, finding me at a second catastrophe?

"Mr. Oldenburg? I'm Dan Riley from the Thirteenth Precinct. The National Arts Club where Mrs. Oldenburg was attacked is in our jurisdiction. Can I ask why the two of you are here?" Obviously he'd been briefed. His words were diplomatic but informative, which is more than some diplomats are.

"I was called because the consulate is always concerned about those connected to it," Lars explained. "Mrs. Oldenburg is my sister-in-law, Dr. Kamimura is part of our family, has been since she was born."

"I understand,' Dan said. "The chief caught me before I left home and suggested I swing by the hospital on my way to the station. I can take statements here but it would be best if you'd both go back to the club. Detectives have begun an investigation there." He paused and thought for a moment. "I'll call the lead investigator and tell him about your interview yesterday, Dr. Kamimura." His nod was businesslike, yesterday's x-ray look was not present.

"We can go to the club together, Yoko," Lars said. "I want to talk to Aldon and Val." Lars looked at me. "On the way, you can tell me what 'your interview yesterday' means."

As we left, the two men exchanged appraising looks. Was it my imagination or did Riley give me an odd sideways glance? Who could blame him? How often did he find the same witness at two bizarre situations, one right after another? One woman shot dead, another in the hospital, unconscious. Would he now ask whether there was a connection between these two situations? Would he begin to believe there was danger? Whatever the detective thought, he didn't say anything about yesterday and I felt too frazzled to revisit that particular issue.

Lars scribbled a note on his business card and left it on the desk in the doctors' office. He pulled out his cell phone when we reached the street. I listened as he told Dag he'd left a message for the staff doctor that Dag was to be kept informed of everything to do with Lanny.

"Connect with the staff doctor and the neurologist as soon as possible. Reiterate that I want you to keep the consulate updated on Mrs. Oldenburg's condition. Let me know the room number when one's ready. Set up round-the-clock supervision in the hall. I want you inside the room, she must not be left alone for a minute."

I knew Lars too well to doubt this would be done.

"All right, Yoko, what did the detective mean about an interview yesterday?"

Quickly, I filled Lars in on the shooting I'd witnessed and the stranger's warning of danger. Lars nodded slowly. I didn't say how worried I was still.

"Yesterday's warning might mean nothing, but what if it's connected to the attack on Lanny?" I asked. "When I was at the police station, the police totally dismissed my concern about the warning of danger."

"I can understand the police would feel there was little to be done about the warning of danger, if you can't think of any reason why you'd be in danger?" Lars looked at me. "Can you?"

"No, none," I said.

"It's hard to see any connection between the two situations. It sounds like a psychotic attacked Lanny," Lars said.

He had found a legitimate parking space for his Volvo on Greenwich Avenue near the hospital, even though he had diplomatic plates. We drove east and turned uptown on Park Avenue and Lars negotiated potholes and jaywalkers with equal care. His face was calm but I knew his insides had to be churning like mine.

"Oh, Auntie Ai," I suddenly said. "We have to let her know, but…." I stopped in mid-sentence. I didn't have to explain to Lars how hard it would be to break the news to Auntie Ai. She was my only living relative and loved Lanny as much as I did. It was going to be a horrible shock for Auntie Ai, whoever telephoned with the news. Auntie Ai's multiple sclerosis had worsened so that these days she wasn't able to get out and about without a lot of planning and a someone to help her. A trip from Brooklyn to the hospital would be impossible, which is why Lanny often visited her and I went out regularly.

Lars understood my sudden silence. "Look, why don't I call her? It might be easier on both of you."

"Thank you, Lars," I said gratefully. "Let her know that we'll both be visiting Lanny and will call her with updates. She knows that when Lanny's out of the hospital, she'll be sure to visit. "

Lars and I exchanged one of those long looks where nothing is said but much passes between two people.

At the club, Lars was immediately closeted with police in the main office. Aldon and Val descended on me.

"Thanks, Val, your message got through. The hospital did have a neurosurgeon who knew about the specialized work of Dr. Ghajar. No, Lanny didn't come round before we left the hospital," I answered Val's query miserably. It didn't bear thinking about, easier to bury the emotion, put on a calm face. "She's scheduled to have surgery as soon as possible."

"A terrible, terrible accident, if it was an accident, given Mrs. Oldenburg's connection with ombudsmen negotiations," Aldon said. "We've police swarming through the club. They'll find out what this is all about."

"Lars thinks the attacker wasn't a professional," I told Aldon and Val, who digested this insight in silence. "And Andy mentioned to me when I came in that he saw someone who followed Lanny and was talking to her. He didn't recognize the guy but said he looked upset. We have to ask Andy again what the man looked like. "

"Of course. But even if the desk attendants don't see everyone who comes in or out, the video cameras *do*." Val was distressed that he or his staff might be to blame for Lanny's attack. "After the ambulance left, I went upstairs and found the sign barring the entrance to the balcony that runs round the dome had been knocked over. It looked as if there'd been a scuffle. Perhaps Mrs. Oldenburg was trying to run away from that…that terrible man? I don't know what we could have done to prevent this tragedy, we try to protect each person who comes to the club, whether they live here or not."

"Val, accidents happen," I said to Val. "Lanny would be the first to defend the club, everyone knows the club is security conscious, always has been."

It definitely was. Partly because of the prodigious art collection that had grown steadily since the club's founding in 1898 and partly for the security of those who lived there, as well as visitors. The double brownstone, originally the home of Samuel Tilden, a governor of New York—best known for losing the presidency to Hayes by one electoral vote after winning the popular vote—had been remodeled to form the club. A modern building with studios and apartments for artists was built on what had been Tilden's garden and stables on 19th Street and was connected to the clubhouse by a long corridor lined with art.

The upper floors of the main building contain the club's administrative offices and those of several other organizations, including the Poetry Club and the National Federation of Press Women. The three bedrooms—bathrooms down the hall—are for members who live sixty miles or more from the club. The club's front entrance on Twentieth Street faces Gramercy Park and is the main access to the club and apartments.

A street door exits onto Nineteenth Street from the apartment building but when the police examined it, they found it locked and undisturbed. Deliveries and staff use a back entrance.

"We checked the tapes from the surveillance cameras for the outside doors," Val said.

I knew all about the row of closed circuit cameras that sat behind the front desk and monitored key areas. One-eyed robots, they'd sat silently on duty when I worked at the club in my student days.

"He must have left by the front door," Val said. "The tape from the camera on the main door shows a man shielding his face with his hand as he left. It was about the time of the attack." Val looked from Aldon to me, his frustration clear. "Why would someone attack Mrs. Oldenburg?"

"Lars thought it probably was a madman but Andy said that man he saw talking to Lanny seemed really angry. Has he told the police about that?" I said.

"The police interviewed Andy earlier, I'm sure he told them what he knew." Aldon said.

"If he was a lunatic, he wasn't so crazy that he forgot to cover his face," I pointed out.

"Survival instinct?" said Val.

Finally, the two left and I sat waiting to be called in by the police. Val reappeared with a cup of hot tea and I drank it greedily. Lars eventually emerged from his interview and I waited as he checked his cell phone for messages.

"Dag called with good news, Yoko," Lars said. "The first part of Lanny's surgery went well. I'm heading back to the hospital. Keep in touch?"

We hugged. I watched him hurry off then reluctantly went in to talk to the police.

The detective who interviewed me was a real Archie Bunker type. Burly body, pugnacious speech patterns. When I was shown in and introduced as Dr. Kamimura, he took one look at me and decided I must have arrived from Tokyo that morning and although I was young for the job, I might have had a hand in the bombing of Pearl Harbor. Hostility oozed out of his every pore. A thoughtful look crossed the detective's face when I said I'd been born and raised in Brooklyn. I didn't say that my dad's father was in World War II, in the 442nd infantry regiment, all

Japanese Americans. Their bravery in combat resulted in the 442nd becoming the most decorated unit in U.S. military history.

Archie let me know straight off that he'd heard from Detective Dan Riley.

"You were at the station yesterday over a street shooting, right?" He headed straight for the jugular. "Think there's any connection between that and this?" He turned on his small tape recorder and made a show of opening a notebook and settling it in front of him. He stared at me, pen poised.

I swallowed hard but didn't let the detective see that his frontal attack shook me up—I still wasn't over the shock of yesterday's murder, let alone the warning, and today's attack on Lanny had sent tentacles of worry deep into my psyche, worry that there was a connection. On some deep level, I was numb. The senses of shock and anger were surface emotions.

"I don't see a connection. I didn't know the woman who was killed on the street and I don't know why my godmother was attacked."

"But you got a look at the man who did this, isn't that true?"

"Yes, I did but it was only a quick glimpse, enough to know I didn't know him but enough to believe I'd recognize him if I saw him again. Did you talk to Andy the front desk clerk? He mentioned to me that he saw a man follow Lanny up the stairs and he seemed to be angry."

"We've talked with Mr. Andy Greer and have a description. I'd like to hear what you saw."

"He had dark hair, lots of it. I only saw him from the waist up because he was standing behind the gallery railing. Mostly it's a blur, it happened so fast—but I could tell he was angry, furious."

"That's it?" Archie asked incredulously.

"Yes, that's all. If I could tell you any more, I would."

I kept my voice neutral but still got a nasty look. Archie decided to move on. He had me watch the morning's security tape of people coming in and exiting the club but nodded, unsurprised, when I said I didn't know the man shielding his face as he left. The videotape held no clues and Archie didn't look too disappointed that I couldn't help identify the man.

"You work where?"

He nodded at my answer, comfortable with the familiar name, State University of New York.

"At SUNY, doctor of optometry, researcher," he muttered, scribbling notes even though his micro-cassette recorder was still whirring. "You research what?"

Sticky question. Sometimes I sidestep it but this time any evasion, however well intentioned, had the potential to backfire.

"Behavioral optometry."

"That is what?" His voice was truculent. It was my fault he hadn't heard of behavioral optometry. Scientifically researched and validated and available in forty countries, it's been around for decades but is still a well-kept secret.

"It's a specialty in optometry," I said.

"Like cardiology versus general medical practice?"

Surprised, I agreed, reminding myself no one ever said Archie Bunker was stupid, just that he veered hard on the side of homophobic. Maybe xenophobic too, like Detective Archie.

"What is it, this specialty?"

This was frustrating. Dan Riley's questions hadn't delved into my optometric background. Then I remembered Riley had grown up next door to Dr. Forrest. I was tempted to ask Detective Archie what any of this had to do with the attack on Lanny but resisted. Maybe clues were uncovered through such questions.

"It's health care for the vision system. Lenses and therapy for youngsters and adults. Helps with learning, health and behavior problems."

The detective glanced at me, raising his eyebrows to show he could.

"If it's a therapy, what are you researching?"

Good one, Archie.

"Currently, my work is mostly helping to write a conference paper about the prototypes one of our professors is developing. Part of what I have to do is compare their value with other types of vision therapy equipment."

"Equipment? There's special equipment?"

"Yes, a lot."

"You work with any drugs?"

Again the police focus on drugs.

"Last year I studied how some prescription drugs affect the vision system, myopia in particular, and how vision therapy can reduce the myopia."

The detective didn't ask about myopia, apparently knowing it was nearsightedness. He looked over his scribbled notes.

"Drugs," he said triumphantly. "Optometrists can't prescribe drugs."

I cursed silently. Had I explained too much?

"Nowadays we can."

This point was often fiercely debated by optometrists but I didn't want to bring that up.

"Therapeutic drugs for the eyes can be prescribed by optometrists who pass state exams."

Satisfied that we optometrists had regulations to follow like anyone else, the detective's questions moved on.

"What time were you supposed to meet Mrs. Oldenburg?"

How often had I run my internal tape about what had happened from the moment I'd arrived at the club? It didn't make any difference. It was always the same. I told Archie what I had seen, step by step, and my frustration built. In the last two days, not much made any sense. I forced myself to concentrate on the man in front of me. He was doing his job and I had to help. Soon enough the questions came to an end and the detective gruffly told me I could leave.

"Will you let me know if you find out who attacked my godmother?"

The detective switched off the tape recorder and snapped his notebook shut. He shrugged, avoiding my eyes. I waited by the door for a moment but he wasn't going to say anything. I left and wandered down to the glassed-in telephone cubby off the grand staircase and called the hospital. Dag answered on the first ring. Voice low, he told me Lanny was expected back from surgery soon.

"Lars is here. The staff doctor did stop by to tell us that the neurosurgeon is optimistic about Mrs. Oldenburg's overall condition."

"Thanks, Dag, I'm on my way."

I hung up, deeply worried about Lanny. What I'd learned in my training was fueling my concern. A lengthy coma means severe brain injury. Coma victims, when they eventually surface from their twilight sleep, can be helped by therapies, from physical to optometric, but the results vary.

My stomach gurgled, reminding me that so far, lunch had been a cup of tea. Something like pizza was overdue. The thought started my digestive juices flowing. I set off to find food. One jogger huffed her way past me. A few locals walked their dogs or carried bags of groceries. Inside the locked gates to Gramercy Park, one of the gardeners raked a gravel path. It was all so normal. I glanced around nervously. It was a few hours since Lanny had been attacked. Even so, that lunatic might be nearby. Would I recognize him? Would he recognize me? My scalp crawled at the idea of meeting that angry man face-to-face. He's long gone, I told myself. All the police buzzing around the club would put off anyone with a guilty conscience.

My mind's eye memory of the attacker wasn't sharp but I'd know him if I ever saw him again. One thing was certain, I'd never forget the fury in his face. The club's videotape of the man shielding his face as he left had shown thick hair. My view of him as he peered down from the gallery was of plenty of dark hair. That narrowed the field to half the men in Manhattan. By now, V. I. Warshawski, the brash Chicago P.I. created by Sara Paretsky and brought to lusty, long-legged life in the movies by Kathleen Turner, would have tracked down the guy and be bashing on his door, waving her gun. But I'm no P.I. and I don't own a gun, only the retinoscope we optometrists use. Hard to intimidate anyone with that.

A warm, yeasty smell tickled my nose. I was outside Ray's Famous Pizza place on Sixth Avenue at Eleventh Street. The three slices I inhaled went a long way to reviving me. When I got back to the hospital, Lanny still wasn't out of surgery.

"I'm staying here until Lanny comes back to her room," Lars told me. "I've arranged for permanent security, three shifts of eight hours each, in the hall right outside the door. Dag will be inside. He's chosen a comfortable reclining chair so he can rest at night. He's a light sleeper so he'll respond immediately to any situation."

I breathed a sigh of relief.

"I'm not convinced security is entirely necessary but I'd never forgive myself if I was wrong."

"I understand," and I did.

"Yoko, what about security for you?" Lars said. "I can arrange that."

"No," I shook my head. "Part of the time I think yesterday's warning means nothing. Now I wonder if it was about Lanny. I just can't come up with any connection."

"The police want to be called when Lanny is out of surgery. They want to question her about the attack."

"So do I. What do you think, Lars?"

"We'll have to be watchful and prepared for any possibility. Lanny will have total security. Beyond that we can only wait. Yoko, you must be exhausted. Why don't you go home, get some rest?"

I shook my head. "I couldn't rest, I'm full of frustrated energy. I think I'll head to the office. Promise you'll call as soon as Lanny returns from surgery? I can be back here in minutes."

"You know I will," and Lars hugged me.

Back at the college, I dropped by Dr. Forrest's office to explain why I'd been absent for more than a long lunch. I kept the conversation brief. I wasn't about to spread the news of Lanny's situation any further, so the afternoon was quiet, which suited me. I didn't want a repeat of yesterday's non-stop flow of visitors. When the phone rang, I grabbed it before there was a second ring.

"Lanny's back from surgery," Lars said.

"I'll be right there."

I speed-walked to the hospital, anxious to see my dear godmother. The sight of a deathly pale Lanny was sobering. She was unconscious.

"The doctors say she ought to have recovered from the anesthesia by now," Lars said quietly. "But recovery times can vary."

We sat by the side of the bed, not talking. Eventually, Lars got up to leave.

"Dag will call me when Lanny regains consciousness," he said. "I can return promptly. I feel useless, as much help as a bump on a log."

I nodded agreement. It was driving me crazy to sit there. I was grateful Lars said *when* Lanny regains consciousness, not *if*. Right now, I didn't want to face the question of *when*. Like Lars, I felt useless and restless. Much better to be at my desk, trying to keep my mind occupied. I could return to the hospital in minutes. I knew the police would want to question Lanny. So did Lars and I. We'd see who got there first.

The rest of the afternoon I spent at my desk, growing more and more worried as time went by and I didn't hear from Dag. Finally I'd had enough of work and I gave in to the temptation to call the hospital. Dag answered immediately.

"Mrs. Oldenburg is still unconscious," he told me quietly. "The doctors are monitoring her closely but there is no news."

My heart sank. I couldn't bear to go to the hospital and see dear Lanny again. I decided to go home. It wouldn't take long to get to the hospital from my apartment if I walked and no time at all if I caught a cab. As I straightened the files and paperwork on my desk, I considered Mary Sakamoto's warning. Was it the key to the attack on Lanny? I had to do some detecting of my own. I knew I wasn't guilty of anything wrong, whatever the detectives might think. Even if the police and Lars thought there was scant evidence of any danger to me, I wasn't going to wait on the sidelines for more trouble to erupt.

"Let me buy you a drink?" It was resident pest Allan.

"Another time." We walked down the stairs, Allan airing his frustration about the lack of funds for the latest technology and for once, he didn't bug me to join him. Outside, we parted amiably, he headed north to the trendy bar he favored, me south to my apartment.

The streets were clogged with traffic and I walked home slowly, glad the day was over. By now, in the normal way, Lanny ought to have come round from the anesthesia. The inescapable fact was that my dear godmother was in a coma and if it lasted, it would only become deeper. I braced myself. I prayed we wouldn't have too long to wait for Lanny to come back to us. Every hour the coma went on spelled major trauma.

At the corner of Tenth Street, I considered what I wanted for dinner before I tackled the long flights to my apartment but I wasn't hungry after the pizza orgy of my late lunch and the emotional turmoil I felt over Lanny put a damper on any interest in eating. The cats and I could share a can of tuna. What I did want, desperately, was a long soak in the tub. My apartment doesn't have a shower, it doesn't even have a real bathroom. The bathtub is next to the kitchen sink in the room you enter from the front door. A piece of plywood covered with oilcloth covers the tub when it's not in use.

The building, turn-of-the-century dilapidated, dates back to the 1900s. The apartments are laid out railroad style, so you walk through one room to reach the next. The first room houses the vintage bath and equally ancient sink, a stove and a noisy fridge. The tenant before me left a round table with three unsteady chairs but the price was right. Two huge windows overlook backyards and the garden of KK, the Polish restaurant. When the weather's good, if I feel like eating al fresco, I take a quick look out to see what tables are empty in KK's pleasant patio.

The front room, my bedroom-cum-living room, looks out over First Avenue. Tucked in one corner is a tiny room, more of a closet really, with a lavatory. One day I may opt out of city life but for now, Manhattan is my speed, even if it's warp speed. Life in the Big Apple may be stressful but I've the antidote: a candle-lit bath in my kitchen-dining-room health spa.

I filled the tub, added lavender salts and lay soaking. I debated whether to call the hospital again but Dag had promised to let me know the minute Lanny showed signs of coming round from the anesthetic. The man had enough on his hands, a 24-hour security detail is no picnic, even if there was always someone in the hall outside Lanny's room.

By the time I climbed out of the tub I felt fairly relaxed. Worry was a waste of energy, I told myself. Opening a can of tuna, I ate a spoonful or two with a handful of pretzels and watched the cats enjoy their share. The relaxation turned to exhaustion, I headed for bed.

Three

My sleep was not restful. In the morning I remembered hazy patches of ghastly dreams. Shimmering spikes of glass chased me round corners and into dark spaces where I tried to hide from the man who'd assaulted Lanny. Mary Sakamoto lurked in the background, repeating her warning. I woke with relief to find the two cats eyeball-to-eyeball with me. Big hint, breakfast time for them. Me, I didn't feel too hungry. I'd have a cup of miso and maybe pick up a bagel and lox at KK and walk up an appetite on the way to SUNY. First, I had to check on Lanny. I dialed Dag's cell phone.

He answered on the first ring with a quiet, "Yes?"

"It's Yoko...."

Before I could say anything more, Dag said, "Will you hold? Lars just arrived, he will be right with you."

I felt a throbbing start at the back of my head and my hands were sweaty by the time Lars came on the line.

"Yoko, Lanny is in stable condition. The doctor says her numbers are good and her vital signs steady. How are you?"

I ignored the query but asked, "Lars, is Lanny still unconscious?"

"Yes."

The rest of our conversation was brief. I put down the phone slowly. It was official, Lanny was in a coma and it had endured through the night. I hadn't cried when Lanny was hurt, but as I spooned out food for the cats, tears trickled down my cheeks. When I combed my hair, the mirror showed my face was calm but tear tracks reached down to my chin. Splashes of water erased them.

I'd run cold at the news from Lars and craved something hot. I dressed in a hurry then made my morning cup of miso from my favorite company, South River. It's the only U.S. company handcrafting miso in Japan's centuries-old tradition. Today's had black soybeans, organic brown rice, sea veggies and koji culture. As I sipped the miso, I decided to eat at home. I debated the merits of instant oatmeal versus mochi, that tasty treat made from steaming then pounding rice into thick squares. Heated, a mochi square transforms into a tasty muffin-like treat with a crisp crust that's meltingly delicious but impossible to eat in a hurry. Perfect for a leisurely morning. This was not going to be a leisurely morning.

Oatmeal won hands down and I raided my stash of those packets you cook in the microwave. Mom hadn't believed in them, she'd given me a rice cooker when I moved to my own place, but Auntie Ai daringly gifted me a small microwave, telling mom it would be handy to warm leftovers. Mercifully, I wasn't on duty at the Infants' Clinic that morning. Just as well. I was on automatic pilot and the youngsters would have picked up on that and goofed off. At times it was tough enough to persuade them to do their vision therapy. Much as I liked the challenge of working with the youngsters, I really loved the intense, often solitary research. The three mornings I spent at the clinic made a perfect counterpoint to working at my desk the rest of the week and many an evening.

The phone rang. I checked the caller ID.

"Auntie Ai, how are you?" My mother's sister was my only living relative since the death of my parents last year within weeks of each other, eighteen months into their happy retirement. A lethally swift heart attack killed my mother before the ambulance arrived. My father lost the will to live; he died weeks after learning he had cancer.

43

"How are you, Yoko? Lars called me with the terrible news about Lanny."

"I'm fine, Auntie Ai," I said. "Lanny's condition is serious but she's in good hands." I decided not to mention I'd seen a woman shot to death on the street. Why pile trouble on top of tragedy?

"If my favorite behavioral optometrist tells me Lanny is in good hands, I believe her," Auntie Ai said.

I smiled, remembering the time when no one in my family had heard about behavioral optometry. No one had been surprised when I decided to study optometry after high school. I'd tested high in science and math, practically a family tradition—Mom had run the science courses at St. Vincent's, a major teaching hospital, Dad was a professor of physics at Hunter College. It was after I finished at SUNY and was a board-certified optometrist that I really surprised them.

"I've got some exciting news," I told my parents after the graduation ceremony, when we were on our way to celebrate. "I've got a scholarship to stay on at college and study behavioral optometry."

My parents looked dazed by the bombshell I'd dropped.

"Study *what?*" my father said. The pupils of his eyes dilated. I'd had six months as an intern at the clinic where youngsters had vision therapy and I'd learned that pupil dilation meant Dad felt really emotional. He had to be thinking, *More tuition bills? She's not getting a job?*

"It's a specialty in optometry," I said.

My mother's eyebrows lifted ever so slightly. Not a good sign. She didn't waste words.

"What about this specialty interests you?"

"It's a valuable health care, Mom," I said. "It helps learning and behavior problems. You know I've been helping at one of the college clinics?" My parents nodded. "Kids of all ages come for therapy and I've seen how it helps their learning problems."

"So you put glasses on them?" Dad said.

"Not always. There are different therapies."

"Therapies? You mean counseling?"

"No, no, exercises for the vision system, not counseling.'"

"Does this really help learning problems?" Mom was interested.

"Yes, if a problem with your vision is triggering the difficulty."

"Problem with your vision?"

"If your eyes aren't teaming, you might have trouble learning to read, plus you wouldn't have depth perception. Even astigmatism might lead to a learning problem." I warmed to the subject. "With horizontal astigmatism, you might not see the horizontal part of the letter E or the edge of the stairs clearly. Vertical astigmatism could mean you don't get a clear view of the vertical parts of letters."

My parents considered this for a moment.

"How does this specialty help someone?" my dad asked.

"It works on the cause of the vision problem. Help the cause and help bring balance to the vision and you help a learning or behavior difficulty that's triggered by the vision problem. Lenses are a big part of the therapy but the exercises are important."

"Exercises?"

"There's a lot. Some of the equipment is as simple as a pencil or beads on a string, some is sophisticated computer software. It depends on what therapy the visual analysis shows is needed. Look, I know this is a huge surprise but I've got the costs covered between a part-time job and financial aid."

"Your plan sounds good," my dad said cautiously. "But where would you work when you've finished?"

"At the college," I said. My parents looked relieved.

"You've been offered a job there?"

"Dr. Forrest—he helped start the Infants' Clinic—told me I'll be working at the clinic as part of the training. When I graduate, I'll continue three mornings a week at the clinic. The rest of the time I'd do research into whatever project the department is working on."

My parents considered what I'd said. Then Dad asked the inevitable question.

"Can you keep up your studies with a job, even if it is part-time?"

"The job's a no-brainer. Lanny found it for me at the National Arts Club. After I finish the shifts, they're in the evening, I can stay with her overnight and walk to college in the morning."

My parents relaxed. My godmother Lanny was family. Long before I was born, our families had been close. Anything Lanny suggested would be fine. I thought about those good old days when I was a student and working four nights a week at the club. It felt light years ago though in reality less than a decade.

"Look at the time," Auntie Ai's words brought me back to the day with a bump "Don't you need to leave for work?"

We said our goodbyes and I promised to visit her soon for some home cooking. I knew Lars would keep Auntie Ai updated about Lanny and I'd visit Lanny every chance I had, even though it was terrible to see her lying in a hospital bed.

I scraped up the last spoonful of oatmeal from the bowl and put it in the sink. As I got ready for work, I wondered gloomily what the next round of questioning by the police would bring. Perhaps Dr. Forrest was right, perhaps it was only routine. Chances were I might learn something from the interview. That encouraging thought stayed with me as I walked quickly to the college. I crossed the lobby full of energy, calling out a cheerful greeting to Mike, who waved, busy talking into his intercom. My good feeling evaporated when I saw Allan lurking in the hall outside my office. He snapped his cell phone shut when he saw me.

"The police are waiting in the staff room," he said. "I've been interviewed again. Ridiculous waste of time. Strange man, sounds like a Harvard professor. As if I had anything to tell them the first time around."

Rather than be dragged into a conversation with Allan, I headed back down the stairs to the staff room. Detective Riley was standing just inside the door.

"Good," he said when he saw me, "I won't have to send out the K9 patrol."

Was that a joke? I played it straight.

"Hope I'm not late."

"We don't give appointments," Riley said. "You never know how long an interview will take."

That wasn't reassuring news. My boss, Dr. Forrest, came out of the staff room.

"Until the weekend, Detective Riley," he said and the two shook hands.

What did that mean?

"Dr. Kamimura," my boss said, "You've met Detective Riley?"

"Yes."

"I'll leave you in his capable hands," and Dr. Forrest nodded pleasantly to Riley and left.

Gloomily I followed the detective.

"You have a great boss," Riley said.

"True."

"We were neighbors when I was growing up."

"I know," I said.

The only person inside the staff room was sitting at one of the smaller tables.

"This is my partner, Detective Zeissing," Riley said.

Was this the man Allan said sounded like a Harvard professor? In contrast to Riley's black windbreaker sporting the white New York Yankees logo over a casual red checkered shirt, open at the neck, and beige slacks—no jeans today—his partner wore an immaculate charcoal gray suit, crisp white shirt and carefully knotted pale gray silk tie. I took the chair opposite Detective Zeissing, who looked a year or two older than Riley.

"Detective Stevens isn't your partner?" I asked.

"No. Detective Zeissing is my partner, but he was not available when you were at the station," Riley said, amiably enough, then continued, "This interview is primarily to ask if you've remembered anything new," and he clicked on the tape recorder. *And for your partner to listen with a fresh ear.*

"If I had remembered anything, you'd be the first to know," I said and dutifully answered the questions, hoping my responses matched those I'd given the day of the murder. I honestly couldn't remember much about the previous interview, only that I'd felt nauseous and irritated and had come away wondering if I was a prime suspect. Riley clicked off the tape recorder, signaling we were done. Before I could stand up, his partner spoke.

"Dr. Kamimura, I believe I have seen you before."

What *now*? What did he mean?

"You were at Ground Zero for six weekends after the September attack."

I was dumbfounded. 9/11 was years ago. The guy must have an eidetic memory, a complete recall of images. Did this man store facts as well? It would be fascinating to examine his vision system for more of an understanding of his abilities, that was the sort of sleuthing I did. When behavioral optometrists examine your eyes with an ophthalmoscope, they are looking at the retina, the lining at the back of the eye. The retina is made of the same tissue as the brain and it's possible to evaluate how the person's brain reacts by the way the retina reacts to the ophthalmoscope's light. A sports team manager who knew the reactions of the players' vision systems might open a baseball game with someone with quick reactions and use a player who takes time to warm up in a later innings.

Riley's partner wasn't wearing glasses and I was fairly sure he wasn't wearing contacts. If the light is right, which it was, you can see the edge of the contact, which is positioned on the cornea, the transparent front part of the eye that covers the iris and pupil. The contact overlaps the white part of the eye—the schleral conjunctiva—on the temporal side, the side away from the nose. Hard lenses are rarely worn these days but if that had been the case, I might have been able to see the round edge of the contact in front of the cornea. No, my careful scan of Zeissing's eyes didn't reveal contacts. Riley didn't look surprised at the factoid his partner had produced out of thin air and way off the subject but Zeissing wasn't finished.

"You were most patient. You stood for hours in the dense and irritating smoke and you irrigated the eyes of first responders thoroughly and carefully."

His words jolted me back to the time I'd gone down to Ground Zero to help. Heart-wrenching yet how could I stay away? Every Saturday and Sunday for the rest of September and much of October, I'd walked down to the gaping chasm where the Twin Towers had been. Once there, I irrigated the eyes of police and emergency workers with a basic saline solution. They stood patiently, sorrow in their eyes, words of thanks on their lips. Two hours in that thick, stinking smoke and I'd needed to treat my own eyes as well. My natural tears, which were plentiful, weren't enough.

"Thank you," I said, fascinated by his precise speech pattern and the accuracy of his comment. Allan was right, the detective did sound like a professor. A smart one. Not many people, unless they were optometrists, would have realized I'd irrigated the eyes of the first responders. This man was beyond observant. If he was eidetic, it was possible he also had compulsive tendencies, one way of coping with the vast storehouse of his mind.

"Anything else?" Riley asked.

I wasn't going to mention the list I'd made but I changed my mind. Perhaps one of the detectives would say something helpful, so I took a chance and I described the three points I'd written down. Riley nodded as if he'd expected me to do something like that.

"Were you looking for anything special?"

"Clues would be good."

"Clues?"

"Like why did that stranger warn me about danger."

"We may never know," Riley said. "We contacted the victim's family but they weren't all that forthcoming, for whatever reason. Remember, this is police business. If you find any clues, as you put it, you must get in touch with us immediately." He leaned forward to emphasize his words.

"Detective Riley is correct, Dr. Kamimura," Riley's partner said gravely. "You must leave this matter in the hands of the police. It is our responsibility now, as is your safety. Your intrusion might jeopardize yourself and others as well as impede our activities."

Good grief. Had the man swallowed a dictionary? I left but my feeling was very different from the way I'd felt after the first interview. Clearly, I was part of a process. Obviously, Riley was dedicated to his work and I could empathize with that. After this second, mercifully brief interview, I didn't feel a suspect, just someone who had to be interviewed. Still, even though both detectives had told me to keep my nose out of their business, I was determined to do what I could to find some answers—it was my business, too. Riley and Zeissing were sworn to protect and serve and they might lay down the law but damned if I'd play the passive part of the hunted. Time for me to do some hunting. How, what and where I didn't know, but I was fairly sure I wasn't going to get any answers or help from the police.

Heading back to my office, I felt a lot better than I had before the interview.

"Are you going to join us at lunchtime, Yoko? "

It was Matt Wahr, the college finance manager. He was in the hall outside Allan's office and the IT specialist himself, Allan Barnes, stood in the doorway directly behind Matt.

"I'm ordering sandwiches. Want your usual?" Allan asked.

Allan's current toy, a Bluetooth earpiece, was perched on his ear. Ever the techie, Allan had gone through a dizzying array of cell phones and other gadgets in his quest to keep up with the latest. He often had several of his latest toys in his pockets or, in this case, on his body.

"Sure," I said.

"Make that two for the egg salad on a hard roll," Allan said, switching off his ear gizmo with a flick of his finger.

I hid a smile at his trick of ordering the sandwich I favored—I never make egg salad. If Allan was trying to ingratiate himself with me, he'd have to think again. The weekly casual lunch, a get-together for most of us, was helpful for catching up with college news plus the food from the deli on Lexington Avenue was tasty. I don't know what they added to the egg salad but it was deliciously different from anything I'd ever had so I could put up with Allan. The food would be delivered at mid-day, so I went in to my office and sat down at the desk. To my annoyance, Allan followed me.

"How's the work with Fred Anders going?" he said, and brazenly started to shuffle through the papers in my out box.

"Hands off," I said and he retreated, holding his hands high in mock deference.

"Reason I ask is that you haven't had a computer crash recently," Allan said.

He was right. Too often, when I was trying to make coherent notes from Dr. Anders' scrawl, my computer would freeze or crash, which meant I'd need to call on Allan's expertise.

"I'm catching up, lots to do." I kept my answer noncommital.

"See you at lunch," and Allan sauntered out.

Not if I could help it. I'd sit next to Matt. He was a good buffer if Allan tried to get too friendly. Not that I hesitated to throw cold water on Allan in public. It just took more time and energy than it was worth, particularly since nothing I ever said slowed Allan down.

Four

Strange how hindsight's a perfect 20/20. The next day, the morning at the clinic was typical, one patient a no show, one cancelling minutes before the appointment, and most of the others arriving late. I hadn't fallen asleep until late the night before, worried about Lanny, and when I woke, I wasn't hungry and made do with a cup of miso. By lunchtime, I was ravenous and devoured a messy meatball sub at my desk, sorting through files as I munched, catching most of the drips before they landed on paperwork. Late afternoon, my phone rang. News of Lanny? I grabbed it

"Yoko, how's your schedule tonight?"

It was Dr. Forrest, my boss.

"Nothing planned, Elliot. Do you need help at an evening class?"

"It's not that simple. I was scheduled to go hear Dr. Forkiotis lecture at the Connecticut Police Academy but I've got a nasty cold, all I want to do is go home to bed. You helped review the journal paper about the work Gus has done on DUI. Would you go in my place?"

I didn't hesitate. "Yes."

"Good. I'll call and tell Gus. You can take a Metro North train from Grand Central, Gus'll meet you at Bridgeport. Dinner's his treat."

"Thanks, Elliot. I hope you feel better tomorrow."

I hung up. I'd heard Gus Forkiotis read his papers at conferences and I never missed reading his cutting edge work, for he was one of the pioneers in marrying forensics to optometry. He and another Connecticut practitioner, Bob Bertolli, had lectured at the Connecticut State Police Academy for decades, bringing the police up to speed on the optometric science behind the ways drugs or alcohol affect our vision, so important in DUI cases. This visit was my chance to quiz Gus on what optometrists needed to know in the way of identifying and profiling techniques when called in to help at crime scenes or disaster sites, something that was happening more and more frequently. The sudden prospect of a trip to Connecticut even helped distract me from my concern for Lanny. How was I to know that later, I'd wish I'd said no. Said I had the flu. Typhoid, maybe.

I scooped up the papers covering my desk and took them over to the filing cabinet, planning to sort them the next day. I had time to finish writing one last memo and still squeeze in a visit to Lanny at St. Vincent's before heading to the train station.

"A question for you, Dr. Kamimura."

I jumped and the papers spilled. My back was to the door and I hadn't heard anyone come in. Guess my nerves aren't in the best shape these days. I bent to pick up the mess.

"Have you had time to read the memo I sent about reorganizing the Infants' Clinic to save costs? Do you think my suggestions will work?"

I caught the familiar undertones of a Southern accent and didn't have to turn around to know it was Matt Wahr. Sure enough, when I turned, he was a few steps inside my small office. In his immaculate navy jacket and sharply creased gray trousers, he was the well-groomed picture of a senior administrator. Did he have rubber soles on those polished wingtips? The man was seriously trim. Might faint at the idea of a meatball sub for lunch. A meager patch of pale brown hair was brushed across a head that showed an expanse of pink scalp, though his eyebrows were strong over blue eyes. It was a relief it wasn't Allan or someone dropping in to shoot the breeze. Today, Matt's normally pleasant expression held a hint of worry.

"Dr. Forrest and I went over the schedule," I said. "You're right, Matt, if we juggle some projects, it looks as though we can keep the clinic open the same number of hours. Dr. Forrest said he'd send you a memo."

"Great," Matt said. "Need help with those papers?" He moved closer.

"No, thanks, I'm leaving soon."

To my relief, Matt nodded obligingly and left.

"Don't be such a workaholic, come have a drink and unwind." It was pest Allan from next door. I didn't mention my plan to visit the hospital but bragged about the trip to Connecticut.

"Allan, I've one more memo to do then I've a train to catch, Dr. Forrest has a bad cold and asked me to go to Connecticut for him, to a lecture by Dr. Forkiotis."

"Now you mention it, Dr. Forrest did sound congested just now when I called. But he suggested I speak to you about a vision exam."

So that's what Allan wanted. The request wasn't unusual. Anyone who works at the college is eligible for an exam, free and gratis. It's one of our few perks.

"I'll be glad to help, Allan. Had problems recently?"

"Yes. I went to someone a friend recommended but I'm not happy with the prescription he gave me for contacts. I'm just not comfortable with them."

"That's too bad. What sort of discomfort?"

It was surprising he'd gone to someone outside the college but I didn't ask for details about the prescription, I'd find those out during the examination.

"A nasty headache now and then, I'm sure it's this new prescription, I don't usually have headaches. Any chance you could fit me in now?" Allan said, not missing a beat.

That was Allan, his schedule was all that mattered. Still, I might as well get it out of the way, I could work on the memo first thing in the morning.

"I guess so. The fourth floor clinic will be free, the evening class isn't scheduled to start until seven."

Allan's smile was a mix of relief and smug satisfaction. He followed me to the main clinic where he settled himself in the examination chair. He took out the contacts he'd been wearing and put them in the container I held out to him.

"Allan, these are monovision, one for near distance, one for far," I said after I'd looked carefully at the contacts. "That's probably part of your difficulty."

"My friend has monovision and likes it," Allan said, eyes blinking as he adjusted to the removal of the contacts. "He uses one eye for reading and the other for looking in the distance."

"That's not really a good idea," I explained. "Our eyes are designed to team, to work together. It's a major strain on the brain to try to use different information from each eye."

"With my IQ, my brain can handle it," Allan said.

"Apparently not, if you're having headaches. Sit back in the chair. Look straight ahead," and I started the exam.

"Have you ever had multifocal contacts?"

Allan shook his head.

'You think I need a different prescription?"

"The prescription you have now isn't wrong. What's not right is that it's been divided. One eye has a prescription for distance and the other for close work, which you knew."

"My close work is very demanding, the college relies on me." Allan sounded pompous, not unusual, he could switch from banter with smarmy sexual overtones in a flash, but I empathized, monovision lenses really are a strain.

"Multifocal lenses would be ideal for your viewing needs."

"If you say so," Allan said grudgingly. "Just what does 'multifocal' mean?"

"The contacts have 'zones.' For close work, like your IT responsibilities, your eyes use the center of the lens. For distance, there's graduated power in the outer zone of the lens so your eyes see comfortably at distance."

"What about in-between?" Allan asked, warming to the possibilities I was suggesting.

"Your eyes will naturally shift to the intermediate zone of the lens if you want to see something at an in-between range. Whatever you want to view, your brain will choose the correct zone in the contact lens. You know how it is when you're in a car, if you look out at the traffic, you see what's outside and the windshield or the wipers don't get in the way? That's because your brain guides your vision and knows what you want to view."

Allan nodded. "Makes sense."

"Do you want me to send the prescription to the lab the college uses?"

"Yes."

"I'll let you know when the multifocals are ready," I handed him the container with his monovision contacts and took a quick look at the time, "I must dash."

I headed down the hall to the stairs, Allan on my heels.

"What time's your train?" he asked, falling into step beside me, jaunty and self-satisfied as usual.

"I'm making a quick stop some place else first." I didn't want to explain I was going to St. Vincent's. God forbid he offered to come along.

"Looks like you're going in the same direction as me. I can keep you company for a few blocks," Allan said.

We chatted as we walked and Allan's company wasn't too irritating. Big plus, he didn't hit on me. If he was this reasonable all the time, we'd get along fine. Maybe Allan had learned his lesson. Maybe he had a girlfriend. Lucky me. I felt a pang of sympathy for any female who'd have to put up with him.

The stop at the hospital was brief and sobering. Lanny had yet to open her eyes. Dag, bless him, was upbeat. "Vital signs are strong and blood pressure's good. The doctors monitor brain pressure regularly and each report says all is going well."

His attitude boosted my mood and I sat with Lanny for a few minutes, explaining why I was riding a commuter train out to Connecticut, even though I knew she wouldn't respond.

"I'm off to hear Gus Forkiotis lecture at the police academy," I told her. "Remember? He's the behavioral optometrist in Connecticut." I almost added that this was the optometrist Lanny'd persuaded to be an Expert Witness at the trial of the drunk driver who'd caused the deaths of her husband, Erik, and daughter, Zembra, but I bit my tongue. Why remind Lanny of that tragedy when she was fighting for her life?

Lanny lay motionless on the hospital bed. It was hard to see if she was breathing, so slight was the rise and fall of her chest but her breaths were steady. I kissed Lanny's pale cheek, reminded Dag to keep in touch and left for Grand Central Station. The weather was as gloomy as I felt after seeing Lanny so still and pale. It was drizzling and the sidewalks were full of puddles although we'd been promised a clear evening.

As I walked, I was heartsick at the thought of the problems Lanny might face when she regained consciousness. Even mild injuries can cause difficulties like dizziness, headaches, poor memory and anxiety. It depends on what part of the brain is hurt. The occipital lobe is the large block of tissue at the back of the brain that receives, processes and retains "seen" information. Damage there plays havoc. Until Lanny came out of the coma, we wouldn't know the extent of her problems.

The vast concourse at the train station was almost empty, acres of Tennessee marble floor free of rush-hour hordes. I craned my neck to look up at the wonder of the celestial ceiling—New York's cathedral for the public. Some years back, the ceiling had been refurbished and the result was glorious. The bright lights outlining the constellations gleamed and twinkled like the stars they represented. New York's masses of buildings and flowing rivers of traffic make it impossible to see the natural splendors of the night sky. Grand Central's starry heavens might be man-made but they're a brilliant facsimile.

A shiver scurried down my back. What a mess if the celestial ceiling collapsed like the dome at the club. I stared up at the Great Dipper and suddenly had the eerie feeling someone was watching me. I looked around the station. Did someone deliberately step back out of sight behind the shelter of the Information Desk? *I'm imagining things. Why would anyone…?* I didn't complete that thought, too many nasty possibilities. Stay positive, that's what the self-help gurus advise.

I walked along to the platform for the train to Bridgeport. The gate was shut but those on either side were open and I walked through one to the platform where my train was. It was one of those wrinkles in bureaucracy, an open side gate. More civilized than the mad rush at Pennsylvania Station on the city's west side, where train platforms are announced at the last moment so the crowd hustles like maniacs in the scramble for seats. Boarding the waiting train, I positioned myself in the middle of the car, away from the doors, and started on the work I'd brought with me but every time someone moved along the platform or boarded the train, I couldn't stop myself looking out the grimy window or staring nervously at each person who walked through the compartment. The train started and I kept my head down and read.

Dr. Forkiotis was waiting at Bridgeport. His hair glinted silver but his face had the youthful determination and vigor that marked his career.

"Change of plans. How do you feel about some hands-on experience?" he said. "The lecture's rescheduled, top brass are off at ceremonies for some bigwig, eulogies for the dead. I only heard the news late this afternoon and when Elliott telephoned and told me you were coming, I bargained with the powers-that-be so you could have a real treat and go on a patrol for driving under the influence, DUI."

I rolled my eyes. "DUI patrol is a treat?"

"You'll be safe, surrounded by armed police." His smile faded as he saw my involuntary shiver. "We can talk over dinner."

Subtle, Gus was not. Perceptive and caring, yes. We ate at a little Greek place where Gus introduced me to *taramosalata*, the Greek caviar spread.

"Carp roe in lemon juice and mayo," he told me. "What do you think?"

"Delicious."

Deliberately delaying the time when I had to explain about the woman shot outside SUNY and Lanny's fall and coma, I asked about the recent visit by Massachusetts state troopers to his colleague, Bob Bertolli.

"I heard they were trying to identify a murder victim."

"That's right. The troopers brought in the specifications of a glasses frame for analysis, forensic optometry at work. Bob and the optician were able to match that particular frame combination to a patient."

"Is that easier than finding out the prescription from fragments of spectacle glass?"

"That's not hard, Yoko. Any fragment of a lens can be measured for the prescription," Gus said. "A frame has a lot of clues. The manufacturer's name, color code, temple size. Usually all that's somewhere on the inner surfaces."

"Wasn't there a famous murder case years back where a murderer was caught because of the glasses?" I asked.

"Leopold and Loeb," Gus said. "Two boys indicted in 1924 for kidnapping and murdering another boy. The horn-rimmed glasses found near the body didn't belong to the victim. It was a common prescription so it was thought the chance of finding the owner was slim. Eight days after the murder, it was discovered that the hinges on the glasses were unique and only three pairs had been sold in the Chicago area. One of those pairs of glasses belonged to Nathan Leopold. Up to that point, Leopold and Loeb hadn't been suspected. The two got life sentences."

I shivered.

Gus looked at his watch. "Before we leave, tell me what's been happening in your life. Elliott said something about two tragedies?"

The words poured out. Gus listened carefully. I started with Mary Sakamoto's killing and then said, "Lanny's in a coma, Gus." I explained what had happened at the club but I didn't mention the eerie feeling I had of being watched at Grand Central. "I'm wondering if Mary Sakamoto's shooting and Lanny's accident are linked."

What Gus said next astonished me.

"Dear God, Yoko. I just spoke to Lanny, it must have been right before the attack! She's working on a major conference about the increase in drunk driving cases and asked me to volunteer to give a talk. Has she been in a coma since the attack?"

"Yes," I stammered.

The hairs on the back of my neck stood up. How could I have forgotten the connection between these two and how fiercely each felt about drunk driving and why.

"It's possible these situations are related," Gus said. "Tell me what happened at the club."

The waiter cleared our plates and I didn't speak until the tea we'd ordered arrived.

"The fury on his face, that's my main impression. The intensity was shocking."

"Could you see the pupils of his eyes?"

The question surprised me although I knew Gus was famous for his analysis of the clues that physical characteristics give about the way your vision functions. His article, "Is that Saddam Hussein Or Are We Seeing a Double?" had been closely read in government circles. The prodding helped me focus.

"Not really, the light was low and he was quite a distance away."

"If they were completely dilated that would mean extreme emotion. In this case, it might have been anger and that led to violence. Such extreme dilation may last all day, even several days. Inhalants or drugs like cocaine cause enlarged pupils."

"All I can say for sure is that he was almost vibrating with anger."

"He'd shut down his peripheral vision under the stress of the situation so his central focus would be intense," Gus said. "You only had a partial view of him, right? His shoulders, were they rolled in?"

"I could see his face and shoulders because his hands were clutching the railing that runs round the gallery, it's about three feet high. His shoulders were hunched. He was medium build and had a lot of dark hair."

"The tension of the moment could account for hunched shoulders but he may be nearsighted, that brings the shoulders forward, rounds them," Gus said.

I nodded. I'd read the analysis Gus had made of Ronald Reagan's vision. Before he was president, Reagan had been one of the first people in the U.S fitted with scleral contact lenses. Back then, contacts could only be worn for two hours at a time, then they had to be taken out to replenish the fluids in the lens so oxygen could reach the cornea. Easy to imagine a Hollywood director yelling, "Cut," while Reagan took out his contacts to top up fluids.

"Yoko, never trust coincidences. Two serious accidents so close, that's alarming. Stay alert."

"I'm going to keep to my daily routine." I sounded stubborn and I felt it.

"Definitely. You can't let terrorists dictate how you live," Gus said. "But don't hesitate to ask for help. Call the police, they're your best defense."

I wasn't going to tell Gus hell could freeze before I called Detective Riley or his strange partner, Zeissing. We were silent on the drive to the police academy and I debated with myself, rationalizing that if it was serious, the police would surface—they had after the attack on Lanny.

At the Connecticut State Police Academy, Gus was greeted by everyone we passed. He had told me ahead of time to thank the platoon commander in charge of the night tour and I did, though I didn't feel at all grateful to be going out on DUI patrol, way too high a level of danger for my frayed nerve endings. The commander nodded pleasantly at my thanks then beckoned one of the officers over, a policewoman only an inch shorter than Gus's six feet. She'd probably had her fill of jokes about the heavy sprinkling of freckles across her cheeks and nose.

"Officer O'Malley, this is Dr. Kamimura."

"Please, I'm Yoko," I said. By now, I was almost used to the swift scanning police give you. *Human x-ray*. This time, the x-ray was followed by a friendly smile.

"I'm Macdara, Mac for short," she told me.

I stifled the impulse to ask someone armed with a gun if she was ever called Big Mac and we shook hands.

Eventually, Mac and Steve Farnell, her partner, another six-footer, as pale as Mac was freckled, took us out to the parking lot. Patrol cars were lined in orderly rows. The doors of the nearest row were marked, "DUI, Driving Under the Influence, Connecticut State Police." Gus and I were shepherded into the rear seat of one of the DUI cars.

"First time out?" Mac asked from the front and I nodded.

Three squad cars had been assigned to the shift and our car eased out of the lot, two others falling in behind us. The Connecticut countryside was tranquil under a low cloud cover. The rain had stopped or maybe it hadn't reached this far from New York. A relaxed Gus sat next to me. I was tight with apprehension. We drove for about fifteen minutes and it was peaceful in the dark of the back roads and my tension eased somewhat. Rounding a double S bend, we pulled over onto the wide shoulder where the road straightened out, a carefully chosen location. It was a tricky turn in good weather, downright nasty if you were high on booze or drugs.

"The police can't stop cars without due cause but at a spot like this, where it's easy to have an accident, it saves time to have a DUI team waiting," Gus explained.

We sat in silence for a few minutes. Then we heard the sound of a speeding vehicle and in the front, Mac tilted her head, listening. Gus nudged me in the ribs and my tension level soared to high. Tires protesting in a rubber scream, a vintage Mustang snarled into sight. It didn't make the bend but slid off the road and jolted to a stop short of a massive tree trunk.

"Lucky not to hit the tree," Steve said. "Now their luck may run out. What a surprise if the driver fails the test."

He opened his door and got out. Mac looked back at me and winked. Gus and I watched as the Mustang's driver, a tall young man, started to get out unsteadily, one long leg then the other emerging from the car. He stood, swaying gently but somehow keeping upright. We couldn't hear what was being said but after a short conversation it was obvious he agreed, somewhat reluctantly, to a sobriety test. Before we left the station, the desk sergeant had warned us not to budge from the squad car unless invited to do so but we had a clear view of the testing. The driver's head moved unsteadily as he tried to follow the penlight that Steve slowly moved from side to side in front of the driver's eyes.

"His eye movements will be erratic," Gus said and I nodded agreement.

Gus was one of the first to train police officers to run the test to detect the jerky eye movement—HGN or horizontal gaze nystagmus. Alcohol or any other substance that affects the nervous system results in HGN. Now the courts accept this test as probable cause of DUI but until the scientific validity of the test was established, drivers under the influence frequently got off because police had no legally acceptable, standardized field sobriety testing.

I opened my mouth to speak but stopped at the sound of an angry shout.

"No way that's legal." It was the driver of the Mustang yelling.

A man erupted from the passenger side of the car, shouting and tugging something out of his pocket. Safe in the patrol car I still trembled nervously. Steve reached the passenger swiftly, turning him against the car and patting him down in fluid moves. The driver lurched for Mac, who sidestepped smoothly and had his arms behind his back and cuffs closed over his wrists in seconds while the man shouted incoherently. I watched in fascination as Steve relieved the passenger of a knife and guided him to the patrol car parked behind us. Still arguing, the two were helped into the car, which left for the station.

"Mission accomplished. Now we wait for another good citizen," Steve said as he and Mac got back into the car. I let out a long sigh and they both laughed.

"Before we had these standardized tests, it was loosey goosey," Steve said. "Some cops threw coins on the ground and said, 'Pick up only nickels or quarters.' Then there was the school of thought that had a driver count backward from one hundred by threes."

"You never know what you'll come up against on DUI patrol," Mac said, turning so she could see us without craning her neck. "Drunks, druggies, run-of-the-mill villains. On this duty, you're either hooked or want to rotate off ASAP. The burnout rate's bad but it can be addictive." She nodded at Gus. "What do you think, Doc? How long before we have an even dozen?"

They laughed at my groan but before Gus could answer, we heard another car coming round the dangerous bend. Steve and Mac switched their attention front and the patrol car was quiet. All told, twenty cars came around the twisting turns in the time we sat there, cats at a mouse hole. Most navigated the sharp bends without problems. Four did not. By the time we'd watched those four drivers take the test, I was limp from the suspense. No one was as much trouble as the first but all would be charged DUI.

By the time we returned to the station, I was exhausted.

"Back to New York City with you," Gus said cheerfully when he dropped me at the train station. "Will you make it to the dedication ceremony? I won't be able to go, it's my daughter's birthday."

The dedication ceremony! That's what Dr. Forrest meant when he said he'd see Detective Riley on the weekend. In the turmoil of the last few days I'd totally forgotten about the dedication of the renovations to the Infants' Clinic, the result of strenuous fund-raising, mostly by my boss.

"Yes," I said. "I'm looking forward to it."

"Let me know when you want to come out for another DUI outing."

Gus laughed at the face I made.

It was after eleven when the train pulled in to Grand Central. Other than a conductor ambling across the station and two hikers with bulging backpacks sitting on the floor by the information desk, the place was deserted. My footsteps echoed as I walked to the Park Avenue exit. After sitting most of the evening full of nervous tension, I needed to stretch my legs and walk. By the time I reached my building I was more relaxed. I scanned the sidewalk, something we city dwellers do. All clear. Shouldering my way through the main door, I headed for the stairs. The door creaked as it slowly began to close behind me and I looked back to check if it was closing. It wasn't. A man had caught the door halfway and come in. He stood in the entrance, staring at me. My neck prickled.

The damn hall light was out again and in the shadowy hall, the man was a faceless outline, gently backlit by lights from the street. A reality nightmare. The pause lengthened. A neighbor or visitor wouldn't stand silently looking at me. I couldn't see if this was the man who'd attacked Lanny, but if it was, he had only one reason for following me. If I ran up the stairs, he'd follow. Better to chance finding my neighbor Larissa home in her ground-floor apartment or maybe someone would come in from the street, scare the guy off. I jumped off the stairs and darted along the hall to Larissa's door. Feet pounded behind me. Throwing myself at the door, I beat on it.

"Help. Call the police, Larissa. It's Yoko," I yelled.

A hand clamped across my mouth and a strong arm grabbed me around the waist, lifting me off the floor. Kicking back, I heard a grunt as my shoe connected with a shinbone. Again I kicked, forward this time, drumming both feet on the apartment door. No response. Total silence inside the apartment. Larissa must not be home otherwise she'd have called out that she'd dialed the police or that her son, the cook at KK next door, would be here in seconds with mace.

The arms round me were tight. My struggles to break free were getting me nowhere. Lashing out at his legs again, I stamped down, trying to bend over, hoping to pull him off balance. In retaliation, my head was bashed against the metal doorframe. Fireworks exploded and a warm trickle started down my neck. I was dizzily aware I was being dragged down the hall. Why was the hall getting dark? *Oh, my vision's fading.*

Through drooping eyelids, I watched lazily as a match flared. A teardrop of a flame floated over me towards the trashcans the super kept lined up by the basement door. The flame flickered and hovered over a large pile of plastic bags then fell on them.

"Careful," I wanted to say, but the word didn't come and the plastic started to smolder. Darkness sucked me to its soft heart as acrid smoke stung my nose.

"She's waking up. Yoko, come on."

One by one, my eyelids came unglued. Groggily, I tried to focus on the two figures bending over me. It was Larissa and her son, Marvin, staring anxiously down. Larissa crooned soothingly as she dabbed at the side of my head. Her mouth set in a tight line as she rinsed the cloth in a bowl of water. I stared in rapt attention as the swirls of water turned pink. Was that my blood? I flinched as Larissa dabbed at me again.

"I'm cleaning your neck, you're not bleeding there," she said sharply. "You've a gash in the side of your head and I'm nowhere near that. What did you do? You let someone in? What were you thinking? A drug pusher or a mugger who hit you then started a fire? We could all be dead in our beds." The outrage masked concern.

"Ma, let her catch her breath," Marvin begged. "Yoko wouldn't let anyone in. He must of pushed in and mugged her. Am I right?"

I nodded, regretting it when my head throbbed.

"Let me get my hands on him," Marvin growled.

"Where…?" I croaked.

Larissa didn't need prompting.

"We came in and found the hall filling up with smoke. So much for that dang smoke detector. Not a peep out of it. You were out cold by the basement door," Larissa said. She stopped dabbing at me and took the bowl of water to the sink, rinsing the rag, wringing the water out of it in angry twists. She came and stood over me, hands on hips, frowning.

"Are you gonna tell us what happened or do we have to guess?"

"Ma," Marvin interceded. She silenced him with a flickering roll of her eyes.

"What'll you have, Yoko? Tea, schnapps?"

I grinned weakly. That was my Larissa. Yell at you and offer comfort, all in the same breath. I knew better than to take the schnapps. Even when I'm in good shape, it blows off the top of my head.

"Tea."

"Schnapps would be better," Larissa grumbled as she poured two liberal shots of the liquid explosive she recommended for every purpose. She and Marvin tossed their shots back. I sipped the tea eagerly and caught a whiff of the acrid smell plastic makes when it burns. I sniffed. Yes, the smell was coming off me.

"Eau de Trash Bag. Liz Taylor, eat your heart out," I said.

After one astonished look, Larissa and Marvin burst out laughing and the three of us roared uncontrollably.

"That's right, kiddo. You smell but good," Larissa wheezed as she wiped her eyes. "You'll need to wash your clothes twice or send them to the cleaner. You were something straight out of a movie in that smoky hallway. Blood trickling down your neck, flat on the floor like you were a dead woman. What happened?"

"I remember seeing a match, after he banged my head on your door," I started, my voice shaky. "The man who grabbed me, he pushed his way in behind me before the door latched."

Larissa sat down on the couch next to me, her face serious.

"I started the fight, but only after he grabbed me. I kicked him."

This got an appreciative cackle from Larissa.

"Was he high?" Marvin asked. "Could you smell booze? Did he rob you?"

The last question took me by surprise but he had a point. Was I so fixated on trouble coming in a terrorist's package of three that I'd overlooked robbery as a motive? Patting my pockets to see what was in them stirred up another acrid smell. I pulled out my keys, my one credit card, the SUNY ID tag and a small wad of dollar bills that added up to the same fourteen dollars I'd had after paying for the train ticket to Bridgeport. It's rare I have a purse or even a wallet on me, I load my pockets instead.

"Yes," I said in relief. "Got everything, I travel light. No, I didn't smell drink and I don't know if he was high, I didn't have time to think, just tried to fight him off." Then I remembered the folder I'd been carrying. "Where's my file?"

"This it?" Marvin held up a limp beige folder, damp but intact.

Relieved, I nodded my thanks and was instantly dizzy. Then I remembered the flash drive, the one I kept exclusively to record the prototype information from Dr. Anders. Had I brought it with me or left it locked in the office file cabinet? I patted all my pockets again. No flash drive. Wait, I was sure I'd left it at the office. That made sense. I wouldn't have time after the trip to Connecticut to go over anything on my laptop. Was that why I'd been mugged, was someone after information about the prototypes? Was I imagining it or did I have a hazy memory of hands groping in my pockets, could the mugger have been looking for my flash drive? But how would there be any connection between Lanny and the work Fred Anders was doing? Serious thinking was beyond me right then and I was easily distracted by Larissa's next question.

"Did he try to fool with you? Was it a rapist? Did you see his face?" Larissa was blunt.

Cautiously, moving my head slowly so as not to get another jolt of pain, I looked down. My clothing hadn't been disturbed, nothing was out of place.

"No," I said slowly. "It wasn't a rapist. I couldn't see him clearly when he came in. That hall light is always on the blink. Only the other morning I saw the super change the bulbs."

"The fixture shorts out all the time, a real fire hazard. Won't matter how many new bulbs get put in. I told the super that last week." Marvin shrugged.

Our building, one of three on the block that the super maintained for absentee owners, was always last for repairs.

"Now the other buildings have gone condo, could be the landlord wants to squeeze us out," Larissa said.

"Fat chance," Marvin told his mother. "We'll get all the tenants together, fight him all the way."

Larissa nodded then went back to her explanation. "We were coming in and a man, not anyone who lives in the building, rushed from the back of the hall and pushed by us," she said. "Smoke was billowing up so that got our attention. Just as well we didn't go after him, the flames from the plastic bags were almost at the piles of newspapers. My boy grabbed the fire extinguisher and I managed to drag you in here. Marvin put out the fire. Couldn't do a thing about the smell, though."

"When you work in a restaurant, you know what to do," Marvin said quietly. "Kitchen fires happen."

Larissa was impatient to get back to the juicy details. "You sure you didn't recognize the guy? You think it was a mugger?"

"Maybe." I didn't voice my fear that it might have been the man who attacked Lanny.

"Why would he start a fire?"

"Ma, you know there's a psycho a day out there," Marvin said. "What about when that subway booth was bombed? With the two clerks inside? What sane person would do that?"

We sat in silence, considering the trouble fueled by rage and frustration. Larissa switched directions with her questioning.

"Did you hear if they caught the man who attacked your god-mother?"

"No," I said slowly.

"I bet you've been worried?"

"Yes."

"Will you call the police?" Marvin said.

"And tell them what?" his mother said. "That something was stolen? No. Someone was hurt? Not badly enough to interest them. Nothing personal, Yoko. The police don't come these days if a car is broken into and the tape deck ripped out."

Larissa was right. Except for one thing. Detective Riley. He might listen. He might even agree there was a possible connection to Mary Sakamoto's warning.

"The detective who interviewed me when that woman was shot in front of me—I could speak with him," I said.

Larissa nodded, satisfied.

"I'll call the super. When I tell him you've got your own city cop on tap, a detective yet, maybe he'll get round to replacing the batteries on the smoke detectors and repairing the light fixture before the end of the year."

She helped lever me up from the couch.

"You want we should walk you upstairs to your place?"

"Thanks, but I can manage."

The two stood in their doorway, watching as I made my slow ascent.

"Call that cop," Larissa reminded me.

You know I will."

Five

I winced my way up the long, uncarpeted flights of stairs to my apartment. Living in a fourth-floor walk-up means I don't need to go to a gym but tonight I could've done without the exercise. My muscles signaled major discomfort with each movement. Sighing in relief, I unlocked the door—home safe. Ivan and Chance, my two brother cats, stood waiting, tails in lazy motion. They always hope for a treat like tuna and when they feel it's overdue, they greet me at the door. Other times, my return is ignored. Cupboard love.

"Come on, guys," I complained. "Let me in."

Carefully I stepped between the weaving bodies. They pressed around my legs, I told them to stop, they ignored me. That was normal. What wasn't normal was that Lanny hovered in the hell of a coma, the stranger shot to death in front of me had warned me of danger and Larissa and Marvin had rescued me from a mugger who'd torched the trash in the hallway after knocking me out. I could have died from smoke inhalation if my neighbors hadn't reached me in time. Was that what Mary Sakamoto had warned me about? Was a killer after me? Why? And who was Mary Sakamoto? I still was certain I didn't know her. And what, if anything did all this have to do with Lanny? Still no answers. I went through the apartment switching on light after light until everything was on. Tonight I needed to dispel the dark. I'll be frugal and help save the environment tomorrow.

The cats stopped begging, smart enough to know treats weren't coming. I checked for messages, nothing. Time to call Detective Riley at the Thirteenth Precinct. I was in luck, he was at his desk. My sore head was almost forgotten until I eased myself into a chair and the room tilted for a mad second.

"I need a professional ear. Something weird just happened. A guy pushed into the front hall after me when I got home, before the door closed, " I coughed to cover the quaver in my voice. Bad move, my head throbbed. "He jumped me in the hall."

Riley didn't interrupt as I told him about my mugger-arsonist.

"My neighbors came in before the fire spread. They think it's a wacko but this is the third time in a few days…." I stopped. Why go over the rotten litany? Riley knew the score. The pause at the end of the line was short.

"Too much of a coincidence," Riley said. "I've not seen any reports about a mugger who plays with fire. If it's arson, it may be your landlord is thinking of torching the building for the insurance dollars but the hallway's not a choice location. I'm betting the three are related. The million dollar question is *why*? Can you describe the mugger?"

"All I saw was a shadowy figure when I looked to see who'd come in behind me. The hall light's out as usual."

"It's rare a victim gets a good look at the mugger."

Riley's voice was reassuring and I almost started sniveling at his caring tone. Until this week, I'd never had a problem keeping a lid on my emotions in public, only letting loose when I'm alone. Now, my emotions were barely below the surface, made raw by Lanny's coma.

"Listen, I doubt anyone will be sent out to investigate," Riley continued. "It's not murder and nothing was taken, right? But I'll make a note in the case file. You did right to call. The more information we have, the more we can help. Never hesitate to call, agreed?"

"Agreed," I said, crossing my fingers. It was a half-truth. I didn't know what information I'd ever get that would help the police.

"How're you feeling? Do you have a headache?"

"No, I've a bit of a bump on my head." I was minimizing the truth, I felt as if I'd been through a cement mixer and that the room tilted if I didn't move really slowly.

"That's not good. How big's the bump? Do you need to go to the hospital for an x-ray? Could be concussion. Is there anyone who can stay with you, wake you up every few hours? Standard procedure for a concussion."

"That's really not necessary. I've aloe vera juice in the fridge, that'll help with the bump. My neighbor, Larissa, would've dragged me to the hospital if she thought it was necessary." I didn't add that if I'd had the slightest suspicion I had a serious head injury, I'd go to the hospital immediately. The truth was that my arms and legs hurt way more than the bump on my head.

Someone called Riley's name.

"Uh oh, more night action in the city that never sleeps," Dan said. "We're short a coupla detectives. Gotta go."

I hung up and sat thinking about the conversation. It actually felt like a decent connection with Riley, maybe because I couldn't see his x-ray eyes. Connections are rare, even in New York with its millions. My social life had been nonexistent for months—OK, maybe it was over a year. Small wonder I often worked late, a habit my mother had often complained about.

"How will you meet someone when you're stuck at your desk late most nights?" Her not too subtle hint that she wanted grandkids. Mom never mentioned my failed marriage to Charlie. He was a charmer, a computer whiz with an impressive job as director of IT at a Wall Street investment house. Trouble was, Charlie was an alcoholic and a dedicated gambler, though you never saw him drunk and he didn't go to the race-track. Online gambling was his obsession. Thirsty work, judging from the number of empty wine bottles stacked in our recycling bin.

Four months after we pledged to a life of bliss, Charlie took off for Las Vegas. Turned out Wall Street suggested he move on. Conveniently, one of the casinos needed their information technology directed. A long-distance relationship would be too challenging, Charlie explained, and when I arrived in Nevada for a divorce, he oozed charm. Charlie didn't dampen my interest in guys, it's just not easy to meet people, even in the Big Apple. Bars aren't my scene, dating services can be weird and as for hooking up with someone over the Internet, I've heard too many hair-raising stories. It was too bad Dan Riley and I had met because of a murder.

When I got up, already the aches were less. I stood and thought about my reaction to the mugger. I'd panicked, I hadn't been mentally ready. From here on, I'd be Annie Alert. I doublechecked the door locks and pulled the shades on each and every window.

Taking the cover off the bathtub, I turned the taps on full then gingerly eased out of my clothes. The toxic smell of burned plastic wafted around me as I stuffed everything I'd been wearing into the laundry bag and put the bulging bag by the door. I'd drop it off at the laundromat in the morning. I stepped gratefully into the hot bath but was too restless to soak for more than a few minutes. I got out, moaning softly as my body reminded me it had been banged and bruised, and patted myself dry then climbed into ancient sweats, my answer to p.j.s.

Comfort food, that's what I needed. I stared at the meager contents of the fridge. Limp carrots, shriveled celery, a batch of rice balls stuffed with umeboshi, the pickled apricots that for some reason are called plums in the U.S., and a few slices of sourdough rye. I eyed the lone bottle of beer. Not tonight. Chamomile tea, that would help calm me. I wasn't really hungry and the ginger cookies in the ceramic jar were beyond stale but dipped in hot tea they'd taste fine.

I wandered through to the front room and sat in the old rocking chair, looking out over a deserted First Avenue. Chance oozed his plump way onto my lap. Ivan sat slender and dignified on the floor next to the chair, his head in easy nudging distance of my arm to remind me to pat him. The tea relaxed me and my emotion spilled up from the depths where I'd tried to hide it. Tears rolled down my cheeks. Chance glared indignantly and jumped off my lap. Ivan stood and backed away. The two headed for the kitchen and I heard crunching sounds as they tackled the dry cat food in their bowls. So much for sympathy.

Leaning back in the rocker, I dozed. When I opened my eyes, salty tears were stiff on my face. Rubbing my face, too tired to wash it, I made for the bed and was asleep before the cats jumped up next to me.

I woke refreshed by a deep, dreamless sleep. My body was a little stiff but my head didn't hurt. I glanced out of the window at the Asher Levy School opposite. Kids were going in, probably for the free breakfast, others were hanging out on the sidewalk. My breakfast was two rice balls and a cup of miso. If I hurried, I'd have time to visit Lanny at the hospital before work. The phone rang as I finished dressing. I grabbed it. Good news about Lanny?

"Yoko, did I catch you before the police?" It was Pat, Gus Forkiotis's wife.

"You're the first person to call this morning."

What did Pat mean, *police*?

"Last night, after Gus dropped you off at the train station, he was hit by a car. He's in the hospital."

"What?" I wailed. "How is he?"

"You know Gus, he's giving them hell in the hospital. Says they need the bed for someone who's ill. The police want to talk to you to confirm the time he dropped you off. Gus says he left the station when you got on the train and went back to the office to pick up something. He was walking back to his car when a minivan came speeding through the parking lot and knocked him down. It didn't stop."

"That's terrible! How badly is he hurt?" I dreaded the possibility that Gus might have serious head injuries.

"Two cracked ribs and a broken leg, a nasty break. He jumped out of the way and was almost clear but the fender caught his leg."

"Did he lose consciousness?"

"No. Somehow he crawled back to the office and called me, you know how he resists having a cell phone. The doctor says the leg break is serious. The ribs only hurt when he yells! I'll let you know when he comes home. Right now, I've got to call Bob Bertolli to see if he can come and cover for this week's patients. Bob was at home today, he and Gus are working on a paper for an upcoming conference." She sighed. "I doubt Gus will get to the OEP conference in England, he'll probably still be on crutches. He wanted me to call you first, he didn't want the news to come out of left field when the police telephoned."

My hand was trembling as I put the phone down. It shrilled immediately. It was the Connecticut police and the short conversation was friendly. I confirmed the time Gus had dropped me at the train station and we agreed that hit-and-run drivers were scum.

"Might've been kids out joy-riding. We found the car later, abandoned. Owner called in this morning to report it stolen," the officer said.

"Officer, I don't know if there's any connection, but in the past few days there've been some…uh…serious problems."

A sigh came over the phone line. Great, now the police in Connecticut thought I was a wacko.

"What sort of problems?"

As briefly as possible, I explained about the murder of Mary Sakamoto and her warning of danger and how, the day after that, my godmother had been attacked and was in the hospital in a coma. The guy in Connecticut didn't make any comment about what I'd told him and didn't sound too interested but he followed through.

"All right, give me the name of the officer in New York who interviewed you about the street crime."

After I hung up, I sat for a moment considering the news. My dad always insisted trouble comes in threes. Mom used to say that's because he expected three. Starting with Mary Sakamoto's shooting, the total was four. Were the four connected? If so, how? It was baffling. Was it a coincidence that Gus had been hit? Was it kids gone wild? Damn, why hadn't I asked the Connecticut officer about hit-and-run statistics? How often did this type of thing happen? At least Dan Riley would receive more news to add to the file when the Connecticut police called. Riley might even think I was cooperating. I was, in a way. I checked the time. I had to leave right away if I wanted to visit Lanny before work. I beat the cats to the door, double-locked and went quietly downstairs.

When Pat called, raindrops had been sprinkling the windows, flattening into horizontal ribbons as spurts of wind hit, but the sun came out as I reached the sidewalk. I scanned the headlines at the newsstand then paid for a *New York Times*. I leafed through and wasn't surprised to find Lanny smiling up at me above a short article on the back page. It was an old photo from her wedding announcement but she hadn't changed much since then.

The headline, "Widow of Swedish Diplomat in Hospital," ran over a few skimpy paragraphs: Lanny's years with the Rockefeller Foundation and charity work with organizations like the League of Women Voters and MADD, Mothers Against Drunk Drivers. It didn't mention the ferocious energy that Lanny put into MADD work after a drunk driver ran down her husband and their daughter. It did note she'd been preparing for a national gathering of experts to speak about the increasing incidents of drunk driving. Dr Foikoitis was one of the listed experts she was wrangling to participate pro bono. It didn't mention why she was in the hospital. It closed with the non-committal sentence that police were investigating the collapse of the historic domed ceiling at the National Arts Club, of which Mrs. Oldenburg was a longtime member and from where she had been taken to the hospital. This was a press release from the consulate. Diplomatically uninformative.

At St. Vincent's, I hurried down the hall to Lanny's room, eager to see her. The guard in the hall nodded, recognizing me from my last visit. Tapping on the door, I pushed it open cautiously, not wanting to surprise Dag, who was sitting close to the door—any unauthorized person who did get by the hall guard would have to get by Dag to reach Lanny. I immediately had Dag's undivided attention and he had me classified instantly—I wasn't a threat. Now there was a man with superior vision processing.

"Morning," he said, his voice low.

"Hi, Dag. Any update from the doctors?"

"Yes. Mrs. Oldenburg's condition is stable," he said. "Here, I can give you the official details." He picked up a notebook and read quietly to me.

"Her vital signs are strong. They monitor brain pressure periodically and have relieved the pressure several times by draining spinal fluid. The neurologist says he's encouraged."

What Dag didn't say was that Lanny's coma still endured.

Sitting by Lanny's side, I took her hand and gloomily scanned the tubes sprouting on all sides. The one-sided small talk I made felt right, even though Lanny didn't show any sign she heard me. Chitchat exhausted, I sat and thought about what Detective Riley had said when I asked about the chances of catching the person who'd shot Mary Sakamoto.

"Do you know how many shootings we have in Manhattan and all we have to go on are the bullets? There are the times we don't even find those. How are we supposed to connect anyone to a crime without the weapon?"

Seeing Lanny lying in that hospital bed finally brought a nagging thought to the surface. Lanny had been working on the conference with Dr Foikoitis and now both of them were in hospital beds. What was the connection? Someone who didn't want the conference to be held? What did that have to do with me? Dag coughed and I saw I'd been there over ten minutes. Kissing Lanny, I left. Dag nodded obligingly when I reminded him to call if there was any change.

As usual, Mike was at the front desk when I arrived at the college. We're supposed to show our passes every time we arrive. Whether he knows you or not, Mike has a random pattern for demanding I.D.

"Checking to see if zombies took your brain," he'll deadpan. Today he nodded me through.

"Morning, doctor."

I grinned in appreciation.

"Morning, Mike."

Mike's use of titles was rare, even with department heads. Niceties completed, I headed for the stairs. The elevators were usually jammed. Gossip had it we'd be moving to a refurbished building somewhere close to Forty-second Street, probably off Fifth Avenue, convenient for commuters. When that day came, I might start taking the elevator, who knows how many floors up we'd be. My boss, Elliott Forrest, another confirmed stair user, was coming down as I started up and I stopped to tell him about the hit-and-run that had put Gus in the hospital.

"I'll call Pat when I get back from this meeting," he said, shaking his head in outrage, and started down the stairs then paused and called back.

"Yoko, Dr. Anders was asking for you. He seemed very anxious. So much is riding on his findings, for his career and for the future of this department. I hope there aren't any problems. Anything you can tell me? Next to Anders, you're the only one who truly knows what's going on in that lab."

"As far as I can tell, everything is on schedule. But you're right, Matt Wahr mentioned something about Dr. Anders asking for an extension on funding. Everything I've seen says Dr. Anders is on track. His creations are really mind-bending, you know," I said. I didn't add that it was a mind-bending challenge trying to grasp the full implications of Dr. Anders' work. I didn't have any doubt that what Fred Anders was doing was revolutionary.

"How's your preparation of material for the OEP conference in England?" Dr. Forrest asked.

"Slowly but surely," I said. *People's careers, the department's future—no pressure, no pressure at all.*

"Good."

My boss waved cheerfully and hurried off and I headed straight to the small lab where Fred Anders was hunched over his workbench.

"Ah, Yoko. Interested in breakfast?" he asked, his British accent as precise as if he'd arrived from Cambridge this week, not thirty years ago.

"I'd love to another day," I said.

Fred Anders was notorious for pulling all-nighters and from the wild look of his thick gray hair this was the morning after one. Brilliant and unassuming, he was widely admired in the field of behavioral optometry. Once I asked him why he left Cambridge.

"Absolutely had to work in New York," he'd said. "American optometrists were making all the significant advances in the field of physiological optics. I read some amazing papers, like Elliott Forrest's on the concept of lenses in vision therapy and one by Gus Forkiotis on the use of prisms and I was hooked."

Fred had come to the U.S. and taken the postdoctoral training in behavioral optometry at SUNY to add to his Ph.D. in physics and had been at the college ever since. My class, like a lot of graduating classes, voted him Most Excellent Professor. Privately, we dubbed him a cool dude but the toughest professor. His doctoral classes in biochemistry, endocrinology and microbiology had waiting lists, even though he drilled students without mercy.

Today, he gave me a sharp glance then returned to his work.

"You look like death warmed over, what's up?"

"Thanks for the confidence boost," I said, before launching into a truncated version of the catastrophes of the past few days. I wound up with the sad story of what had happened to Gus. When I reached the end of the tale of woes, Fred put down the scalar microscope he was retooling and swiveled to face me.

"How bloody awful. I agree with your detective chappie that there's a possible connection between the shooting death and the attacks. As for the brute or brutes who careened into Gus, that could be unrelated. What does the detective say about that?"

"I haven't talked to him since Pat called this morning. The police officer from Connecticut was going to call him."

"So what did he say *before* the hit-and-run?" Fred wiggled his eyebrows.

"He did say not to trust in coincidences," I mumbled.

"Even more important in life after September eleventh," Fred said.

He pushed his chair away from the lab bench and stood, stretching and yawning.

"If I don't eat soon, I'll be gnawing fingers, mine or those of anyone who's close by," and he waggled his fingers under my nose. "Here are my latest notes. I managed to do a fair bit last night. I apologize, there are some changes. Hope you can make sense of my scribble. You're doing a splendid job so far."

I flipped through the pages he gave me. It helped I knew the existing equipment but it was a struggle to keep up with the way Fred expanded the capabilities of the various pieces. Once he'd finished his current revisions, I hoped to have enough information to make sense of everything. Right now, even though I'd spent week after week on this work, it was an intricate jigsaw puzzle. Even with many pieces in place, the big picture was tantalizingly elusive. Now changes! I'd need to fill the flash drive and take it home with me to look over the work. Not the best security but the conference was coming up fast. I'd heard through the grapevine that a three-letter branch of the government was waiting in the wings for Fred to finish. I didn't want to know if it was the CIA or the FBI. I knew Fred's sole focus was vision therapy to help people. Mine, too. Trust the government to think of other uses—what they might be I didn't want to consider. Tucking the latest pages of notes under my arm, I looked more carefully at what Fred Anders was tinkering with right then.

"Is that the macro lens attachment you used on the digital camera? The one that can see through cloudy corneas?" I asked.

"Yes. Infra-red reflectography when used with conventional IR film."

"And videography if electronic?"

"Correct."

A few days ago, I'd written up his report on this macro lens attachment. I couldn't believe he was revising it.

"You're making *more* adaptations?"

Fred Anders looked thoughtfully at his littered workbench. "I believe I can expand the range considerably," he explained.

"That's incredible," I said.

"The potential for treating vision problems is wonderful," Fred said.

A wide smile lit up his tired face and he left in search of breakfast. Hurrying up the stairs, I headed for my office and was surprised to see Allan coming out of it.

"Hey," he said breezily, "I thought I'd see if you were ready for a coffee break."

"Way too early," I said, irritated when he casually wandered in after me and stood watching as I dumped my armful of papers on the desk and settled down to work.

"Don't you have something to do?" I said and bent my head over my notes. It was a relief when Allan sauntered to the door, the picture of a man of leisure. At least he hadn't hit on me or suggest we have a drink after work.

"Huh," I muttered as I shuffled through the latest batch of Dr. Anders' notes. "That's puzzling."

Allan, just at the door, caught the words. "Want to run something by me?" he said eagerly.

The offer was hard to resist. I vented and Allan listened and even made a helpful comment about a technicality that had bothered me. Was Allan growing up or was I? Something he said gave me pause.

"What you're working on with Dr. Anders is really important," and he gave one of those nods that goes with a meaningful stare to indicate something crucial has been said.

"Back up, Allan. You can't say I'm working *with* Dr. Anders, he's the genius."

"Don't play modest, everyone knows you're the only one who can translate his notes. That means you understand what he's doing. Besides, you researched and co-authored the journal articles about most of the equipment he's adapting."

Allan left and I considered the implications of his remark. How was it that people managed to ferret out details of work supposedly under wraps? Who, I wondered, would be talking to Allan about confidential work? Other than me, of course, and I'd been careful to keep to general terms. Perhaps no one had leaked information, perhaps Allan had seen e-files when he was unscrambling problems on our computers. Technically, that would be either my computer or the two Fred Anders used, one in his office, another in his lab; like me, Fred used a flash drive to back-up everything, though the final interpretation was on my computer and the flash drive I used. Of course, other people, like the dean and my boss, Dr. Forrest, exchanged e-mails about the work as it progressed, but their e-mails were more overviews and comments on the schedule. It was puzzling and deserved serious consideration.

I promised myself that when I had time I'd go over the notes again. What, for instance, were the non-vision therapy uses for the equipment?

The phone rang. "The Infants' Clinic started ten minutes ago, Yoko," it was Dr. Forrest. "You're on this morning, right?"

"Oops, be right with you," and I hurried off, shelving thoughts of sleuthing.

The clinic was hectic, nothing unusual about that. Lunch was a virtuous salad from the corner cafe, rounded out by a Larabar with the intriguing name of Cashew Cookie. It consisted of cashews and dates. Mouth-watering, totally satisfying, even healthy.

In the afternoon, I settled into more work deciphering Fred Anders' scrawl. The afternoon ground on until the sun went down and I was still not done. It was late enough, I needed some real food. On the way out, I stopped by Fred's lab.

"I'm still working on that last batch of changes but I'll finish it up tonight at home or tomorrow morning when I come in," I said.

Fred, engrossed in maneuvering the delicate wires of what looked like a pair of goggles, nodded, not looking up.

"Swing by early tomorrow. I'll have some more ready, all right?" he murmured, intent on the work in his hands.

"Right," I said and left.

I decided to stop at the Elephant and Castle for a meal. The restaurant was deserted and I sat at a window table. A waiter took my order and while I waited, I pulled out my notebook. Before I left for work that morning, I'd scribbled down a timeline of events from Mary Sakamoto's shooting and the attack on Lanny to the mugging-arson attempt on me and the hit-and-run on Gus. It was demoralizing to see it written down and possible reasons or connections didn't jump out at me.

My food arrived, a welcome interruption, I was starving. Even a Larabar doesn't last through an afternoon of hard work. I slathered ketchup on my turkey burger and fries and chewed thoughtfully, looking over the timeline again. The guy who'd attacked me in the hallway of my apartment building had taken a serious risk, someone could have come in at any moment. What motivated him? Was this the danger Mary Sakamoto had warned about or was the mugger just a psycho who couldn't put a lid on his temper?

Optometrists take psychology courses, so I knew it might have been classic, post-offense behavior or sustained aggression. The city has a lot of people on the streets with that mindset. I could rationalize the attack on Lanny and myself as the work of psychos except for one disturbing fact, Mary Sakamoto's warning about danger. Always I circled back to that.

Lars had assured me Lanny wasn't involved in any of the various fractious factions at the National Arts Club but did he really know? Had Lanny been attacked over one of the problems at the National Arts Club? Where to start? Who poisoned the pigeons with Avitrol? Apparently that's an illegal pesticide and its use raises all sorts of questions. Then there was the furor over trees in the park being axed.

I racked my brains for connections. A possible link between Lanny and Dr. Forkiotis might be the conference Lanny was trying to plan, that certainly did connect her to Dr. Forkiotis right now. But why would that have caused all the trouble? Perhaps psychotic anger had motivated the man who attacked Lanny and the hit-and-run could have been just that, a hit-and-run.

The media carried stories about tax evasion and grand larceny at the National Arts Club, although the ongoing litigation by members who say they were forced to vacate their apartments hadn't been aired in public. Any one of these situations could have fueled the rage I'd seen on the face of Lanny's attacker. But how were any of the troubles at the club connected to me? By the time I finished my meal and put the timeline in my pocket, I wondered if anything would ever become clear.

Much later, when I was brushing my teeth, I started to consider in all seriousness the fact that Fred Anders' work might hold clues to the bizarre events of the past days. I was too tired to try to write anything down or even think more about it but for sure I needed to search for answers. I wouldn't get in the way of any official investigation, if there was one, which I doubted. If a government agency really was interested in the prototypes, and the underground news was certain about that, then other groups—and not legitimate ones—might be also, and not for therapeutic purposes.

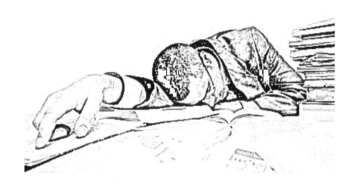

Six

The next week was wonderfully boring—nothing remotely terrible happened. It was a string of days when life cooled to placid routine despite my anxiety about Lanny, which wasn't eased despite regular visits to the hospital. Then, one evening, yet another of my late sessions, the tedious work of sorting through the giant stack of files on my desk was eased by a tuna salad sandwich. The mayo dressing had a serious zing, more like wasabi than Grey Poupon. The phone rang and I swallowed a mouthful hastily, eager to answer. Most likely a personal call, evening classes were almost over by now.

"Yoko, Lanny's come round. She's out of her coma."

"Lars!" I managed to say.

The news was stunning. The nerve-shredding wait was over.

"The doctors say Lanny will need therapy but to see her awake—she recognized me...." His voice broke, faltered to a stop. I waited for him to catch his breath.

"She's taking liquids with a straw, not a tube."

The news of Lanny's return to consciousness was a beautiful end to the day. I listened eagerly to Lars, cramming the tag end of the sandwich into my mouth in my excitement so that I had to cover the speaker end of the phone to muffle the sounds of chewing.

"Dag called from the hospital to say Lanny was conscious. I broke a few traffic laws getting there. Lanny was groggy but she recognized me right away. When the neurologist is satisfied with the results of the tests he's ordered, she can leave the hospital. Yoko, it's over, Lanny's going home soon."

The joyful news silenced us both for a moment.

"The doctor said Lanny will need—how did he put it?—cognitive rehabilitation with a speech pathologist," Lars said. "Why? I didn't have a problem understanding what she said. It wasn't that clear but for God's sake, she just came out of a coma."

"The clue is the word 'cognitive.' What the therapist does goes way beyond speech," I explained. "Therapy will help Lanny."

No need to say other problems might have been caused by the brutal attack and the fall. Lars didn't let it go.

"What problems?"

It was time to be blunt.

"It depends on what part of the brain was damaged. Her recovery will take time, Lars."

"You sound like your mother, you forgot to say, 'Little steps.'"

"Infuriating but true," I agreed. When had I started to turn into my mother? "I'm coming to the hospital right away."

I was too elated to stay at my desk any longer, I had to see Lanny. I gathered the files I'd been working on and dumped them in the file cabinet, locked it and set off for the hospital. As I walked, I considered what Lars had told me. A coma is serious but already, on the meager information Lars had given me, Lanny's situation sounded more positive than I'd dared to hope. My level of worry had held constant at high but now it went down a notch or two. Obviously, Lanny's long-term memory was reasonably intact if she'd recognized Lars. The days ahead would reveal the state of her short-term memory.

I recalled classes when Dr. Forrest had outlined how our brains work.

"The left half of your brain is the analytical, dominant side, where we do our logical thinking and reasoning. It's where our speech areas are and where we process and understand and store words. The brain's right side is the creative side, the visual-pictorial side that stores visual memories. As for interpreting language, that's the domain of our temporal lobes, the lower lateral cerebral hemispheres."

We'd turned to the pages in our textbooks with the gruesome account of the first documented case of brain injury. A railway spike had gone into the eye of an engineer working on the railroads out West, hundreds of miles from a doctor. Pictures showed the spike protruding above the victim's eyebrow. Astonishingly, the man survived. However, damage to the injured part of the brain had shocking results—it literally altered the victim's personality. The good-mannered, dependable, well-liked engineer was transformed into someone who drank heavily, cursed constantly and was totally unreliable.

In the short time since Lanny had been conscious, Lars said she'd sounded like and behaved like her usual self. Time would tell just how her brain had been affected. I reached the hospital in record time and found Lars at Lanny's bedside. My godmother moved her head slowly to look at me and smiled, it was a small smile but my heart soared, Lanny recognized me. I hugged her gently and felt the light pressure of her arms as she hugged me back. I wanted to ask her about the attack, but decided to talk to Lars first. Had he asked Lanny already? What about the police? They'd want to interview Lanny. When would that interview take place? A nurse came in to monitor Lanny's blood pressure and vital signs, so Lars and I moved away from the bed and quietly I asked if he'd spoken to Lanny yet about the attack.

"Yes, but she doesn't have any memory of it."

And that was what Lanny told me when the nurse left and I sat beside my dear godmother, holding her hand, talking in a matter-of-fact way.

"Do you remember what happened to you at the club?"

"Dear heart, I remember nothing about the past few days. Nothing."

I patted her hand lightly, not too surprised. I'd hoped Lanny could shed some light on a reason for the attack but I knew she probably had amnesia.

"Don't worry. I'm just so glad to see you looking much better."

Dag cleared his throat, the signal that it was time to leave. Lars and I smiled at each other. In his unobtrusive way, Dag was a mighty presence.

Outside the hospital, Lars and I chatted for a few minutes then I set off for home. Once I got over my excitement at Lanny coming out of the coma, I discovered I was hungry, I needed a little something after the sandwich I'd been eating when Lars had called with the good news. I decided I had every right to skip a healthy choice, which would be salad—who ever heard of salad for a celebration? I bought Purely Decadent's Cherry Nirvana. I won't tell you how much was left in the container by the time I finished celebrating. Let's say it was enough to top a brownie. Right, we're talking a spoonful. OK, a teaspoon.

The next morning I woke from a luxurious sleep, feeling optimistic. Hard work faced Lanny, rehabilitation takes time, but she'd survived and she was awake, I was encouraged by these facts. Slathering almond butter and blueberry jelly on a bagel, I reflected happily on how life had changed. Lanny had come out of her coma and was coherent. Life had been calm for day after tranquil day. I was still worried about my godmother but she was started on the road to recovery. I turned my thoughts to work. I was on schedule with everything. Yes, things were looking brighter than they had for some time.

Eager to finish the changes to Dr Anders' paper before I was due to start at the Infants' Clinic, I arrived at the college early and walked into an uproar in the lobby. Mike at the front desk was on high alert. He gave me his fish-eye stare. You'd have thought he'd never seen me before today. This translates roughly to, "Show me your ID even if you are the dean." I whipped out my ID and he waved me through with a nod, no pleasant chat today. His face was serious, his attention divided on listening to what one of the security guards was telling him and keeping a watchful gaze on the people milling around in his territory.

Puzzled, I looked around but didn't see anyone I knew. SUNY is one of several tenants in the building and I only know college people. Clearly Mike wasn't in the mood to answer questions. If it was an anthrax or bomb scare, the building would be closed. Couldn't be fire, either. Shrugging, I went on up the stairs.

I decided to drop in on Fred Anders before heading for my office. He'd been away for a few days visiting the Ohio company that was to manufacture the equipment he was developing. I was looking forward to the latest news. I might even finally fully grasp what this brilliant man was doing. Odds were that Fred was already at his lab bench, would have been for hours.

He wasn't. Two strangers were in the tiny space. One, a slender woman, twenty-five-ish, in black jeans and a light jacket, was busy with something on the top of the crowded bookcase. The other, a dark-suited man also in his twenties, was bent over staring in fascination at the littered lab bench. He looked up and held out a hand in warning.

"Sorry, this is off limits."

The woman swung round and muttered something about technicians late with the tape as usual. Both stared at me intently.

"Is Dr. Anders around?" I asked.

"When did you last see him?"

"Not for several days, I guess it was just before he left for Ohio."

I stopped. Something was strangely familiar. The way the two had taken over, their tight focus on me, the question instead of an answer. Had that woman been dusting for prints? I was willing to bet my retinoscope these two were police. Non-uniforms meant detectives. What the hell was going on?

"You are?" the man said curtly.

"Dr. Kamimura."

"You work here?"

"Yes, I'm on the faculty."

I stared at the man. Detectives could only mean an accident or major trouble. My mouth dropped open as I made the connections. It didn't bother me that I must look like a stranded fish, I felt like one.

"I'll take you to the staff lounge. We're gathering people there." Detective Dark Suit ushered me out and down the hall. My stomach knotted and my palms were wet with sweat but I walked steadily beside him. My heart skipped a beat when I saw Dan Riley in the lounge, this definitely had to be trouble. He and his partner were talking with two senior faculty.

"Dr. Kamimura, I thought you might be in early."

Detective Dark Suit looked inquiringly at Riley, obviously wondering why I merited any comment.

"Bad news?" I said, annoyed at the undertone of fear in my voice. It crossed my mind that Riley might think I attracted trouble—did he think there was any danger yet? It had to be serious for police to be swarming around the college like bees buzzing around honeysuckle.

"Yes. I'm sorry to tell you that Dr. Anders was found dead early this morning," Riley said, his voice sympathetic, his eyes intent but concerned. Detective Dark Suit watched me carefully, maybe to see if my pupils dilated. Maybe he knew the eyes are a treasure trove of information. Dilation could indicate I was going to faint or tell a lie.

"What's the cause of death?" I heard myself ask.

"We don't have the autopsy results yet."

Riley nodded at the other detective, who took the hint and left, heading back to Fred Anders' lab.

I shook my head. This was going too fast. Riley indicated a chair but I didn't want to sit down, I wanted to know what had happened.

"Did Dr. Anders have a heart attack? What time did he log in?"

"He signed in around ten PM. The cleaners' log shows he was working in his lab when they stopped by at eleven last night. He asked them not to bother to clean, told them he'd been away and the place was fine. The front desk doesn't show him signing out."

Riley hadn't answered my first question. Usually, I have enough self-control to wait until I'm sure there's no more information. Not today.

"He often pulls all-nighters. Probably couldn't wait to get back to his lab bench," I babbled. "His wife is very understanding of his long hours. She's a biochemist at…." My voice trailed off as I thought of Fred's wife.

How understanding would she be when she heard her husband was dead? She'd be devastated and confused, like me, like everyone who knew Fred Anders, but she might not be suspicious. I was. This was one too many coincidences. Mary Sakamoto's warning was clear in my head. *Danger. Be careful.* Perhaps Fred's death was natural causes, people died of natural causes all the time. On the other hand, my scientific self questioned if this was something to do with Fred's work. His prototypes could be used for a lot of purposes, not only for vision therapy. Somewhere, somehow, I slotted into the equation. But what in heaven's name was the connection with Lanny? And what about Gus's accident? Okay, that could be kids running amok. Then and there I knew I had to get serious about sleuthing. No more putting it off because of work overload. Riley might have a badge and this might be official police work but I had a need to know, a personal need to find out for myself what was going on. I owed it to my godmother and now, to Fred Anders. I definitely owed it to Mary Sakamoto. Riley coughed and I jerked out of my thoughts back to the stark reality of Fred Anders' death.

"This is a shock, Dr. Kamimura," Riley said. "I'm sorry. One of the technicians came in early this morning and found him."

"Could it have been a heart attack?" I repeated, almost to myself.

"We don't know yet. Until the cause of death is established, we can't rule out murder."

"I understand."

Sad to say I did.

Riley pulled a micro-recorder out of his pocket and a notebook.

"We need to cover a few questions. Timing of your day yesterday, when you left, when you came in this morning. Last time you saw the deceased. You know the drill."

Hell's bells, yes. These days I know the damn drill.

The day went down in flames. Everyone, from students to faculty, shed tears, some surreptitiously, some openly weeping as they tried to get on with their work. Depression shrouded us like heavy dawn mist on the Hudson. Our sorrow was palpable. Fred Anders had been a beloved professor, universally liked, respected internationally. We'd lost a good, decent man. Gone was one of optometry's greats.

The police poked around gathering information but not releasing any details. I admired the skilful way they coaxed answers out of stunned people but sidestepped sharing any information. Staffer after staffer came out from interviews with dazed looks, unsure exactly what they'd said but certain they'd learned nothing significantly different from the official line. It was a relief to retreat to the Infants' Clinic for the rest of the morning and concentrate on my patients and their needs. I suppressed thoughts of the tragedy. One of the patients, super-aware the way city kids are, asked why I looked sad. I leveled with her.

"A dear friend of mine died."

She patted my arm to comfort me. That silent reassurance given with such sweet innocence almost undid me but I managed to hold it together. It wasn't until the last patient left the clinic that I could head for the bathroom and gave in to the luxury of sitting in the stall and sobbing at the loss of a dear colleague, mentor and friend.

When I shakily emerged from the bathroom, I ran into weepy clusters of people mourning the loss of Fred Anders. We were all in shock but that didn't stop rumors flying. Until the police released a statement about the cause of death we were in limbo. I didn't voice my thoughts. Although I wondered if it had been a heart attack, I also questioned whether it was yet another act of violence to add to the bizarre events since Mary Sakamoto was shot. My logical self tried to scoff at this but my creative side flitted restlessly through a forest of doom.

At my office, I found Matt and Allan standing in the hall outside Allan's office. "We're ordering pizza," Allan said. "Join us?"

They both looked quite calm and when I stared in surprise, Allan said, "You need to take a break, Yoko, while the police are here. They've locked up Anders' lab and office as tight as a drum until they figure out if it was a murder or not."

That did me in, to hear Allan talk in such a casual tone. I dug in my pocket for a tissue and frantically mopped at my wet eyes. The two men stood there, embarrassed, and the tears stopped as soon as they'd started. One tissue was enough.

"Let's go and eat. You gotta eat." Allan said.

I stifled a laugh, covering it with a cough so that guys wouldn't think I'd flipped out. But Allan sounded like my Auntie Ai, who always offered food when there were problems. Incredibly, now that Allan mentioned it, I really was hungry. The queasy stomach I'd had when I'd learned about Fred Anders' death had been quelled by two charcoal tablets. The infuriating truth is that sorrow as well as joy turns my appetite up a few notches.

"Lead on," I said, and the two smiled in relief.

Allan's right ear had his Bluetooth gizmo perched on it and as we walked down the hall to the staff room, he ordered two large pizzas, one double cheese, one sausage and peppers. Not surprisingly, the staff room was jammed. Right then and there we had an informal celebration of Fred's life. No rumors, no speculation about how he'd died. Instead, tale after tale of his beguiling English humor, his eccentric work habits and his creative genius. It was cathartic. People drifted back to their offices with obvious reluctance.

Matt and Allan and I left together and walked slowly down the hall.

"Some time I want to hear more about your retirement plans, Matt," Allan said as he turned to go to his office.

"Retirement?" I was surprised.

"A dream for the future," Matt said. "I'll sail the seas, anchor in hidden harbors."

Matt's passion for sailing, I learned, included having a boat big enough to live on. As yet he didn't have even a small boat.

"What he does have are a lot of funny stories about sailing mishaps," Allan said.

"Where do you sail?" I asked Matt.

"New Jersey mostly."

"With your cousin whose son is a better sailor than the two of you, right?" Allan asked.

Matt was quiet for a moment, then said, staring at the floor, "You know my nephew's dead."

We were silent in embarrassment, then Allan muttered an apology and changed the topic, asking if it was true that the college was scheduled to move uptown. This piece of gossip wasn't new to me but I was interested in what Matt had to say. Uptown sounded good.

"Between rent hikes here and the wish to have a location closer to Grand Central and Penn Station, it looks imminent. Still, you know politicians, a lot of talk, another committee, plenty of plans but not always any action."

"You're more a man of action?" Allan jabbed.

"I try," Matt said but the look he gave Allan was cold. Allan blinked in surprise then backtracked.

"I know you are, Matt," he said. "You organized the food drive for the homeless and keep it going year after year."

Eventually, I was able to escape to my office. Finally alone, it was impossible to stop thinking about Fred's death. If he'd died from natural causes, my worry was pointless. Was I way off track, imagining trouble where none existed? The only way I'd be satisfied was to search for the truth, but I didn't have any ideas on *how* to start. Fred's death was a terrible wake-up call. One fact I knew for sure, I'd keep any personal snooping confidential, particularly from Detective Riley.

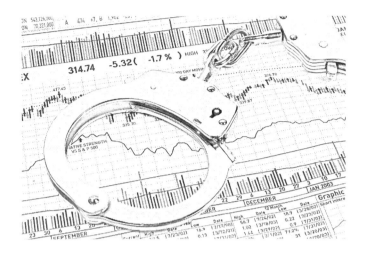

Seven

The afternoon dragged but I stuck it out until about seven. Most everyone had gone home and the place had quieted down. The mound of work still on my desk was depressing and I was ready to call it quits when the phone shrilled. I almost didn't answer it.

"Yoko, glad you're there, can you come to my office now?"

It was Dean Jackson, someone so high up the ladder that I usually met him only at official functions. Basically, after welcoming me when I joined the staff, my contact with the dean was limited to brief, impersonal conversations at gatherings for visiting dignitaries. You know the type of exchange, "How are you?" "Good speech, wasn't it?" Nonetheless, we all knew the dean was fully informed about everything that went on in the college. This was my first telephone call from him.

"I'll be right there."

What now? Must be serious.

The dean was alone. He didn't beat around the bush.

"Yoko, I know this is unexpected but we need someone to attend the conference next week in England in place of Dr. Anders. We hope you will agree to go. None of the senior faculty can get away at this time and you've been closely involved with the research and the writing of his paper for the conference. Dr. Anders told me more than once how much he valued your help."

Astounded, I stared at him for a moment and then blurted, "I don't have a passport."

I realized I'd accepted, albeit obliquely.

Dean Jackson smiled. "Not a problem. The passport office will expedite it for an extra fee." He must have remembered my modest salary because he hastily added, "SUNY will cover all expenses for the passport. Conference fees, the hotel and meals are already paid. My secretary called the travel agent and a ticket will be issued in your name. She'll make sure it reaches you promptly."

I nodded my understanding. The dean delivered a second bombshell.

"You'll have to present Dr. Anders' paper at the conference." He smiled. "Don't look so alarmed, I've every confidence in you. We're not sending you into the lion's den alone. I've spoken to Bernell, the company developing the prototypes. Dr. Steve Farge, who's leading that work, is already scheduled to attend the conference and he's agreed to join you at the podium. He will be especially helpful during the question-and-answer session."

My nod was half-hearted. The rationale behind the dean's request was understandable. However, it left out the human element, me. The thought of presenting a paper to an international audience was overwhelming.

"Can you go to the passport office first thing tomorrow?"

Again I nodded and the dean settled back in his chair, mission accomplished.

"Keep in touch with my secretary. She'll help sort out any details."

I mumbled my thanks and the dean stood. I was at the door when he spoke again.

"Yoko, I know this request is a shock. None of us has had time to come to terms with Dr. Anders' unexpected death but he'd be the first to say you're the right person to go in his place."

"Thank you, Dean Jackson," I said.

No way could I go home now. I needed to focus on the paper. I'd been working on it for so long and I wasn't entirely clueless but a burst of enlightenment would be useful. Part of the difficulty was that there was more than one prototype and I wasn't sure if I'd interpreted the last-minute changes Fred had made. Everything had taken more time than I'd anticipated. The review by several senior practitioners had also generated a little more work. I sat at my desk, sorting papers mechanically, my thoughts racing. My emotions were wildly conflicted. I hated that the opportunity came because of the death of Fred Anders, even though I knew that he, ever the pragmatic scientist, would have cheered me on. I'd felt a fraud accepting the dean's congratulations but excitement was growing in me.

The words, "When you get to England," played over and over in my head—I was trying to blot out the part about giving the paper. Thank God two of us would handle that. Farge's help with the question-and-answer session would be valuable. What a rite of passage—first time to an international conference, first trip to England, first time giving a major paper. The state meetings I'd attended were small gatherings, mostly for continuing education. I'd made presentations but I'd rather poke a sharp stick in my eye than speak to large groups. Remember, I'm an optometrist. I know the damage a stick in your eye can cause.

I looked over my schedule for the days before I had to leave for the conference. Apart from a final editing of the paper and the three mornings at the clinic, the only unusual event was Saturday's dedication of the renovations to the clinic. Rooting around in my desk I found munchies, crackers, rock-hard cheese and, joy of joy, a Larabar. I labored over the paperwork and sooner than expected was heading home, exhausted. A sense of eager anticipation mixed with dread at the thought of the upcoming trip and I decided to stop thinking about the downside of the conference and look forward to the pleasure of a visit to England. It wasn't till I reached my building that I returned to earth with a bump. Cautiously I scanned the street. Just a few pedestrians hurrying by, not remotely interested in me.

The hall was bright, the overhead fixture replaced and sporting a high-intensity bulb. No menacing figure followed me in off the street. I relaxed and took the stairs to my apartment. Tired as I was, I knew I wouldn't sleep unless I ate something more substantial than the leftovers I'd found in my desk. I microwaved a package of mac and cheese and ate while running a bath. I added a few drops of rosemary oil to the steaming hot water to ease my muscles and nerve endings and climbed in. Gradually my body unwound but now my mind picked relentlessly at the beginning of the murder and mayhem, the shooting of Mary Sakamoto and the puzzle of her warning.

Would the police ever reveal any helpful information—if they ever had any? I doubted it. I considered the question of why anyone would target me? It was true I had a stock account, all of two thousand dollars, money from the sale of the family home in Brooklyn, after my parents moved to Arizona. They had gifted me funds to pay down my college loan, insisting I invest what was left over. For weeks, I'd scanned the *Wall Street Journal* at the library, finally putting half the money into stock in Bausch & Lomb, the other half into Apple. Lenses and computers would always be useful. Maybe that investment would grow enough in a few more decades for someone to want me dead. Not now. Not enough money.

A shudder shook me. What if Mary Sakamoto's death and the attack on Lanny were related because of Lanny's connection to me? Was the death of Dr. Anders as simple as a heart attack? My sleuthing had better get off the ground fast if his death was suspicious. By now, the bath water was tepid and my hands were like prunes—time to stop obsessing. I climbed out and was putting the wooden cover back over the tub when the phone rang.

"Almost too exciting," I told Lars when he asked about my day. "The dean's sending me to a conference in England,"

"Congratulations. When do you leave?"

"Next week, on Monday. I fly back on the Saturday."

"Is it in London?"

"No. Some city on the south coast. It has a new conference center so the optometric foundation that plans these meetings got a deal."

The good news from Lars was that Lanny was holding her own. We talked for a few more minutes. The cats were curled up on the bed, anticipating my next stop. Joining them, I lay listening to their even breathing. Sleep was impossible. My mind ticked on wearily as I slipped between patches of sleep and dozing and wakefulness. The phone ringing in the kitchen brought me fully awake to morning brightness. My eyes were gritty from lack of sleep. Blearily, I focused on the clock's digital display: 7:10. An early bird. Then I heard the caller's voice. It was Lars again and he sounded really cheerful. Dashing into the other room, I picked up, yawning as I greeted him.

"Yoko, it looks as if Lanny can go home tomorrow. Any chance you can stay there, even if it's only for a few days? She'll have a nurse with her during the day, someone who is also trained in security, and I'll be there overnight for a while. I know she'd love to see you, so would I."

"Lars, that's a great idea, I'd love to," I whooped, coming awake with a surge of happiness.

The cats looked up from their food bowls, blinking in annoyed surprise, then went back to crunching dry Friskies.

"Wonderful. Look, I want to talk to you about what the doctors told me," Lars said. "I'd rather not go over it at Lanny's when she's home. Can you spring free for lunch today, meet me at the club?"

"I'll be there with bells on. I'm going to the passport office first thing this morning but after that, I'll be at the college. It'll only take me a few minutes to walk to the club."

After I dressed, I scribbled out a note for my neighbor, Larissa, asking her to look after the cats while I was at Lanny's and also when I was at the conference. She had my spare key and joked that time with my cats was her "pet fix." I decided to pack when I got home in the evening. That way, I could take my suitcase to work so that when Lanny went home, I'd go straight over to her place from the college.

It helped that I was second in line at the passport office. The process, from taking a photo to filling out forms, was speedy.

"This will be ready in forty-eight hours," the clerk said.

I arranged for the passport to be sent to the college, which the dean had suggested, saying that the college would pay any extra fee.

It was barely ten by the time I got to SUNY and settled down to some serious deskwork. Lars and I were to meet at one and it was almost that when I left to walk the few blocks to the National Arts Club. How different from the day I'd hurried to meet Lanny, the day she'd been pushed over the balcony. Today felt good because Lanny would soon be leaving the hospital. It really was beautiful, sunny and mild. The trees in Gramercy Park were unfurling tender leaves the vivid green of Granny Smith apples. Bright pansies edged the flowerbeds in the park.

Lars was walking briskly down the street towards the club as I reached its front door. I waved my arms like a maniac, not minding the stares of passersby.

We went into the lobby and up the wide marble steps of the grand staircase, passing the club's latest acquisitions, a massive nineteenth-century Japanese wood carving of a lion and tiger cavorting happily. Peter Dalton's contemporary marble of a lush-limbed female nude was close to the toothy jungle duo, a strange pairing. Lars unhooked the red velvet rope barring the way into the members' main lounge and we walked across the expanse of Persian rugs and into the bar lounge where we stopped to gaze curiously at where the iconic glass dome had been. A pale aqua silk canopy draped in graceful pleating over the gaping hole left by the dome's absence was the temporary replacement.

Val Sangrassio glanced up from behind the bar where he'd presided with tender sophistication for decades.

"Mr. Oldenburg, Yoko, welcome."

Val came hurrying to greet us, shaking our hands, relief and pleasure softening his craggy face when Lars told him Lanny would soon be leaving the hospital.

"The dining room isn't crowded," Val said. "This nice weather, more people come in of an evening."

"Special news calls for champagne, agreed, Yoko?" Lars asked.

"Twist my arm! But only one glass of bubbly, I have to go back to work."

Lunch turned into a mini-celebration with staff and a few members stopping by our table as the good news about Lanny spread. She'd been active on various club committees over the years and had a reputation as a hard worker, not a socialite prima donna but a woman who was warm and honest. Her connections had landed me the front desk job here when I was a student and I watched the familiar faces, remembering who had sharp tongues and hot tempers and who were genuinely good natured. Was anyone here involved? Had Lanny been attacked because of something she knew about one of the members or some of the behind-scenes problems forever brewing? Lars had said he didn't think so but I wasn't totally convinced.

Lars filled me in on the doctors' reports then added, "You know that the police questioned Lanny. She doesn't remember that, she doesn't even remember that you and I asked her about the attack. She doesn't remember anything about being at the club or what she was doing in the days before the attack."

I kept quiet. Words wouldn't help right now.

"The hospital is running more tests. So far, the news is good. The exact words, if I can remember them, was that 'prompt monitoring of brain pressure and the draining of excess brain fluid greatly reduced the potential effects of the injury and coma.'"

"That's good news."

"Lanny's in fair shape but the other day you mentioned possible problems. What did you mean?"

I chose my words carefully. It wouldn't do to play fast and loose with the facts and gloss over potential problems. Better that Lars knew what to expect.

"It depends on what part of the brain was damaged," I said slowly. "Problems will be neurological and Lanny may complain of blurring or double vision."

"Will they keep her longer in hospital because of that?" Lars asked.

"That's unlikely. The sooner she goes home, the sooner she can start on therapies. The good news is that the brain is often able to create new pathways, it's called neural plasticity."

I didn't dwell on the not-so-good news, that too often problems like double vision went untreated. People usually thought it would disappear as the patient improved. People were dead wrong. If double vision seemed to vanish, it was frequently the brain playing tricks and suppressing the input from one eye. I'd thought about what Lanny would need once she came out of the hospital. Top of my agenda was a thorough exam of her vision but that had to wait until she was home and started on rehabilitation.

"Any news yet on the homecoming?"

"Today or tomorrow, if there aren't any setbacks." Lars hesitated. "The doctor said she'd had several small seizures so she was put on anti-convulsant medication and has to continue that for a few more days.

Then there are the headaches. Lanny says they are terrible and nothing she's been given helps for long. I asked the doctor and he said she may have to live with them because the headaches are partly from neck strain."

"Among other things," I said, thinking of the myriad symptoms, physical and psychological, that vision dysfunction can trigger. "Give Lanny time to settle in at home. Trust me, when the time's right, I'll suggest a vision evaluation. Have the doctors explained what to expect, what adjustments may be necessary or what treatments might be appropriate?"

"No. Other than prescriptions, we don't have any special instructions."

"You said a speech pathologist was recommended?"

"Yes."

This was no time to hold back, not that I ever did. Anyone who knows me will tell you I'm outspoken, I've been that way since I was a kid, even though it goes against my parents' mantra, the one from the Japanese adage, "The nail that sticks out is hammered down." In other words, "Don't speak out. Go along to get along."

"Has anyone said that Lanny's behavior may be different?" I asked.

"No. Isn't it early to make judgments? At the hospital, they said the best thing was to make her comfortable. Relax and wait, they said. It's mild TBI."

"Mild TBI is a bit misleading. It doesn't always mean mild functional loss. What may seem like minor injury can cause serious, lasting disability."

"What do you mean, disability?"

"Dizziness, headaches, poor memory."

Lars nodded, looking more and more uneasy. I sighed. James Brady, President Reagan's press secretary, had helped raise awareness of brain injury to a national level, but most people still don't have a clue about the terrible impact TBI can have on someone's functioning.

"What exactly does 'function' mean?" Lars asked.

"Even the simplest part of Lanny's day, from brushing her teeth to dressing, may now be complex and confusing to her. Some brain cells respond selectively to faces and eyes. Damage to those cells means visual memory is impaired. It's thought that doing something for the first time may prime the brain's visual system to deal with useful information. But if it's damaged, information that was stored there can be lost."

Lars stared, puzzled. "But she *can* see and she *does* recognize me."

"True, Lars, and that's good! Still, daily chores we take for granted, showering, washing your hair, deciding what to wear, can be terribly difficult if you don't have stored memory of those functions. Sometimes, what happens after TBI can be like dementia. President Reagan had been riding horses for years, but eventually he literally forgot how to ride because dementia changed the way his brain functioned. You have to prepare for a learning curve on Lanny's part, we all do."

I suggested Lars check out the New York chapter of the Brain Injury Association of America, I knew he'd find a lot of helpful information there. We talked more about what Lanny's convalescence would involve. Only once did Lars show real anger. That emotion had been a long time coming to the surface, overlaid by another emotion, deep fear that we'd lose Lanny.

"If I ever find the man who attacked Lanny...."

I didn't say a word. From a purely selfish point of view, I didn't want to think about that man finding me. I wasn't sure what I'd do if I ever saw him again, for sure I'd call the police—after I stopped running. I'd deliberately not mentioned my pyromaniac of a mugger to Lars, he had enough to worry about. If the man who tried to set me on fire in the hall of my apartment building was the man who'd attacked Lanny, he'd found me. If so, would he return? Obviously he now knew where I lived. Lanny's tragic encounter, chance or not, had left her with TBI. It was a hair-raising prospect to consider how I might fare a second time, given the violence shown Lanny and the vicious setting of the fire in my hall.

At some point, when Lars had less to deal with, I'd talk to him about my niggling suspicion that the equipment Dr. Anders was developing might be the reason Mary Sakamoto had warned me of danger. Trouble was, it didn't make much sense. Who—other than a select few at SUNY—knew about the prototypes? And they were for vision therapy, a health care. Still, plenty of creations designed to help and heal have had their uses perverted. I'd have to think carefully about the prototypes. Beyond that, where were the connections? It was a hell of a leap to get from Mary Sakamoto to Dr. Anders. Right now, Lars needed my full support. It was crystal clear Lars and Lanny were more than good friends and that might make his adjustment to Lanny's condition all the more difficult. Many TBI victims are so different, their relationships are forced into unwelcome changes like separation and divorce.

I steered the talk to a safer place. "I'll bring you a book, *Endless Journey*, by Dr. Janet Stumbo. She was in a horrendous car crash and partially blinded and told she was TBI, with 'no hope' for change." Lars frowned and I shook my head at him. "That's not the end of the story, I'm glad to say. A learning disabilities specialist referred Dr. Stumbo to a behavioral optometrist and she got back much of her sight and vision."

"She did?" Lars said.

"It took time but once she had hope, nothing stopped Janet."

"Will I be able to understand the book?" Lars asked. "I have to ask the doctors to speak English and your field is hardly better, such techno-speak."

"Stumbo's book is user friendly," I promised. "It's written for the families of TBI victims." I glanced at the time. "I'd better get back to work. Can I do anything to help with Lanny's homecoming?"

"I've stocked up on groceries. Tina, a private nurse—and trained in security, only keep that under your hat—is coming to spend days with Lanny, help her with everything, take her to doctors' appointments and therapy and shopping. We'll try that for a few weeks, see how it goes. Lanny will be so glad to see you." He paused, then said, "I'm still inclined to believe the attack was random violence."

"Do the police agree with you, that it was random violence?" I asked the question deliberately, knowing it was vital that I was objective, open to what others thought. If I wasn't careful, I'd be seeing problems and connections where none existed.

"They seem to. I can't think of any reason why she'd be attacked. Can you?"

"I don't know, Lars. But so many crazy things have been happening, it's hard to know what to think. I'm glad you're keeping someone on the security detail." I hesitated then went on, consciously choosing my words, mindful of the effect they could have at a time when Lars was dealing with so much.

"Lanny needs rehabilitation. It will take time, Lars, don't expect an overnight recovery. Lanny's a fighter, she'll give it her best and then some. Your support will mean so much to her, even if she isn't able to tell you that for a while."

We parted outside the club and I walked the few blocks back to SUNY thinking about the drastic changes TBI victims go through.

"Nothing will ever be the same for me again," Janet Stumbo said after her terrible car accident. But she'd done more than survive, she'd prevailed and created a new life for herself. A shining example of what is possible despite TBI. I was glad Lars had suggested that I stay for a few days at Lanny's before I left for the conference in England. I'd be able to see for myself how Lanny managed her daily routine, a critical first step for any TBI victim. My happiness that the coma was over was a jubilant tidal wave that carried me through an afternoon of challenging work on Fred Anders' paper for the upcoming conference. I was finally grasping the full meaning of the equipment developed by the man who'd been the college's resident genius.

As usual, I ignored my own advice and sat for hours pecking away at the keyboard till my neck was stiff and my eyes sore, clear signals I'd put my vision system under pressure. It's simple enough to look away from the screen and into the distance every twenty minutes for a minute or two to relax your vision but who remembers? Not me, not most of the people I know. At the end of the afternoon I called the hospital.

"Any news?" I asked Dag.

"Tomorrow's the big day," he told me and laughed when I cheered.

"Tell Lanny I'll come by soon," I said. "I'm almost finished here."

On the way to the hospital, I thought about the talk Lars and I'd had at lunch. Even mild TBI means there's injury to the speed and efficiency of the way the nervous system works. On top of memory loss and lapses, it can be so hard for someone who is TBI to remember how to get from one place to the next or even remember what food one likes. Lanny would need time to develop coping skills. That's where the care-giving would come in, helping to evaluate her needs, devising ways to work around limitations. She faced a long hard road ahead. Even though I knew all this, I was filled with joy as I pushed open the door to Lanny's room.

My godmother was propped up against a mound of pillows, looking tired but awake. Her curly brown hair framed a pale face dominated by wide brown eyes. She was not tethered to any machines, they'd been pushed back to the wall. She recognized me instantly and held her arms out for a hug.

"Are you taking me home?" Lanny asked. "It's impossible to rest here." Her voice was low but clear and her words understandable but ever so slightly slurred. Medication perhaps. "I've a terrible headache and they won't give me anything for it," she was plaintive, not a tone I'd ever heard from her.

Behind us, Dag cleared his throat, probably a signal to steer away from the subject of pills for headaches.

Several times Lanny asked why she was in the hospital yet she didn't question me further when each time I told her she'd been in an accident.

"Do you remember anything about the accident?"

"No," she said.

"We were meeting at the club for lunch," I tried to prod her memory.

"Were we?"

"I came in just after you'd gone upstairs to one of the offices."

Lanny looked at me and didn't say anything.

"Andy at the front desk said some man who'd probably been to see the current show was on his way out but turned back and followed you in. He was a stranger, not a member, and Andy said he couldn't hear what was said but the man seemed angry."

"My dear, I truly cannot remember anything or even think about anything right now," my godmother said.

She closed her eyes wearily, and was asleep instantly. I kissed her cheek and fussed with smoothing her covers, reluctant to leave. Finally, I walked over to where Dag sat.

"I guess everyone's asked every possible way if she remembers anything about the attack?"

"Yes," Dag said. "Lars even suggested I ask a few questions if I thought there was a good time to do so but I'm afraid there hasn't been one yet."

"It's a relief to see Lanny awake and unhooked from all the equipment. Has she been given something for the headaches?"

Dag nodded. "Whatever they try, nothing lasts. Her headaches must be terrible."

"That's not good," I said, filing the information away. Something other than medication might help. Chiropractic work or shiatsu, the Japanese version of acupuncture. No needles in shiatsu, only skillful finger pressure on the body.

"Tomorrow's the big day, homeward bound?"

"If she continues stable, Mrs. O can leave then."

"Welcome news."

"Tina, the private nurse, was in today—you know she's trained in security, also?"

I nodded.

"Tina's been on rotation with me for several days so she and Mrs. Oldenburg can get to know each other. Tina'll come back tomorrow and help take Mrs. O home if all goes well. As you see, rest is needed." He hesitated then continued, lowering his voice. "Her attention span is, well…fractured is the word that comes to mind. So far, she doesn't remember the attack. She definitely has amnesia about that day and the days before it, and she rarely remembers what she's told, even a moment later."

"That's classic with TBI," I said. "If there's frontal lobe damage, it's the short-term memory that's affected. Rehabilitation takes time and work but it's possible."

I told Dag I'd call the next day to see if Lanny was actually going home and thanked him for all he'd done to look after her while she was in the hospital.

"It's one of the quietest duties I've ever had," he confessed. "The consulate can be hectic between visiting dignitaries and UN activities. While I was here, I read a lot."

The next morning I was at my desk just before 8 AM. Minutes after I settled down to work, the call came from Lars.

"Lanny has the doctors' blessings to leave. Tina and I will take her home soon."

"Fantastic. I'll see you tonight. I've got my suitcase so I'll come over after work."

That evening, I was anxious to leave. Even though I had more to do to prepare for the conference, it was mostly revisions and polishing. As I thought about what other uses there might be for the equipment Fred Anders had created, I realized I probably had information the police did not. Ought I to call Dan Riley and mention my suspicions? It was possible he'd dismiss my suspicions the way he'd dismissed my concern about Mary Sakamoto's warning of danger. I certainly didn't have any evidence. No, I damn well wasn't going to call the police, why waste time, mine and his? Then it struck me. If I really was serious about this suspicion, I ought to do something to protect the information about Fred Anders' work. Usually, I'd back up everything I'd written about the prototypes on a flash drive and lock that in the filing cabinet in my office or, if I had time of an evening, I'd take the flash drive home to see if I could get some more work done. From here on, I'd always take the flash drive with me when I left the college. That decision felt satisfying, almost as if I'd made some progress, though all I'd done was take a precaution. What was it a precaution against? Probably nothing, time would tell.

By now, it was five, and although often I worked late, I was eager to see Lanny back on home turf. It was time to leave. Staying at 34 Gramercy Park, the first cooperative building in New York, would be like old times, when I was a student, working evenings at the club. Back then, I'd leave the club after my shift, walk the half block to Lanny's and stay overnight. In the morning, I only had to walk the few blocks to college. A perfect arrangement. The spacious apartment where Lanny lived alone since the death of her husband and daughter was one of the few that remained true to the architect's 1895 plans. Most of the original units, which had rambled grandly, three to a floor, had been carved up into smaller apartments. Ceilings in the Queen Anne style building still soared magnificently and windows and the ornate, brass-hinged doors had matching proportions.

The original staff quarters on the top floor, small, low-ceilinged rooms, had been converted into an apartment for the super and his family. The super, who ran the place with meticulous care, loved the personal side of the building's history and was proud of former residents like Margaret Hamilton, whose most famous role had been as the Wicked Witch of the West in "The Wizard of Oz." The locals said she was charming in person. As for James Cagney, turned out he definitely was not a tough guy in real life.

When I rang the front door bell, the doorman peered out from his cubby at the opposite end of the cavernous lobby. He recognized me and buzzed the door open, not bothering to amble the length of the hall. He stepped into the elevator after me and prepared to take me up. The place, built by the man who developed Gramercy Park to induce people to move downtown and into the building, still had an Otis hand-run elevator, the last in the country, a gem of inlaid wood and mirrors. All the operator had to do to run the elevator was tug gently on the cable. Usually the takeoff or landing was silk-smooth, unless you got the old timer who enjoyed a jug or two of wine of an evening. Then you were guaranteed a bumpy ride. Every ride had background music of clanks and wheezes as you rose or descended at a leisurely pace.

Lars let me in and I took my case to my old room. The apartment was in the shape of a capital *L*. The enormous, formal living room on the short stroke of the *L* overlooked Gramercy Park, so did the two small rooms next to the living room. These were opposite a bathroom and a small butler's pantry. The long part of the *L* had a vast kitchen and next to it was a cozy family room. Then came two generous bedrooms and a second bathroom. The furniture was warm wood, Scandinavian style, the curtains, chairs and couch in the brilliant fabrics Swedes use to brighten their long, somber winters. After I dropped my case in my old room, I found Lars in the kitchen, snacking on dark bread coated with blackberry jam, no butter—his country's national memory of food shortages from centuries of war, nothing to do with calories or cholesterol levels.

"Lanny went to bed right after she got home, she was exhausted. She's been resting ever since. Tina left some time ago," he told me. "For some reason, I'm exhausted, too. How about I whip up a cheese omelet?"

I watched as he moved around the kitchen and my nose twitched at the aroma of butter sizzling in the pan. We ate and talked more about Lanny's rehabilitation.

"When will we get the old Lanny back?" Lars asked.

"Give Lanny time to settle in, she'll be different in many ways," I said, rather than give him the bald truth that we might never see the old Lanny. "I put that book, *Endless Journey*, by Janet Stumbo, on the hall table for you."

Lars stared at me for a long moment then nodded in tired acceptance.

The next morning, I left before anyone else was up. Lars and I had both gone to bed early and I woke at the crack of dawn, enthusiastic about starting the day. SUNY was tranquil at this time in the morning, not many people in yet, and I was deep in work when the phone rang. It was Beth Bazin. We'd graduated together and kept in touch, although she was in private practice in New Jersey.

"Is the place crawling with government types?" she demanded.

"Here? Government types?" I was at a loss.

"You haven't heard about Matt Wahr?"

My heart sank. Someone else out of commission?

"Beth, it's not even nine. News circulates later when people gather for coffee. What's up?"

"Some Albany politician was picked up in a sting operation. He's given Matt's name in return for an immunity deal. Story is a lot of fiddling was going on, books being cooked. The auditors swooped down on the college late yesterday afternoon with agents from the Department of Finance and checked Matt's office and found discrepancies in the records. It looks as though he's the only person who could be responsible. Matt denied it but he's been locked out of his office, told to wait at home until they finish going over the files. Didn't I always say he had unplumbed depths?"

The news took my breath away. I couldn't remember anything remotely like it happening at the college. Beth's source had to be her husband. An ad executive, he worked in mid-town and car-pooled in from the suburbs with one of the college administrators.

"As I recall, you always said Wahr was a dreamboat and you were sorry he was married," I teased Beth. "What sort of discrepancies?"

"Major. Fiddling the taxes. Big question is, who was getting the loot? I'm relying on you to check out what people are saying. It doesn't seem possible, does it? We always thought Matt was one of the best, we all did. Whoever did this, it's a disaster for the college."

I agreed. Theft, if that's what it was, would hit hard. Our budget was perennially anemic, every dollar stretched thin. Was I ever glad my responsibilities were clearly defined. I wore two hats. As one of the optometrists at the Infants' Clinic, I examined patients, gave them vision therapy and kept their charts current. As a researcher, I worked on whatever projects my boss assigned me. I had absolutely no connection with administrative or financial matters and always had pitied those involved with the college's budgetary workings.

Promising Beth I'd get back to her as soon as I had any news, I headed for the staff lounge on a scouting mission. Coffee was a good enough excuse to mingle. How had I missed the arrival of the auditors the previous day? Then I realized that usually Matt Wahr or Allan were my sources of news and gossip and I hadn't seen either after lunch.

I didn't have to go far. Halfway to the lounge, I caught up with Martin Collins walking down the hall deep in conversation with Len Preston. Both were senior faculty. They stopped talking when I caught up with them but read the knowledge and query on my face.

"You've heard," Dr. Collins said gloomily. He waved us into his office and closed the door firmly.

"The dean's preparing a statement. Until further notice, no one's to fraternize with Wahr."

'Is it definitely Matt?" I asked.

The two men exchanged looks.

"It looks that way," Dr. Preston said finally. "It's alleged, you understand."

White-collar crime. I thought of all the patients who could have been helped, all the corners we'd trimmed, all the equipment we could have afforded with that money.

"Any idea how much is involved?"

"Too much. Yoko, we must keep a tight lid on this. Some details will be public knowledge soon enough but beyond that, do your best to neutralize any rumors, particularly with students."

I walked back to my office, leaving the faculty lounge for later. The sooner I gave Beth accurate news and the all-important warning, the sooner the grist mill would have truth for grinding. She was busy and our conversation was short. All afternoon, students stopped by my office with questions. I let them ramble but corrected flights of fancy. Predictably, people were upset, outraged and titillated in equal part, most defending Wahr, certain he could not have done wrong. He was well liked and it was hard to believe he'd steal from the college.

Allan kept popping in and out like a damn yo-yo. Fact-finding missions, he said, but before he'd share his news, he'd quiz me about what I'd heard. Only then would he tell me what his latest visitor had said. He alternated between sad and angry.

"How could Matt do this? We thought he was a man of integrity. How terrible to steal from us."

"Allan, it's not proven," I reminded him. "Remember, innocent until proven guilty."

"You're too generous, Yoko. From all I heard, there's little doubt that Matt is implicated in fraud." He tapped his nose knowingly. He wouldn't say more and for the nth time I wondered how he always had the latest news.

By the time the day was over, I was starving and I was down to pretzel crumbs. I was eager to get back to Lanny's to see how she'd coped with her first day at home. I called and left a message on her answering machine that I'd bring in deluxe subs, one sausage and cheese, the other grilled veggies. Foraging for breakfast that morning, I'd spotted salad makings in the fridge so dinner was set. I let myself into the apartment quietly and as I walked through to the kitchen, a young woman came out of Lanny's bedroom at the end of the corridor, closing the door softly behind her.

"You must be Tina, is Lanny resting?" I asked, introducing myself.

"Sleeping, she's exhausted," Tina answered. "It's a combination of being home, welcome though that is, and medication. Plus she has a definite tendency to try to do too much."

"Doesn't want to give in and admit she's tired?"

"Exactly," Tina agreed. She eyed the packages I held. "Smells good. Salad's ready in the kitchen. I ate with Lanny but I can sit with you and tell you what happened today. Lanny managed really well. She handled the move from the hospital to home base with a minimum of fuss but she does complain a lot about serious headaches."

The details were much as I'd expected. Tina, a nurse as well as trained in security, had experience caring for other TBI survivors and was prepared for the bursts of bad temper and frustration over even simple tasks. When Tina was ready to leave, we tiptoed down the hall and peeked in on Lanny, who lay fast asleep, her face tranquil and relaxed.

Lars arrived as Tina was on her way out and I left them to their quick conversation.

'Lanny, you, and extra-long subs, my lucky day," Lars said when he joined me in the kitchen. We sat rehashing what Tina had told us. Lars admitted he was dismayed at Lanny's spotty memory.

"She forgets the simplest thing almost immediately. She always had a good memory. When will it come back?"

"That's a tough one," I said. "She's on a learning curve, a re-learning curve. Give her time. She'll start therapy soon and you'll see changes."

"You warned me," Lars said. "It's so hard to accept the difference in her. It's like she's another person."

"She really isn't the same and may not ever be the person you once knew. Accepting that is a challenge for her and everyone else."

There, I'd said the dread words, that Lanny might never be the same person that we'd known and loved. I had faith that Lanny and all of us who knew and loved her would surmount the challenges of her TBI.

"Yoko, would you mind going up to the super's apartment?" Lars asked after we'd rinsed the dishes. "Let him know it's okay to fix the disposal unit in the kitchen sink tomorrow, any time he wants. Normally, I'd not bother him after five but he left a note asking me to let him know this evening. I think he really wants to hear about Lanny. Besides, he'll be glad to see you."

The resident super, Ian Campbell, a gruff-sounding Scot, ran the building with an iron hand conspicuously lacking a velvet glove. Yet underneath his brusque manner was the proverbial heart of gold. He went fishing once a month and moist parcels of the day's catch appeared on your doormat if you were in his good graces. His father, a World War II veteran, had spent time in Japan with MacArthur and passed on to his family a liking for soba noodle soup and sushi. I always had a warm welcome from Mr. Campbell.

When I reached the hall, I could hear the hum of the elevator on its way up. It stopped on the floor below and then someone rang for it from the ground floor. Rather than wait, I took the stairs. The elevator didn't go to the top floor anyhow, since that had originally been maids' rooms. The super's wife said her husband was in the furnace room. After I'd told her Lanny was home and doing well, I clattered back down the stairs to the basement. The super was coming out of the enormous room where the furnace, a goddess of heat two stories tall, was housed. Lars was right, the super wanted to know about Lanny.

"I'm very happy to hear the news," he told me, his r's a purring resonance. "Give Mrs. Oldenburg and her brother-in-law my regards. I'll stop by tomorrow for that sink unit, lassie." I hovered, hoping for one of his historical gems. Over the years, the super had entertained me with stories of the building's famous residents. Apparently, Jimmy Cagney had owned a ground-floor apartment that backed on to the small courtyard where the trashcans were stacked "Must have been infernally noisy when they picked up the trashcans," the super had mused, "but that man never complained."

He didn't disappoint me this time. "Did I ever tell you that we had Albert Schweitzer visiting in this very building for several days? Truly a fine man. Perhaps he'd have recommended something to help Mrs. Oldenburg." The r's rolled magnificently.

I left the super and walked down the long corridor away from the furnace room. The faint echo of the elevator buzzer was audible, someone in the entrance hall ringing for a ride. I decided to take the stairs back to Lanny's, this way I'd get the exercise I was missing by not being at home. I was on the last flight up from the basement when a man rounded the corner from the entrance hall. He began to descend the stairs, I continued up. About half way, we drew level with each other and I was about to step around him but my heart damn near stopped when I glanced up and saw who it was on the stairs—it was the man who'd attacked Lanny at the National Arts Club.

What the hell? Was he after Lanny again? Or had he tracked me down?

Eight

His silhouette had been etched deep on my mind's eye from the day I'd seen Lanny callously pushed over the gallery railing at the club. That menacing shadow had moved dimly, terribly, through my nightmares. Here was harsh reality. The man raised one hand and I didn't wait to find out what the gesture meant. Atavistic rage burst out of me in a piercing cry and I surged forward, pounding the man's chest. We careened against the wall and fell heavily on the stone stairs in a tangle of arms and legs. I struggled to get free, suddenly mindful I was being beyond foolish. What was I thinking, tackling such a dangerous man? I took off for the basement and met Mr. Campbell hurrying up the stairs, all bristling energy.

"What's wrong?"

"Man…knocked me down," I gasped, pointing up the stairs.

Ian Campbell didn't hesitate.

"Never on my watch," he said and took off. A ripe Scottish curse floated behind him. I hung on to the heavy brass stair rail as I labored back up the stairs, fuzzy-headed but not in serious pain. My exploring fingers found a tender place on my forehead but I wasn't bleeding. I made it to the hall to find the super and the doorman standing by the open elevator, flanking a third man.

When I saw the man I'd taken for Lanny's attacker, I stared incredulously. It was Matt Wahr. This was not the jaunty figure from SUNY's halls but a disheveled, disconcerted man. We eyed each other in surprise and Wahr asked, concern on his face.

"Are you all right, Dr. Kamimura? I'm not sure how we collided."

The super looked curiously from me to Wahr and the three men waited for my answer. Staring at Wahr, I saw how I'd made such a colossal error. Wahr's build was similar, even the shape of his head was identical to that of Lanny's attacker. Trouble was, an awful lot of Manhattan's male population fit that mold. The differences between Wahr and the brute at the club were glaringly obvious in the strong light of the hall. Wahr's head was balding, his hair wispy, Lanny's attacker had a curly thatch, which I'd seen when he and Lanny were struggling above me in the gallery. I'd also seen the attacker's head from the back when I viewed the video of him exiting the club and the man definitely had a full head of hair. Now that I'd literally crashed into Wahr in a place where I never expected to see him, it was clear my perceptions were jittery and had played tricks.

What a blunder. I felt a total dummy.

"You know this man, Dr. Kamimura?" the super asked.

"Yes," I muttered.

"Are you here to visit Dr. Kamimura?" the super asked Wahr, his tone polite but not pleasant.

I frowned. Good point. Exactly why was Wahr here?

"No, I'm Matt Wahr. Are you Mr. Campbell?"

The super nodded.

"I telephoned earlier and you suggested I drop by around this time," Wahr said to him. "I headed for the basement like you said and Dr. Kamimura was on her way up. Somehow we collided."

Now it was my turn to stare from Wahr to Ian Campbell. Was Wahr planning on moving into the building? 34 Gramercy Park was a coop, not a condo, residents bought their apartments but not the land under it. It was against the rules to rent out your place but it did happen now and then. The typical cover story was that a relative or close friend was conveniently staying in the apartment while you were on a trip. If Wahr was planning on hiding at 34, it was a strange place to choose, so close to SUNY, now that Wahr was officially not welcome at the college.

Wahr watched me uneasily, perhaps wondering if I was going to say anything about the fraud charge hanging over him.

"Are you thinking of moving in to this building?" I asked.

"No. I'm here to see Mr. Campbell about something else," Wahr said.

I made one of those split-second decisions that sometimes rear up later and bite you in the ass big time. I didn't want to hassle the guy. Innocent till proved guilty is good enough for me.

"The dean wants to hear from you."

That was all I said. I didn't offer an apology or an explanation for charging Wahr on the stairs. I moved towards the elevator, making it clear I was done. The super took charge.

"I'll walk you to the door," Mr. Campbell said and put one large hand under Wahr's arm and set off for the front door.

"Best get yourself upstairs, put some ice on that head," the super called to me. He and Wahr walked to the street door, where they stood talking. I got into the elevator, glad to collapse on the bench against the back wall.

"Mr. Campbell's right, you need something cold on your head," the doorman said as he started the elevator.

One look at me when Lars opened the apartment door and he saw something was wrong. He searched the fridge for the aloe vera gel and gently spread it on the swelling on my forehead. It felt tender to his touch but I knew from experience the gel worked wonders.

"You look as if you've seen a ghost," he said.

"That's just it," I said, holding an icepack wrapped in a kitchen towel to my forehead when Lars was done smearing on aloe vera. "For one dreadful nanosecond, I thought the man who attacked Lanny at the club was right here, on the stairs when I was coming up from the basement."

Lars sat down heavily. "Dear God."

"I was wrong. The lighting was low and I guess my nerves are still stretched tight," I said and reminded Lars about the full head of hair on

Lanny's attacker. "Matt Wahr doesn't have a full head of hair, just a few straight wisps."

"It must have been a terrible shock," Lars said as he made us comfrey tea, a remedy Swedes recommend for soothing the nerves. Sipping the warm tea, I filled him in on how I'd mistaken Wahr for the attacker, then I told Lars about the news of Wahr's white-collar crime.

"It's alleged but since the problem with the financial records was discovered, he hasn't been at the college. He was asked to stay away and is supposed to be at home but apparently he's been AWOL."

Before Lars could comment, Lanny walked into the kitchen, a cherry red housecoat snugly belted round her waist. She smiled at us.

"Mind if I join you?"

Lars and I scrambled for cookies and another mug, happy to see her, but she only lasted a few minutes.

"That awful headache is back, I have to lie down," and Lanny walked slowly out of the kitchen.

"Let me help you with the pain pills," Lars poured a glass of water and hurried down the hall after her.

"They're useless," Lanny said.

"Why don't the pills help?" Lars asked me when he came back to the kitchen.

"I suspect the cause could be structural," I answered. "See if Tina can take Lanny to the chiropractor you went to for the back trouble you had last year."

I didn't want to make promises, but if medication wasn't helping, possibly a chiropractor could make changes for the better.

At college the next morning, the bump on my head wasn't noticeable. It had shrunk to almost nothing through the magic of the aloe vera gel, which also stopped any bruising. The mountain of work I had to get ready for the conference in England was almost complete so I settled down in front of the computer for what I hoped was the final tweaking and polishing of the paper about the prototypes. The peculiar encounter with Matt Wahr was the last thing on my mind but it flooded back when I had a surprise call from Detective Riley.

"Morning, hope you're enjoying your home away from home? How's Mrs. Oldenburg?"

How weird that he knew I was staying with Lanny. Had he talked to Lars? Was I under surveillance? I hid my surprise.

"She's doing well, considering."

"I'm calling because we have some new information about Mary Sakamoto."

I took a deep breath. Was there finally some light on the mystery?

"Occasionally, she worked for several of the execs who were top aides to Ken Lay of Enron fame. Even after that scandal, those guys are living high on the hog. Mary Sakamoto went from one home to the other, fitting cocktail dresses, tuxedos, that sort of thing. Ring any bells?"

"Not one," I said. "I still can't fathom what connection she thought she had with me or why she'd think there was danger."

"Let me know if something does occur to you," Riley said. "How's life at the college? The fraud squad say the finance manager is in trouble."

"Yes, it's hard to believe. Matt Wahr has always seemed a regular guy."

"The usual candidates, money, revenge, sex, any one can turn regular guys inside out,' Riley said.

I decided to tell him about the bruising tangle with the college's discredited man of finance. Perhaps it would make me feel better about not mentioning my suspicions that the prototypes might be the cause for some of the strange events in the all-too recent past.

"I'll make a note in the file," Riley said. "It might help to see if there's a pattern. Why don't you ask the building super why Wahr visited him? If Wahr's a crook, maybe he didn't tell the truth about not moving into the building, though now that you've seen him there, it's not much of a hiding place."

I said I'd talk to the super and that was the end of the conversation.

In the cold light of day the mishap with Wahr was more like an unsettling mistake. Shrugging, I turned back to my preparations for the conference. My revisions to Fred Anders' paper were as good as they were going to get. It was ready for review by the dean, who'd have some of Fred's peers critique it. The equipment Fred had created was worthy of prize-winning attention and it hurt to think that the man who'd labored so long had died before he saw his work put to practical use. He'd known the tests promised well and he'd told me a few weeks earlier that Bernell, the Indiana manufacturer, never took on any project without independent analysis.

"Too much money at stake," Fred had said, adding that the company's president had called to share the glowing recommendations of a panel of behavioral optometrists from colleges in California, Pennsylvania and Illinois. "Peer review pleases me more than commercial interest," Fred said.

The rest of the week before I was to leave for England was a blur. Days of intense work were balanced by quiet evenings with Lars and Lanny. Lars and I listened carefully to Lanny's comments about what doctor she'd seen, what hurdle she'd crossed. Lanny's trauma was considered mild but that didn't make her rehabilitation straightforward or easy.

Lanny had started the rounds of specialists. She tired easily but was cooperating with Tina, who made sure Lanny had plenty of rest. TBI victims can sometimes be difficult to persuade to tackle the hard work of rehabilitation, not Lanny. Part of this was the type of injury to her brain, part it was her relationship with Lars, which was wonderful motivation. Lanny was determined to meet the enormous challenge of regaining a normal life.

Her excruciating headaches, the ones she'd been warned she might have for the rest of her life, had been eliminated by a chiropractor. X-rays showed that the top vertebra of her spinal column was almost dislocated. Skilful chiropractic manipulation sent Lanny home in happy tears. As is often the case in TBI, Lanny's long-term memory was vivid but her short-term memory was almost non-existent, which worried her and she was working hard to learn how to cope.

"The most important thing in my life right now is this notebook," Lanny said, holding up a small black book. "I keep it with me all the time and write down my schedule so I know what I have to do."

We finished our meal of green beans and Swedish meatballs, ✉ the house specialty that Lanny had no problem remembering, although putting together the ingredients and making the meatballs was hard for her. Lars discreetly helped Lanny find and measure ingredients. Something as simple as setting the oven heat baffled Lanny but Lars was there, ever ready to help. As soon as we'd finished eating, Lanny hugged me and went to bed, tired from her day.

"I'm just so damn glad she's out of the hospital. She's coming along, isn't she?" Lars said.

"Yes, she is," I said, full of gratitude at Lanny's progress.

"What about the visual analysis you said she might need?"

"It's early days yet," I said. "Lanny's going through a developmental process. She has to redevelop the tone and function of her gross musculature before she gains control of the fine muscles."

"How long will that take?"

"It's hard to say. Right now, the physical therapy is what she needs. The simpler the activity, the more frustrating for her when she finds it difficult. That's why she can be cranky sometimes. It's tough having problems with coordination and balance when you're an adult. Perhaps she'll be ready for a visual exam in a few more weeks, she still needs plenty of rest."

Lars nodded thoughtfully but didn't let the matter drop.

"What will you learn from that exam?"

"It'll help us understand how she's functioning," I explained. "The visual system is a relationship of sensory-motor functions throughout the body. Because the brain is the organizer and control center, if you insult the cortex, you cause problems with the way you function."

"I didn't know vision was so complicated," Lars said. "Lanny's not permanently disabled, is she?"

"No, thank God," I said, grateful Lanny had been spared that. "But her life has been changed. Some TBI survivors go back to the work they were doing before, some don't or can't. So much depends on the individual and the rehabilitation."

"You're easier to understand than the medics and a lot more positive."

"That's because I've seen TBI rehabilitation fly in the face of zero hope predictions. The specialists are often reluctant to talk about the future. I believe Lanny can regain a lot of her old lifestyle. It takes patience and perseverance and a strong support system. Lanny has all that."

At last it was the day before I was scheduled to fly to England. The conference material was ready and I had one task left, the pleasant one of going to the dedication ceremony. All I had to do was show up, enjoy free food and listen to speeches thanking donors. The Infants' Clinic had been able to replace equipment and chairs and refurbish the treatment rooms, all long overdue, and the fund-raising committee had organized a sit-down meal. I found the staff room transformed by flowers and table-cloths. The long head table was filled with bigwigs and there weren't many seats left at the six small tables. Dr. Forrest came hurrying over when he saw me.

"Yoko, I need your help, will you keep an eye on the rep from the police? They raised quite a donation. Besides, you two are the only ones here under the age of sixty." He took my arm and led me to where a tall man sat at a half-empty table.

"Dan Riley, I believe you've met my colleague, Yoko Kamimura." My boss pulled out the chair to the left of Riley, courteously ushered me onto the seat and abandoned me. Riley grinned at my obvious surprise.

"Dr. Forrest said you'd be here," he said. "Shall we get some food before it's too late?"

The x-ray look was gone, the voice was friendly. Fine, two could play that game. We filled our plates at the buffet and returned to the table, small talk all the way. Either Dan Riley was a good actor or he was genuinely relaxed and glad to be at the dedication. I was tempted to ask if there was any new information about the woman who'd been murdered but decided not to go there, why spoil a pleasant meal? Riley didn't have any such qualms.

"Any insight into what's been going on since the street shooting?" he asked, casually enough, eyes steady on me.

"I wish I did," I said. The tone of my voice was believable and Riley nodded acceptingly. I felt somewhat guilty at not sharing my suspicions, nebulous though they were, but I reminded myself I didn't have a shred of proof. If I did find out something to back them up, I'd tell Riley, I promised my conscience.

"You're off to a conference in England?" the detective asked.

It no longer surprised me that Dan Riley had a handle on what was going on in my life. Between Dr. Forrest and the various police departments, he probably had regular updates on my daily activities I thought gloomily.

"Yes," and I smiled at the thought of the upcoming trip.

"You can e-mail me if you remember something about any of the various, ah, situations," Riley said. He gave me his card—again. The speeches began and we were quiet. The ceremony was a success and as soon as I could, I slipped away, leaving Dan chatting to my boss.

The evening at Lanny's apartment was peaceful and when Lanny headed for bed early, so did I. My flight didn't leave till 6 PM but I had to be at the airport by mid-afternoon so I spent most of the morning with Lanny and Lars then walked downtown to buy more cat food.

"You won't starve," I told the cats, "I'll only be gone a week but there's enough food here for a month." The cats still stared reproachfully so I opened a can of tuna and gave them each a huge spoonful. Larissa, my neighbor, had promised to spend time with them each day and I scribbled her a note, asking her to give them the rest of the tuna the next day.

Finally I was on the plane and heading across the Atlantic. The meal had been cleared away and cabin lights turned low. A lucky few were napping. The optometrists on board were scattered in different rows. I recognized several from the photos with their journal articles, Steve Gallop from Pennsylvania and Sam Berne from New Mexico. I watched our flight path develop on the individual screen in front of me and relaxed. Lanny was home and doing well, I'd be out of the country for a week, what a welcome change from recent events.

Someone tapped on my shoulder and I looked up into the friendly eyes of Bob Bertolli. He was attending the conference in place of Gus Forkiotis, who was still on crutches. We stood in the aisle and talked. First thing Bob asked about was the financial scandal at SUNY—good news travels. I gave him the party line and said that the chances of recovering the money were slim but insurance would cover the loss.

"The fact that there's insurance makes the theft a federal offence, so the financial manager could get a prison sentence," I explained.

"Really? I heard Wahr disappeared, true?"

"His wife says she doesn't know where he is, apparently he's not living at home."

I'd told Lars and Dan Riley about Wahr's unexpected appearance at 34 Gramercy Park but had put that strange encounter out of my mind. The police knew about it, that was good enough for me. The past few days had been so hectic as I prepared for the trip to England, I'd forgotten to ask the super why Wahr had been visiting him.

"I don't see any one else from SUNY, are you the only representative?"

"Yes, no one else could spring free at such short notice after Dr. Anders' death. Final exams and state boards are coming up. Do you know Steve Farge?" I asked. "He's head of research and development at Bernell."

"Only by reputation. Most of the companies that sell visual training equipment and supplies have booths and sales staff at these conferences. Why?"

"He's involved in the manufacture of Dr. Anders' prototypes and is going to help me present the paper on the prototypes and handle questions and answers."

We chatted about the journal papers he and Gus were preparing and then, satisfied we'd caught up, Bob moved on down the aisle to chat with someone else. I looked over the information about Bournemouth. Aerial photos showed curving sandy beaches and cliffs dotted with palm trees from the tropical Gulf Stream that blew over that part of the coast. Swimming weather it wasn't but beach walks would be a pleasant change from Manhattan streets.

The outline of the eleventh-century Christchurch Priory was dramatic against the sky in one photo. My interest kicked up a notch when I read that one of the tours went to a cemetery where Mary Shelley's grave was located. When I was ten, I'd discovered *Frankenstein*. I've moved on from monster tales, now I'm into mysteries like those by Naomi Hirahara, whose writing beckons me deep into my roots, the worlds of the *Issei*, *Nisei* and *Sansei*—the first, second and third generations of Japanese born in America.

I drowsed for the rest of the flight.

Nine

Stark predawn greeted us at Heathrow, where it was barely 6 AM. My biorhythm was still set on New York's 1 AM, but fatigue was easy to ignore in the excitement of being in England. The airport officials were courteous but like us were in a state of borderline wakefulness. We shuffled along, first producing passports then waiting to claim luggage. The suitcases came out quickly, though I may have catnapped as I stood drowsily watching the cases slide by on the conveyer belt. Passengers around me yawned and stretched, glad to be off the plane. A bright-eyed courier whose nametag identified him as Stuart stood waiting for us as we exited. He flourished a sign, "OEPF Conference." Gathering the nine optometrists who'd been on the flight, he shepherded us to a small bus.

"We'll take the M25 out of London then head south on the M3," Stuart said as he slid into the driver's seat. "It's ninety miles to Bournemouth."

The motorway was modest compared to American freeways. The vehicles zipping by looked as if they were part of a giant's play set. I wasn't bothered they were on the other side of the road, I didn't have to drive. Traffic was heavy as the bus wove through London's outskirts but few pedestrians were out this early on a windy morning. Gradually, the buildings dwindled. In their place were fields, some covered with brilliant green grass, others were dotted with horses or sheep. Occasionally, I saw dark furrowed earth through which the tips of young crops showed. Hedges bordered the mosaic of fields.

Gentle snores came from Horrie Humphreys next to me. A Canadian, he'd been inspired by the forensic optometric work of Gus Forkiotis and Bob Bertolli. After visiting them in Connecticut, he'd taken a postdoctoral course in behavioral optometry at Yale's Gesell Institute. Offered a position at the institute, he'd stayed. His snoring was soothing and my eyelids drooped in Pavlovian response but I resisted sleep, too much to see. For the first time in weeks, I wasn't worrying about Mary Sakamoto's warning of danger. Lanny was home and recuperating and I could relax and enjoy the trip.

Around 8 AM a radio message came over the bus's intercom. I caught some of the words, "Major accident... detour."

The courier told us there was a multi-vehicle accident ahead on the A31.

"We're approaching the outskirts of Bournemouth but there's a tailback," he said. "Articulated lorry tangled with a horse van."

Horrie Humphreys woke with a start at the radio's crackling and heard the message.

"Traffic's backed up," he translated. "A tractor trailer crashed into a horse trailer."

"We'll reroute through the New Forest, the scenic approach," Stuart said cheerfully. "It's off the motorway and a bit slower but better than twiddling our thumbs for hours on the A31. We're too early for the heather, by late July the heath will be purple with it, but the early rhododendrons are almost out. My daughter and her husband live in the New Forest, on Buddle Hill. He's one of the verderers."

"What's a verderer?" someone called out.

"Comes from the Norman word, "vert" or "green." It refers to woodland. The verderers are the officials who deal with the care of common land in areas that are the Crown's. The Royal Court of Verderers was founded in 1877."

He waited for the murmur of interest to fade and added, "My son-in-law's family has grazing rights for ponies and other animals."

"What does the Royal Court of Verderers actually do?" was the next query.

"They watch over the habitat and the health of the animals, we've got everything from donkeys and ponies to cows and other cattle."

"Cattle grazing? Like a cattle ranch?"

"Not rightly a business, more like extra income. The family's got ponies in the New Forest near Fordingbridge. In August, the verderers hold an annual pony sale."

We turned off the motorway and onto a narrow road that wound through open land of gentle hills, clumps of ferns and windswept trees. At one place, our way was blocked by four or five small ponies straggled across the road and our bus came to a stop. The ponies paid no attention to our vehicle but stood companionably nose to shoulder, their shaggy coats and rough manes the soft grays, browns and blacks of the downs. Stuart didn't touch the horn and soon the ponies ambled to the side of the road and we drove slowly past them.

"Don't the ponies get hit by cars?" Amile Francke asked.

"Accidents do happen, though the ponies have right of way," Stuart said. "In busy parts of the forest, fences have been put up so the animals can't cross the roads there. They don't venture near where it's built up, round market towns like Ringwood. Mind you, quite a few ponies have been hit by golf balls but they still wander close to the golf courses."

"How is it the ponies have right of way?" I asked.

"This is the New Forest. It was created by William the First in 1079 for a royal hunting ground. Royally offended the farmers, he did. They were mostly tenant farmers and crofters, and Rufus—the king's nickname because of his red hair—kicked people off their farmland and planted trees so he could go hunting. In return for taking the land, certain rights were given forest people. A stray arrow killed Rufus, so you could say that hunting caused his death. Course, there's some as says the arrow was shot deliberately, which would make it treason."

"It's an historic riddle, like who killed Kennedy?" Bob Bertolli said.

"Perhaps," Stuart allowed

"If the forest belongs to the queen, are we on royal ground?" someone asked.

Stuart shook his head. "Not necessarily. The New Forest is just over a hundred square miles. Forty-four belong to the crown. The whole place became a national park in 2005."

"The land is so open, doesn't look much like a forest."

"We're in an open area, part heath, part bog," Stuart said. "The crown's land is the most wooded, beech and oak, trees that provided timber that built a royal navy so strong Nelson won British control of the seas for more than a century."

Our tour guide explained that houses were few and far between because building had been restricted for decades and remodeling was allowed only at the back of existing homes. The few cottages we passed were picturesque, some had thatched roofs and hanging baskets of flowers. A young boy leaning over the garden gate of one cottage was feeding carrots to the donkeys crowding around him.

"You're not supposed to feed the animals," Stuart said. "The donkeys get downright pushy. Backed one fellow into a pond last year." He navigated a sharp corner and at a crossroads took the road heading away from the open heath. "Here's where we pick up the A35 into Bournemouth."

Twenty minutes later we pulled up outside a contemporary hotel next to the modern, glass-fronted conference center and people gathered their bags and got off. Soon I was the sole passenger left on the bus.

"So you're the one going to the other hotel," Stuart said. "You got the better part of that deal."

Minutes later we pulled up at the elegant Royal Bath Hotel, a venerable building from a different era. Cream-colored and turreted, it sprawled luxuriously on the East Cliff. My room had tall windows overlooking a wind-swept Atlantic and the bed was queen-sized. No bed ever looked more inviting but even though I desperately wanted to lie down, I resisted. Lars, a veteran globetrotter, had warned me against this particular temptation.

"Don't nap on the first day, you'll have trouble adjusting to the time difference. Stay up till evening, go for a walk, drink lots of tea."

It was just after 9 AM. I had a quick shower to dampen my drowsiness. Refreshed and in clean clothes, I wandered downstairs. Today was free, the conference proper started tomorrow. Tonight we'd gather at 5 PM for an informal cocktail get-together at the conference center. Tours were offered each day and I'd signed up for the 11 AM tour of the Shelley family tomb at St. Peter's Church and Cemetery. Not that I'm much of a poetry lover but as a major fan of Mary Shelley's *Frankenstein*, I knew the feminist document her mother, Mary Wollstonecraft, wrote, *Vindication of the Rights of Women*, was the first of its kind. I was intrigued with the idea of seeing the tomb of such historic figures. The receptionist at the front desk gave me a handful of pamphlets and told me the conference center was close to the hotel.

A waiter with a loaded tray hurried by and at the rattle of china I was immediately hungry. It was hours since the breakfast snack on the plane and suddenly I craved a real meal to make up for the lack of sleep.

"Is it possible to get breakfast now?"

"Certainly. The dining room is open," and I was pointed in the direction of a large room with tables of people enjoying breakfast. French doors led to a flagstone patio but no one was eating outside. The waiter who brought me a menu explained that kippers were smoked herring and bangers were sausages. I couldn't resist the kippers. A pot of tea arrived first and I looked over the pamphlets as I sipped strong black tea. I learned that a few years after it was built in 1838, the Bath Hotel added Royal to its name because it was "much frequented by royalty." The first hotel in Bournemouth, it was opened on Queen Victoria's coronation day in 1838. That made it a few decades older than 34 Gramercy Park, where Lanny lived.

"Here's freshly baked Hovis," the waiter said, when he returned with a full tray.

The small loaf, a cross between whole wheat and multigrain, was warm and wonderful. The kipper was crisp and delicious and soon only its backbone was left on my plate. Now I really felt sleepy. I set out to find the way to the conference center, hoping that fresh air would wake me up. The day was breezy and sunny, no clouds.

"The entrance to the Pleasure Gardens is straight ahead on this road, Westover Road," the porter had told me. "Walk across the gardens and you'll see a big glass building, that's the conference center."

One side of Westover Road was lined by pine trees and budding rhododendrons, the other by expensive looking shops. "Upmarket," according to the porter. I found the entrance to the gardens, the British version of a park, and went down a path bordered by pansies and begonias. A stream meandered through thick green grass, its banks grooved deep by time. It wasn't the city's namesake, the River Bourne, but one of the many Avons in England, a really small Avon. I sat on a bench, people-watching. French, German and Italian filled the air as well as an astounding mix of English accents. Students, I'd read in one of the pamphlets, came from all over Europe to study English at Bournemouth's language schools. The crowd thinned for a moment and there, opposite the bench where I sat, was the glitzy conference center.

My tour bus wasn't due for another hour so now that I knew how to reach the conference center, I decided to follow the stream to the sea. It felt good to stretch my legs. The gardens ended close to Bournemouth Pier. Grouped at the pier's entrance were rides, an arcade with beeping electronic games and kiosks selling balloons and souvenirs. The boardwalk was paved, not wooden. The winter must be temperate enough that roads didn't heave and grow potholes like New York's.

I walked leisurely back through the gardens to the conference center. The tour bus hadn't arrived so I went inside to check conference information in the lobby. I was studying the floor plan when my name was called. It was Bob Williams, the longtime director of the OEP Foundation, the international association for optometrists. Bob and his staff ran the foundation in California, publishing books and journals and coordinating conferences like this one.

"Are you taking the tour to Christchurch Priory?" Bob asked.

"No, I signed up for the literary shrine."

"Good choice," and he hurried off to the exhibit hall.

As Bob entered the exhibit hall, I blinked in surprise at the sight of the man coming out. What I could see of the man's face under his Boston Red Socks cap, it looked uncannily like Matt Wahr. The man walked quickly to a waiting elevator and the doors slid shut before he turned around, so I didn't get another glimpse of his face. I had to be mistaken. Wahr couldn't possibly be in England. He'd never been scheduled to attend the conference and after the financial mess at SUNY, alleged or not, money was missing and he was suspect. Besides, why would he even want to be here? I'd totally forgotten to ask Ian Campbell, the super at 34 Gramercy, why Wahr had been at 34. No, surely not Wahr, not at the conference. But I deflated like a punctured balloon. Ugly memories of the trouble in New York surfaced. *So what if someone looks like Wahr? A lot of men do.* I managed to shrug off my reaction, it had to be jet lag.

Outside, people were boarding a bus marked, "Literary Tour," and I joined them.

I knew one or two practitioners from state meetings. Three cheery Australians from the Australasian College of Behavioural Optometry introduced themselves. I recognized Lesley Vedelago of Queensland and Simon Grbevski of Sydney, featured speakers at the conference. People from Sweden, Belgium, Italy and Switzerland called out greetings. It was difficult to hear names clearly, tags would help at the evening get-together.

The last to board were English, Owen Leigh and his wife, though later, I learned she was a transplanted Dane. The British don't call their dentists or optometrists doctor, so it was Mr. Leigh. The Leighs, who lived about two hours away, confessed this was their first visit to Bournemouth.

"It's an interesting seaside resort," Owen said.

I smiled. Atlantic City was an interesting seaside resort. Bournemouth was an elegant Victorian dowager sailing grandly through her second millennium.

At St. Peter's we walked through the impressive church then wandered around the cemetery, trying to read the headstones through the grime of centuries. The Shelley family tomb housed three generations. The poet's heart was also entombed, according to the church pamphlet, "…saved from the funeral-pyre (after he drowned in the Gulf of Spezia)…." I could have done without that gruesome detail.

Two shadows fell across the mottled façade of the Shelly family tomb. The dark outlines on the moss-covered stones looked sinister and I caught my breath. It wasn't trouble, it was the Leighs. Jet lag playing more tricks?

"Ready for lunch?" Owen asked.

"Yes," I said. "I had a kipper breakfast a few hours ago but I'm hungry again."

Our group ate at Bobby's, one of the big department stores in the town center. The upstairs restaurant with its panoramic view of the city's shopping center was crowded and the buffet was mouth-watering. I chose pork bangers with grilled tomatoes and mashed potatoes. Not as meaty as American sausages, the bangers had herbs and bread stuffing and were very satisfying.

After the meal, the group broke up, some heading for their rooms for naps. Bleary-eyed but determined to follow Lars' advice and not sleep, I set off across the gardens to the pier, glad to walk off the heavy meal. I'd see how far along the beach I could get from the pier. The sea was calm and the wind had died down. The cafes were busy and the boardwalk was crowded with walkers enjoying the mild day.

The crowd had thinned by the time I reached Boscombe Chine, a ravine, according to one of the pamphlets I'd read. As I walked, the hackles on my neck started to rise and I had the uneasy feeling I was being followed. Physicists say this is a response to the reality of the unseen world. The few times I risked a look back, I didn't recognize anyone and no one showed the slightest interest in me. It had to be fatigue and my overly vivid imagination.

Boscombe's pier was shorter than Bournemouth's but because the cliffs had steadily risen to hundreds of feet, there was a chair lift for trips up and down the steep incline. A zigzag path snaked up the cliffs for walkers. I had time to go farther, perhaps see the rest of the front before the get-together. A tanned senior in neat overalls was painting the front of a small beach chalet a brilliant blue. I stopped and asked about it, casually glancing back, not seeing anything worrisome.

"People rent 'em for the summer." He looked me over. "The family spend the day, make a meal, enjoy a cuppa, change their clothes in private. I own this one and another at the end and rent to holidaymakers. It's my retirement fund, these places start at a hundred thousand."

I knew he meant pounds, not Euros, because the English had kept their own currency when they joined the European Union in 1973. I did the math and whistled. A hundred thousand pounds wasn't chump change. At the current exchange rate it was close to two hundred thousand dollars.

"Thanks, I'm here for a week, at a conference."

"Come for a holiday next year," he said and went back to his careful painting.

I sat on one of the benches along the front and stared at the ocean. Waves crept languidly up the empty beach. Farther out, the heaving water was a rich green, wave crests stretching in curling white ripples. As they came to shore, the waves paled to a sheen of silver darkened by strands of seaweed. Behind me, the cliffs rose imposingly. A cactus-type of succulent creeper was spread out over much of the sandy bluffs and small palm trees were dotted here and there. I consulted the pamphlet. Southbourne Beach came after Boscombe in the eleven-mile expanse of curving shore that stretched to a place called Hengistbury Head.

I decided to try and walk to Southbourne and set off, glancing back occasionally. I wouldn't have noticed anything if it hadn't been for the abrupt movement of a man who looked like he was deliberately ducking back by the zigzag's stone wall. Was he trying to avoid being seen? The only other person in view was the man painting the beach hut. I kept my eyes fixed on the spot. Was it the man at the conference center who looked like Matt Wahr? Was I turning into a Nervous Nellie? The trouble in Manhattan had seemed never-ending but now I was three thousand miles away and I didn't have to jump at every falling leaf.

Time to be bold. I walked quickly back and saw that whoever it was must have turned onto the zigzag walk and started up the cliff. The first zig was empty and bushes hid the rest of the path. Whoever it was had to be a good way up by now. Had I misinterpreted the hasty movement? Nervous tension swamped me and I set off east again, arguing with my-self about light and the distortions of shadows.

Minutes later, in Southbourne, the pedestrian walkway ended. Deep golden sand stretched ahead but I decided to leave the beach and return to the hotel along the cliff top. Some way back I'd seen a second chair lift and I decided to take it. The ticket seller poured heavy coins in my hand in exchange for my crisp pound note and the ride up the cliff was quick and smooth. The lift unloaded right by a bus stop and the sign on the waiting double-decker read, "Bournemouth Centre." Impulsively, I jumped on the bus and climbed to the open top deck after handing over some of my coins to the driver. No one boarded the bus after me and I breathed in relief as we left the bus stop. Sandy dunes lined the cliff side of the road. On the opposite side, small hotels faced the sea, their hang-ing baskets and courtyards gay with flowers but no billboard. So far, what I'd seen of the area was free of ugly commercialism, even though I'd read that the south coast's main industry was tourism.

Back at the Royal Bath, I had another quick shower and put on my one suit, a light taupe wool Lanny had gifted me a year ago. Perfect for an English spring evening. A black silk blouse and dressy flat shoes and I was ready. I looked around cautiously as I crossed the gardens but no one dodged out of sight. I made record time, propelled by twinges of angst. The buzz of loud talk at the party spilled down the corridor. I took a glass of red wine from the bar and a cheese snack from a waiter and circulated. The noise escalated beyond comfort level and I joined Bob Williams and Earl Lizotte, who were chatting on the fringe of the crowd.

"Did you see Steve Farge from Bernell yet? He's looking for you," Bob Williams asked. "Leave a message at the front desk if you don't catch up with him here. How did you like the literary trip? I've heard rave reviews about the trip to Christchurch. I'm told the eleventh-century priory is impressive."

"I can recommend St. Peter's, the graveyard was fascinating," I said. "Are you going on the Christchurch trip?"

"I'd like to go but probably you need to include me out," Bob said. "I rarely have a free moment at meetings like this." Right then, I was sorry Bob didn't have any free time but with hindsight, it's doubtful his presence could have changed the outcome of that disastrous excursion.

I wasn't due to give the paper until the third day of the conference and by then I'd enjoyed several nights of deep sleep. Butterflies fluttered in my stomach when it was time for the presentation but with Steve Farge's help at the question and answer section, it went smoothly enough. Over dinner that evening, a small group of us sat and talked. Decoding Fred Anders' work needed time but the implication of his prototypes was profound.

"Once we finish building the units, we start testing," Steve said. "We'll send prototypes to four of the major colleges and they'll check them out. This equipment is so innovative, it goes far beyond anything like the second Visagraph Taylor and Nystrom designed."

"That measured how well you process information as well as sampling eye-movement positions as much as sixty times a second, correct?" someone asked.

"Yes. It checks a lot of things, including your span of recognition and understanding," Steve said.

"Fred Anders was a genius. The prototypes test and evaluate the vision system in such depth," Horrie Humphreys said.

"True," Steve replied. "The possibility of remote analysis is exciting."

"How's that done?" someone asked.

"With a video feed. You can check on breathing, posture and eye movement. Even small expressions. Everything but the focusing."

"Why not focusing?" Paul Harris queried.

"It's possible there's a way," I said, remembering something Fred Anders had told me. "Usually, if the person is still, you can visually monitor the video."

"Incredible," Horrie said. "Remember when Westinghouse developed an armchair that automatically measured blood pressure, heart rate and various other facts about whoever was sitting in it?"

"Never heard of it," I said but Bob Williams nodded.

"It looked like a regular wing-back armchair, the sort you'd find in anyone's living room," he said.

The one question that Steve was not able to answer was when the units would be ready for testing.

"We're behind schedule but this isn't work that can be hurried," he explained. "We don't have Dr. Anders to answer questions so there's a certain amount of trial and error."

The rest of the conference kept me busy. Lectures were followed by evenings of informal discussions. I didn't skip anything and most days I started with a short walk on the beach. I never caught sight of anyone ducking out of sight again and I didn't get another glimpse of the man whom I thought had looked like Matt Wahr. I persuaded myself that fatigue had deceived me on my first day and concentrated on the conference. Any time I looked in to the exhibit hall it was so jammed that I skipped it. I slept deeply, courtesy of Bournemouth's soft air, notorious for putting people to sleep.

"Bournemouth was known for TB sanitariums at the turn of the nineteenth century," the hall porter told me. "The patients slept on open porches to benefit from the smell of pine trees. The truth is, sea-level air reduces the corpuscle count of red blood."

Maybe my lowered corpuscle count was why I didn't have any strange dreams the way I had after Mary Sakamoto was killed. Maybe I just didn't remember them in the morning. The conference was winding down and I was disappointed to find the tours were over. Two Californians, Bob Sanet and Beth Ballinger, had raved about Christchurch, enchanted by the quaint town that was long on charm, tearooms and swans gliding on Christchurch Bay.

"Don't miss it," Beth said. "Go round the priory first and be sure to stop in at the rose garden, it's beautiful."

Horrie Humphreys hadn't been on any of the tours either.

"Nothing to stop the two of us taking a trip to Christchurch," he suggested and we agreed to go after the conference ended. A decision lightly taken with irrevocable results.

On the last day of the conference, I listened to a panel of European practitioners discussing activities in their countries, a far cry from my sheltered world at SUNY. After lunch, I sat in on Bob Bertolli's presentation about drug-testing detection and sobriety tests by Gus Forkiotis.

"When defense lawyers read about Dr. Forkiotis' experience as an Expert Witness, they plead their DUI clients guilty," Bob said and the audience clapped loudly. The questions ran long and I was beginning to think we'd have to forget the trip to Christchurch but finally the presentation came to a close and Horrie and I were free to leave. The conference really was over, it had been a wonderful experience and now it was time for some sightseeing. The main hall at the center was crowded as people started to leave. A few were returning home, many were setting off on trips around England. Horrie and I went outside to look for a taxi.

"Let's walk down to Bournemouth Square," Horrie suggested. "Too many people ahead of us here to get a taxi for quite a while."

He was right. Even though there was a long line of taxis, the line of people waiting with their luggage was longer. As we were walking away, a crowded bus at the head of the line pulled out slowly. Someone in the rear seat glanced out of the window in my direction and I stopped cold in my tracks, appalled. This time, I knew I was definitely seeing the man who'd attacked my dear godmother at the National Arts Club. We stared at each other for several agonizingly slow seconds. Then the coach accelerated and he was gone, leaving a trail of exhaust and questions in my mind. *What was that look on his face? Satisfaction? Was he satisfied he'd avoided me at the conference? He didn't seem concerned that I obviously recognized him. He does look a little bit like Matt Wahr but perhaps I'm wrong about that. Why was he here?*

"What's wrong, Yoko?" Horrie asked. "You're shaking, are you all right?" He stared after the departing coach then back at me. "Did you know that man?"

"Yes, that is, I mean no, I don't know him but I've seen him before and…." I took a deep breath as I thought back to my sensation of being watched during my time in England. So my reactions <u>had</u> been to something external, not nerves or jet lag. *So he was here and knew I was here and now he's leaving.* I felt enormous relief and knew that as soon as I got back to New York, I'd find out who the man was and then—yes, then—I'd contact the police. No way would I try to track down the attacker by myself. Now I had more than suspicions.

"He was in the exhibit hall," Horrie said. "I don't remember which vendor, but he was one of the two reps for a company that always comes to OEPF conferences."

"I need to find out the name of that company," I told Horrie, "if you think of it, let me know." As we walked to Bournemouth Square, I told him about the bizarre events that had started with the warning of danger from Mary Sakamoto.

"I just don't understand what connection there can be between the shooting on the street, then the attack on my godmother and the mugging."

Horrie stared ahead, considering what I'd told him. "I don't know about connections," he said slowly. "But is it too much of a stretch to ask whether the prototypes Fred Anders developed might be the cause for the attacks? You know there's talk of government interest in them?"

"That's true," I said. *And who knows who else might want be interested in the equipment.*

"You're going home tomorrow, it'd be a good idea to talk to the police when you're back in New York," Horrie added.

"Yes," I said and this time I meant it, I'd give Dan Riley a call. Even if I hadn't been able to uncover any real clues, finally I had more than suspicions. I'd be able to find out who the man was, either Horrie would remember or I'd ask Bob Williams at the OEP Foundation. He was sure to have a list of all the vendors. My satisfaction was mixed with resolution—what a difference from the weeks of mayhem and mystery when I'd worried and wondered and not found any answers mostly because I didn't now where to start.

We found an empty taxi at Bournemouth Square without any trouble and by the time we reached Christchurch, it was late afternoon. The taxi dropped us a few blocks from the priory and as we walked along the main street, the cloud cover lifted.

Small shops, bakeries and cafes lined High Street, so different from Bournemouth with its large department stores and trendy boutiques. Sidewalk stalls were piled with fruit and vegetables, clothes, toys and souvenirs. It was casual and gay and crowded, less than ten physical miles but light years away from Bournemouth's cool sophistication. Cars, busses and bikes streamed by in a nonstop flow. That changed when we reached the street to the priory grounds. The thirty yards of the cobblestones leading to the open gates was too narrow for cars and we walked through the massive gates on to a wide flagstone path that wound through a tranquil graveyard to the priory.

Inside, sunlight deepened the vivid colors of the magnificent stained glass windows. I dropped coins in a box for a pamphlet, "The Priory Church," and flipped through it. "The eleventh-century priory took four and a half centuries to build," I read to Horrie. "Do you feel like climbing seventy-five steps to the museum in St. Michael's Loft? It was a school for novice monks. Or we could take one hundred and seventy-six steps up a spiral staircase to the top of the bell tower and look over the town and harbor."

Horrie rolled his eyes. "The last OEP conference I attended was in France and someone bet I couldn't climb the bell tower in Notre Dame. I won the bet but my legs were sore for days. Why don't we walk to the harbor?"

We retraced our steps and took High Street to the right, away from the town center. The entrance to Abbot's Walk was a broad sandy path that meandered along beside the shallow river. When we reached the harbor, it was deserted, the cafes closed and the car park empty. A few sailboats were dropping anchor, joining the boats already moored. We walked leisurely round the bay then returned the way we'd come. The round trip took less than thirty minutes, a peaceful walk marred only by my uneasy sense that we were being watched. I shook myself mentally, I'd seen Lanny's attacker drive off. I almost asked Horrie if he had the same feeling but held my tongue. Didn't want him to think I was a space cadet.

Ten

The sun was low in the sky but we had time, the dark of summer nights comes leisurely in the south of England, far later than in New York. Horrie and I walked slowly in the gathering dusk, the murmur of the stream a soothing background to the gravel that crunched under our feet. We'd reached the High Street when I remembered the roses.

"Let's take a quick detour. Beth said the entrance is just past the lawn bowling club building."

Horrie nodded his agreement and we retraced our steps and found the entrance.

The rose garden was larger than I expected. Oblong beds of roses were surrounded by neatly cut grass that was in turn circled by a wide sandy path. Benches were evenly spaced along the path. The priory loomed, an aloof, austere backdrop on a crest of high land immediately behind the garden. Stepping onto the grass, I walked to the nearest flowerbed. The dozen bushes in it were covered in half-open roses, petals luminous in the growing shadows. Leaning close, I sniffed the delicate fragrance.

"These smell heavenly," I said, turning to Horrie, who stood on the path. Dusk had drifted in but I could see him clearly, relaxed and smiling. With equal, awful clarity, I saw a man moving stealthily towards Horrie.

It was Lanny's attacker right here in the rose garden—he hadn't left after all. The man raised his arm high, some sort of thick stick in his hand.

"No!" I screamed and lunged forward.

Horrie, oblivious to the danger behind him, was startled by my mad rush and stood staring at me. Before I could reach Horrie, the stick crashed down on the back of his head and he dropped to the ground without a sound.

Now I was face-to-face with the attacker. I kicked out, deliberately aiming for the man's groin but missed. He swung the stick at me. I twisted to one side and the blow landed on my shoulder with painful force. I danced wildly to avoid another blow and kicked at his knees. Yes, contact! I heard a gasping grunt but I hadn't slowed him down. The stick swung again and smashed onto the side of my head. My legs buckled. Through the pain I registered that the eyes of Lanny's attacker were the chilling gray of cold slate. The resemblance to Matt Wahr was striking. *Why hadn't he left?* I slid away from that puzzling thought into nothing.

When I came round, velvety darkness was complete. A leather strap gagged me and my hands and feet were bound tight. My hands were tied in front of me and I was able to reach up and feel my head to check for damage where the blow had landed. The blood around the bump was a sticky trickle, not quite dry, so I hadn't been out long. I didn't have a headache, so I didn't think the blow was serious. What was serious was the situation. I was wedged on my side against the grassy edge of the rose bed. I took inventory. The first blow had been glancing and my shoulder hurt a little, the other blow landed with some force, but nothing was broken, I didn't have a headache and I was thinking clearly. What about Horrie? The nauseating sound when he was hit worried me.

Now I'd seen Slate Eyes clearly, one fact was clear: he looked too much like Matt Wahr for it to be a coincidence. Too old to be a son, perhaps a brother? Horrie thought he was a rep with a company that made vision therapy equipment, so that was one puzzling question answered and it explained why he was at the conference. But what possible connection could there be to Lanny? Why had she been attacked? Obviously, something in this man's mind linked Lanny to Gus Forkiotis, tenuous perhaps but there again was the optometric angle and the conference that Lanny had asked Gus to address. Horrie and I had been deliberately ambushed. The attack on me had to be because I'd seen Slate Eyes at the National Arts Club. Was Horrie attacked because he was in the wrong place at the right time? Mary Sakamoto's warning of danger echoed in my mind. The *why* was still ever elusive but her prediction of trouble had come true over and over.

I lay staring at my side view of the night sky. My stomach heaved now and then. God, I hoped I wasn't about to throw up. In a movie, I'd have wriggled free of bonds by now. Welcome to the real world, Yoko. I lay on the damp earth longing to hug Lanny one more time and to tell Auntie Ai she was the best Auntie anyone ever had. Someone bent over me. I shut my eyes.

"You and your buddy Forkiotis, who's calling the shots now?" A kick landed on my side. Nasty but not lethal. "You optometrists think you're so smart. Put your pants on one leg at a time, don't you? Who does Forkiotis think he is, giving evidence at court cases? It's bogus, all of it."

The bitter words brought a staggering answer to part of the puzzle. At last, clarity about some links. Dr. Forkiotis, wearing his Expert Witness hat in some court, had roused this devil. Gus traveled all over the U.S. at the request of state prosecuting attorneys so it was hard to know where the offending case had been prosecuted. A second kick landed. Dazzling lights burst behind my eyes and the world vanished.

When I regained consciousness, I was jolting sack-like over the man's shoulder, flopping against his back. The leather gag was sodden with saliva, a real gourmet treat. I wasn't dead but escape was a fragile concept. Where were the lovers out for a moonlight stroll in the garden? Better yet, how about a policeman making rounds? I couldn't remember if the rose garden had gates at the entrance. If it did, someone might come to lock up and spot what was happening.

We didn't go far. I was dropped carelessly on the ground. Swiveling my eyes a fraction, I could see rose bushes close by but tree branches blotted out much of the night sky but at least I knew we hadn't left the garden. When Horrie and I had arrived, I'd noticed a hut flanked by trees at the far side of the enclosure. Was it a public lavatory? No lack of them in Bournemouth.

"Don't go anywhere." The voice mocked, gloating at the control, the license to hurt.

The sound of his footsteps faded into silence. I strained to look around, hoping to see Horrie. No sign of him. Twisting and tugging at the bonds on my hands and ankles got me nowhere. My hotel room card with my wallet was in the zippered pocket of my light jacket, half a Lara-bar in the other pocket. That was it. No knives or files. I had folding scissors in my bag but the bag was in my hotel room. I heard a trundling noise. Slate Eyes returned but didn't speak, just hoisted me up and roughly bundled me into a wheelchair. That explained the trundling sound but where had he found a wheelchair? If he stole it from the car park, would someone miss it and call the police?

A hat was jammed on my head and a blanket draped round me. In-sane perhaps, but this man was also resourceful. My vision was blocked by the hat, which he'd pulled low over my face. He tucked the blanket up round my chin to complete the picture of an invalid protected from the night air. Off we went. What if I threw myself out of the chair? If people were around… I felt a sharp prick at the back of my neck.

"Keep still and real quiet or I'll cut your throat."

I promptly discarded the idea of creating a commotion. Where were we going? We reached Christchurch High Street. Streetlights were on but we didn't meet anyone walking. Cars drove by. They'd see a man pushing some poor soul in a wheelchair. We covered the few yards to the en-trance of Abbot's Walk and turned in, heading to the harbor. Had he taken Horrie there already? I shivered. We didn't pass anyone and when we got to the bay area it was deserted. Boats neat under canvas covers bobbed at their moorings. None had lights on to show people were aboard.

"Quiet as a tomb, eh?"

He bent down and stuck his face close to mine.

"We're going out on the water. Hope you don't get seasick."

The voice was not solicitous, the face was that of a predator. The wheelchair was pushed to stone steps that led down to a small wooden dock where a rowboat rocked gently. I was hauled out of the wheelchair and carried down the steps. If anyone was watching, it would appear reasonably normal. He hadn't thrown me over his shoulder this time, not wanting to look suspicious. He dumped me in the rowboat with a thud that rattled my teeth. I landed up against a hard, unyielding mass that felt suspiciously like bricks. Next to it I felt something larger, softer. I wriggled myself about until I could look. It was Horrie, silent and unmoving. Slate Eyes clambered in, settling on the seat across the middle of the small boat. He fiddled with the oars until they slotted into the oarlocks then untied the mooring rope. The rowboat moved slowly away from the dock, oars plish-plashing.

"Nice night for a swim." His voice was breathless from the rowing.

I strained against the bonds on my hands and feet but they stayed tight. I wanted to know why this was happening. If he'd only take the gag out of my mouth, I'd ask. Horrie and I were crammed in the front of the boat and I couldn't see Slate Eyes. The soft rocking of the boat would have been soothing if I wasn't on a deadly sailing trip with a madman. Cool water dribbled over me as the oars rattled free of the oarlocks and clattered into the bottom of the boat. Had we reached our destination?

"Got to give you some weight." He pulled my jacket zipper down and began wedging in bricks.

"Ow," I mumbled round the leather gag.

The jacket's thin material ripped. Too bad. I was banking on that happening when I was in the water so the bricks would fall out and I'd keep myself afloat till a boat came by. On to Plan B. Slate Eyes muttered angrily and fumbled at my ankles. I strained to see what he was doing. He threaded the cord of a canvas bag through the rope around my ankles and started shoving bricks into the bag.

"You first, then your friend. You're getting off easy, you deserve to be hung," he said.

"Why?" I said but it was an indistinct mumble through the soggy gag.

Once the bag of bricks was fastened tightly, he sat back and looked at me in pure satisfaction.

"What did we do to you?" I said but it was the same indistinct mumble through the gag.

"Say your prayers," he said, ignoring the mumble and stood cautiously, waiting for the boat to steady. Bending, he grabbed me under the arm, starting to lift me. Time for Plan B. I lashed out with my legs and the bag of bricks shifted, rolling against his feet. Slate Eyes cursed and staggered sideways but didn't let go of me. The boat tilted and he pushed me to its edge and stuck one foot on the far side of the center seat to prevent us capsizing. My breathing was ragged as I dangled over the side of the boat. One more heave and I'd be in the water. The boat wallowed then steadied. I heard an engine. It got louder. Would they notice us?

"Ahoy, coastguard here," someone called.

Our small rowboat rocked in the waves from the motorboat as it puttered close. A searchlight slid across the water, chasing away the dark. We were hailed again. Slate Eyes ignored the call. Grabbing my legs he launched me into wicked cold water. I wriggled like crazy, trying to free myself of the bag of bricks. Suddenly, a windmill of arms and legs landed heavily on me, forcing me down deeper. Had Horrie been thrown on top of me? What the hell was going on?

I struggled to get out from under the various limbs thrashing around on top of me. It couldn't be Horrie, he'd been trussed as tightly as me. All at once, the windmilling stopped and strong arms gripped me. Up we went, surfacing into glorious air. Lightheaded and limp, I was pushed by my rescuer and pulled up by two men leaning over the side of the coast-guard's boat. I landed on the deck spluttering feebly around the gag in my mouth. A circle of faces looked down at me, their expressions a mix of surprise and outrage. Quick hands undid the gag and my bonds.

"Stark raving mad," someone said.

"Too damn true," I said and managed a weak grin.

The coastguard, I discovered later, had been alerted by a fisherman who'd been surprised to see his brother's rowboat slipping out of the harbor. His brother was in the hospital and no one else ever used his boat. When the coastguard saw me heaved overboard, one of the crew jumped in to retrieve me. Slate Eyes immediately leaped over the side of the rowboat, landing on the crewman, who was propelled onto me. The would-be murderer did his best to prevent my rescue, fighting underwater like a maniac. Another crewmember jumped in to help.

"Between us, we managed to overcome him," one of the men told me. I nodded cheerfully, on a euphoric high, convinced the end of a horrendous rollercoaster ride had been reached, that danger was over. It didn't matter that I was a sodden mess.

Someone went over to the rowboat to check on Horrie.

"His pulse is strong and he's breathing steadily, let's get him on board."

Anger had me gritting my teeth as I watched the crew send a hammock over to the rowboat. Horrie was swung to safety and willing hands swiftly cut his bonds. One of the crew brought a first-aid kit and dabbed antiseptic on the dried blood on the back of Horrie's head. Horrie groaned and opened his eyes.

"My head hurts."

"You took a terrible whack on the head," I said. "You dropped like a lead weight."

"We were in the rose garden," Horrie said.

"Yes," I said, relieved he was coherent.

"We'll get him to the hospital," the crewman said as he put away the first-aid kit. "They'll keep him for observation, see if he has a concussion."

Revulsion filled me at the brutality of that vicious blow to Horrie's head. The boat turned in a tight circle and headed back into the harbor. Someone tapped my shoulder.

"Come below, Miss, we'll find you some dry clothes and take a look at any scrapes you may have." I followed the crewman, trailing drips. It didn't take long to climb into dry trousers and a thick sweater, both baggy but warm and comfortable and then I sat quietly while my bruises were gently cleaned with antiseptic.

Stuffing my wet things into the plastic bag I was given, I followed the crewman up on deck and my anger flared again at the sight of the man who'd first attacked Lanny then vented his spleen on Horrie and me. He was stubbornly silent, avoiding the crew's curious stares. He gazed into the distance, face blank. We neared land and the crew got busy, preparing to dock the boat.

Slate Eyes erupted into violent action, seizing a tiny window of opportunity, precious seconds when no one's attention was on him. He rammed the man next to him and scrambling to the shore side of the motorboat, took a daring leap onto the dock, staggered but caught his balance and sprinted off into the dark. In the confusion of a crowded cockpit where we'd been sent sprawling like dominoes, it was a long minute before someone took off after him. Racing clouds sped across the moon and soon a veil of misty rain made it hard to see. We could hear feet thudding on the wooden dock. The sounds changed as they reached what was probably a pathway. Two more crew jumped ashore and joined in the chase, shouting to the first man that they were coming. Then the air filled with the screeching of brakes followed by the ominous sound of the impact when flesh meets metal. By now we were securely docked but when I went to clamber ashore, firm hands held me back.

"Best not to go yet, Miss." Unable to move, I waited.

The men who'd taken off in pursuit of the runaway came back, faces grim. The van coming to meet the coastguards' boat had collided with Slate Eyes. He'd been running so fast neither had time to swerve.

At Christchurch police station, my story was heard with assiduous attention and a certain level of puzzlement that bordered on disbelief. Admittedly, the explanation of why I'd been bound and sent to play with the fishes was fractured. It sounded strange, even to me, especially when I backed up and gave them a thorough rundown of the bizarre events in New York and explained that the man who'd jumped off the boat and run to his death was the man who'd attacked my godmother. The wallet found on the body had a name I didn't know and a New Jersey address.

A police surgeon arrived to examine me.

"You're lucky, it's not serious," he said as he finished his thorough exam. He'd already seen Horrie, who was being kept at the hospital overnight for observation. "I believe Dr. Humphreys will be able to leave in the morning," the police surgeon said, reassuringly.

Then it was back to police questioning. It was repetitive but overlaid with British politeness that took the sting out of it. The detective who first interviewed me was a young man with bright red hair and a habit of blushing scarlet when I asked him to repeat questions. I didn't have the heart to explain I had a hard time following his accent. The chief inspector, a walrus of a man, radiated calm even though I knew he'd been called out of a sick bed.

"A heavy cold," he said pleasantly, waving a hand dismissively at my apologies. "I'll live." He turned serious. "Let me be frank. Your account is, ah, somewhat unusual. An autopsy will show if the man was on drugs. He certainly behaved as if he was deranged. It would be helpful to talk to the New York police, try to get a full picture."

That way you can check on my story.

The chief inspector didn't want to contact anyone at the Swedish consulate, he wanted to talk to his U.S. counterpart on the police force. Happy to oblige, I gave him the number for the Thirteenth Precinct.

"Detective Riley has a file on everything that happened up to when I left New York," I explained.

It was 11 PM in England, 6 PM in New York. I waited, nursing a mug of hot chocolate. The chief inspector returned to let me know he'd spoken with Riley's boss.

"It was quite useful," he said in his ultra-correct voice. He didn't say he'd checked up on me but his manner switched from cool to cordial. "I have a message from Detective Riley for you. He'd appreciate it if you'd e-mail him, here's the e-address." He passed me a slip of paper.

"Thanks," was all I said, though as I took the paper, I relished the thought that finally I had something to tell Riley, something that wasn't just a suspicion.

"I'll have you driven to your hotel," the chief inspector said. "In the morning, if the police surgeon is correct, Dr. Humphreys will be able to leave hospital. We'll make sure he is taken back to where he's staying. We'll be in touch."

I nodded gratefully. I couldn't wait to telephone Lars and tell him that Lanny's attacker wouldn't bother anyone again. Life would be peaceful now, right?

The front desk clerk at the Royal Bath was too polite to raise even one eyebrow at my overlarge clothing or the soggy bundle under my arm.

"I trust everything is all right?" he asked.

"Yes, it really is," I said and went upstairs to dial long distance. It was extravagant but I had to let Lars know the danger was over. E-mail wouldn't do for this particular call. Lars answered almost instantly and the story poured out of me. Shaken as I was by the attacker's gruesome end, I felt safer than I had for weeks.

"His driver's license is in the name of Lou Kralle but he looked so like Matt Wahr, he must be related in some way, it can't be a coincidence."

"Wahr is the financial manager at the college charged with fraud?"

"Yes," I said. "I was with Horrie Humphreys when I saw the man and Horrie said the guy is a rep with a company that sells vision therapy equipment, which explains why he was at the conference in England."

"I'm not sure it fully explains the attack on Lanny, even if this man had some sort of vendetta against Dr. Forkiotis," Lars said.

"I know. And it doesn't explain why I was attacked in the hall of my apartment building."

Lars was silent and I realized I hadn't ever told him about the mugger-arsonist so I quickly filled him in.

"Are you sure that's everything?" Lars asked. "Any other trouble?"

"No, really. I didn't tell you because I didn't want to worry you."

After the phone call, I hurried down to use the hotel's computer. My e-mail to Detective Riley was brief and I felt almost virtuous that I was communicating with him.

"Lanny's attacker is dead. I survived his attempt to drown me. I believe this is the end of all the trouble. I telephoned Lars, he'll fill you in. British police talk funny but are very pleasant." I resisted adding, "…and the Brits didn't make me feel like a suspect."

Riley couldn't have known my reaction to that first interview at the 13th Precinct and by now I was way past the sense of outrage I'd felt back then. I'd been deeply shaken by Mary Sakamoto's death and worried about the warning of danger. Now that I'd survived more than one dangerous scene and several encounters with Dan Riley, I knew he wasn't such a pain after all—just a guy doing a tough job.

The police surgeon's prediction was accurate, Horrie Humphreys was well enough to travel. We were lucky, Horrie and I got to go home. Lou Kralle would not. Now I was free of the fear of the last few weeks. Lanny had paid a terrible price for reasons still not totally clear. Would they ever be known? But emotional scars can heal and her rehabilitation from TBI would happen, even if it took time. The British police asked me not to discuss Lou Kralle's death with anyone and I had no problem following that request. If the British media picked up on the gory details, I never knew. Soon I was winging my way home across the Atlantic.

Lars and Lanny met me at the airport, looking happy and relaxed. Words weren't necessary for me to know she was making good progress. I promised to visit soon and they dropped me off at home. I climbed the stairs to my apartment, glad to be back in New York. It was the Saturday of Memorial Day weekend and I wanted to catch up, get my conference notes in order. My brother cats gave me a cool reception but mellowed when I opened a can of tuna. I'd almost finished unpacking when the phone rang. It was Riley.

"I'm on duty at the moment, but thanks for your e-mail. Do you have time to talk to me about what happened in England? It's probably a major piece of the puzzle. Be helpful to slot it in to place. Perhaps we could meet for a drink or a meal?"

Was this a good idea? I heard my voice say, "Yes."

Since when do the police invite you out for a meal or a drink to talk about a case? Truth really is stranger than fiction. We settled on lunch at the Elephant & Castle the next day. It felt strange, the prospect of a meal with Dan Riley although I was way past any irritation I'd ever felt with him. The fact that my boss looked on him favorably said a lot. Besides, my social life had been nonexistent for months—OK, maybe it was over a year. No wonder I often worked late.

"By the way, Matt Wahr has officially skipped. His wife says he's not been home for days. He missed a preliminary court hearing and his wife is upset because bail was set and it's forfeit if he's a no show."

"How did he get bail?"

"His lawyer made the case that Wahr isn't a threat and he's known in the community. A bench warrant is out for him."

"What does that mean?"

"It's a technical term that simply means the warrant is issued by a judge."

This was not good news. Matt Wahr was the one chance we had to learn about Lou Kralle.

"Did you ask Wahr's wife about Lou Kralle?"

"We tried. She won't go into any more details other than the basics. Said she'd had enough trouble. But you were right, Matt and Lou are related, they're first cousins, their moms were sisters. Mrs. Wahr told us she'd never wanted anything to do with Lou," Riley said. "Sounded final.

Who knows, there may have been problems with the marriage before the embezzlement charge."

"Where does she live?"

"Don't get ideas," Riley warned. "Leave it to us."

"I can look for the address without your help."

"No need to get mad with me. It's for your own good."

That was so patronizing I couldn't stop a sarcastic comment. "I must have jet lag. I haven't seen anyone die for several days."

"Okay, okay. The Wahrs are in Brooklyn Heights. Oh, just found this in my notes—They—Lou and Matt were, quote, 'close, too close,' according to the wife."

"Kralle's address was in New Jersey," I said. "Twenty minutes from Manhattan. They could easily get together."

"Wahr's wife didn't seem surprised when I told her about Kralle's death. She was, well, resigned is the word that comes to mind. She did say he was a wild guy with a violent streak."

"She say anything else?"

"No. I told you, she didn't want to talk. She couldn't get us out of the house quickly enough."

"Us?"

"My partner, Detective Zeissing. Remember him?"

"Oh, right."

Riley and I agreed to meet at 12:30 the next day for lunch.

As I hung up, I wondered what would happen if I visited Matt Wahr's wife? Would she speak to me? Was she worried about her husband or glad to see the back of him? What would Dan Riley's reaction be to my going to see her? Quickly, I decided he need never find out—for sure I wasn't going to tell him. That's if I did get to visit and talk with Matt's wife. I shelved more speculation about visiting Mrs. Wahr in favor of getting ready for bed. The flight back had been smooth but now I was on home turf, I was unwinding from the emotional burden that had accumulated steadily since the day Mary Sakamoto had been shot.

Overriding my feeling of relief was a set of niggling queries I couldn't get out of my head. Was Matt Wahr also dangerous, like his cousin? Was the fact that he was on the loose an indication of trouble to come? Was I doing the college finance minister a serious injustice? What if the charges of fraud against him were wrong? I wrestled with the possibilities until sleep lulled my mind to silence.

Eleven

The next day dawned tailor-made for picnics. Lars invited me to the consulate's annual celebration but was totally understanding when I begged off the day's activities.

"I need to catch up, go in to the office for a bit," I explained.

"Then come over for an evening meal?" he said. "Lanny's been asking for you."

"I'll be there," I promised.

At breakfast—ah, the pleasure of sipping a cup of miso as I planned the day—I thought over the puzzling questions I'd had the night before and discarded them. Why anticipate trouble? I indulged in mochi to follow the miso, heating an entire package in the toaster oven. I ate half and wrapped the rest for a snack. The cats graciously accepted the treats I put out and showed I was forgiven by purring and rubbing against my legs. Larissa was home when I called and happy to hear I had the teapot she'd wanted instead of cash for looking after the cats.

"I'll bring you the teapot on my way to the office."

"Stop for a cup of tea," she said. "Help me christen the teapot."

"Let's make it another day."

I stuffed my snack and conference notes in my backpack and tucking the teapot under one arm, set off downstairs. Larissa threw open her door eagerly and beamed as she took the package. Fending off another invitation to have tea, I promised we'd get together soon so I could tell her about the trip and I left for SUNY. My feet registered the familiar hardness of the sidewalk, so different from the shifting texture of Bournemouth's sandy beaches.

A peaceful silence blanketed the college. I made quick work of the report to the dean, thanks to the daily notes I'd taken at the conference. I sat back, feeling reasonably ready for the coming week. Sun still filled a cloudless sky and I had the rest of the morning before I was due to meet Riley. I chewed on the last of the mochi squares and decided there was nothing like the present to see if I could talk to Wahr's wife. I needed an address. Riley had deliberately not mentioned it and I hadn't asked outright, though I'd hinted around. The hell with politically correct games.

Riley had mentioned Brooklyn, and over the years, Matt had talked about riding the subway home to that borough, so I leafed through the Brooklyn phone directory. I didn't plan any strategy, just jumped in cold and dialed the phone number I found for Matthew and Sylvia Wahr. A woman answered on the second ring. Quickly I introduced myself to reassure her I wasn't the law or a legal beagle in pursuit of her husband.

"This is Yoko Kamimura. I'm an optometrist at SUNY. Is this Sylvia Wahr?"

A faint gasp was the reply. I waited out a long silence.

"Are you the one who was in England?"

"Yes, I was there."

"What do you want?"

Ambiguous reply. I'd take it she was Sylvia Wahr.

"Mrs. Wahr, I'd like to come see you to ask you about Lou Kralle." I paused, not wanting to jeopardize the chance of meeting with her, reluctant to rub salt in the wound by mentioning the fact that her husband had forfeited bail and disappeared.

"I told the police I don't know what Lou was doing, he was a crazy man." Her voice broke and I could hear the soft sounds of crying but she didn't hang up.

"I could be at your place in less than twenty minutes, it doesn't take long by subway."

Acid roiled in my gut at another long silence but she doubtfully agreed and gave me directions to her home from the station. The train jolted its way out to Brooklyn and I reviewed my skimpy options. I wanted to know the connection between Matt and Lou. Did they have a business relationship? If so, about what and did it involve SUNY? The only option I had was to ask her. Above all, I wanted time with Matt Wahr. I was kicking myself for not talking to him when he'd barged in to 34 Gramercy Park. I never had asked Mr. Campbell, the super, why Wahr visited him. How I wished I had.

The Wahrs didn't live in one of Brooklyn's many apartment buildings as I'd somehow expected. Their home was on State Street, in an elegant and spacious corner brownstone. Wide steps led to an ornately carved front door. An intercom was set in the wall to one side of three mailboxes. I pushed the button for Wahr. The static crackling that came with the answer almost took my ear off and I had to call my name twice before the lock to the massive front door was buzzed open.

A petite woman stood in the doorway of the first-floor apartment. She looked exhausted, her eyes rimmed red. Lack of sleep or crying? She pulled me in to the apartment, pushing the door shut hastily, as if outside threats could be stopped by locking the door. This was one nervous woman.

"Mrs. Wahr, I appreciate you seeing me."

Matt Wahr's wife held up her hand commandingly, like a traffic cop.

"The college didn't send you?" Her voice was low with the trace of a Southern accent like her husband's.

"No one asked me to come. I'm here because of Lou Kralle. He…"

Again Sylvia held up her hand. It was shaking. Too much coffee or too little sleep, perhaps both.

"Matt said that's why you wanted to come all the way out here. I don't know anything about what Lou was involved in or got up to." Her voice was defiant.

"You spoke with your husband after I called?" I kept my tone low, conversational, but my heart jumped in an excited rat-a-tat-tat.

"On the telephone." Her lips trembled. "He calls when he can."

I didn't comment that the police would want to know about the phone call from a man who'd skipped bail. I tried to bridge the awkward pause.

"I thought he was a Brooklyn boy but sometimes his accent was like yours, not a typical city voice."

"That's how we met," Sylvia said, eyes looking away at happier times. "His mother died when he was little and he lived with his aunt in Virginia. We went to the same college."

"How long did he live in Virginia?"

"Until he left for two years in the military." She slid a sideways look at me. "He's not in Virginia now. His aunt doesn't know about this…this trouble."

"It must be hard, the problems at SUNY."

Sylvia mopped her eyes with a handful of soggy tissues. Anxious not to outstay my lukewarm welcome, I hurriedly continued my questions.

"I was hoping you could tell me whether Lou Kralle had any business dealings with the college?" I got a blank look. "He sold vision therapy equipment so he had that connection to optometry. I'm wondering if Matt worked with him, like a second job."

"I told you, I don't know what Lou got up to, he was a terrible man. I'm sure Matt never worked with him on any second job. SUNY kept Matt busy."

I nodding understandingly then asked the important question.

"Would you ask Matt if he'd talk with me? Tell him it's nothing to do with SUNY. I'm trying to find out why Lou Kralle attacked me and the man I was with in England. There was another, a previous attack, a terrible one on…." I stopped. Although I'd seen Kralle at the club and was certain he was Lanny's attacker, there was only my word and now the man was dead. I had no real proof Lanny had been attacked by him— these days, I knew proof was important. "There was an attack on someone else," I finished.

Sylvia rubbed her eyes hard again and I bit my lip, not wanting to say anything to irritate her but if she didn't stop that, she'd hurt her eyes. To my relief, she nodded in agreement.

"Here's my home and work numbers," I said.

Sylvia stood. I didn't need a second hint. I made my escape, exhausted by the tension vibrating from Matt Wahr's forlorn wife.

I barely made it to the Elephant & Castle by 12:30, reminding myself that I wasn't planning on mentioning my visit to Brooklyn to Dan Riley. The deliberate omission made me feel just a little guilty but I buried the feeling. The restaurant was quiet and Dan sat at a window table, watching the door. When he saw me, his wide smile reached his eyes, no x-ray stare there. It felt good to see him, more than comforting. This man was someone I could relate to and not in a brotherly way. We both ordered burgers and fries, no picky eaters here.

"Sorry, I can't stay long," Dan said after we'd demolished the burgers. "I called in a few favors so I could spring free for lunch but we're short a couple of guys."

I was relieved and disappointed all at the same time. My personal space was secure. Darn, what's a girl to do?

"What are your plans for the rest of the day?" Dan asked.

"I'm heading home until dinner tonight with Lanny and Lars."

Dan looked at his watch. "I've time to walk you back to your place, okay?"

"Okay."

We shared the bill, over Dan's objections.

"I asked you out," he said. "Next time, no arguments, please?" He smiled disarmingly. *My head said Irish blarney, my pheromones circled wildly.*

On the walk home, without any prompting, Dan told me he was divorced.

"Aren't we all?" I said, aiming for the noncommittal. "Do you have kids?"

"No, married young, divorced fairly recently, still fairly young. How about you?"

"No kids and I'm divorced."

"Here's your building."

We came to a standstill on the sidewalk. I held out my hand to establish boundaries.

Dan shook my hand cheerfully then pushed the boundary line and bent to kiss me. The short kiss on my cheek was light but his fingers touched my face gently and lingered intimately. It was sexy and caring and I melted. Larissa came out and caught us standing so close we were touching at all the right places.

"See you later, Yoko," she called knowingly as she walked by.

Dan waved goodbye, grinning at both of us.

All the way up the stairs, I worried that this was happening too fast. Then I thought about what lingerie to order from Victoria's Secret. My cotton bikinis aren't what you'd call a major turn-on. Important decision, red or black? Lace or satin?

Dinner with Lanny and Lars was low key. I didn't mention my trip to Brooklyn, Lars would not approve. I did mention lunch with Dan and that news garnered approving smiles from Lanny and Lars.

"You're looking well, Lanny," I said. "How are you feeling?"

"Good, though I still get tired. Something as simple as showering can be overwhelming. I stand in the shower, wet and soapy, but can't remember if I washed my hair," Lanny said, watching me scoop out a melon to go with the pineapple Lars was cutting into chunks.

"Lanny's doing everything the therapists ask her to do," Lars said.

"That's the best news. Don't worry, Lanny, it will all smooth out." I said and meant it.

The three of us made solid inroads on the first course, a sinfully rich crab and spinach quiche. When it came time for dessert, I protested weakly when Lars suggested pouring *aqua vit* over the fruit, transforming it into a decadent delight.

"The walk home will help you get rid of the calories," Lars said.

Lanny was tired, so I left soon after I helped Lars clear up after the meal. The streets were quiet. A lot of people had left town to celebrate the Memorial Day weekend, the rest were at Central Park, hanging out in the warmth of the May evening. No humidity, a slight breeze, a perfect ending to pleasant day. At home, the red light was flashing on the answering machine. One message, from Dan. It was short but to the point.

"Here's hoping you call when you get in," Dan said. "I'm stuck at the precinct till late tonight and have early starts all week, but from Friday evening I'm off for forty-eight hours. A whole weekend. I was wondering if you had any plans or if the two of us could think of something."

I didn't waste any time dialing the precinct and Dan picked up promptly. We dickered amiably about what to do on the weekend, finally leaving it open at starting with a meal somewhere and going from there. Exciting not to know. So far, I was enjoying his company. No need to blow it up beyond that.

By mid-week, I hadn't heard from Matt Wahr. No point contacting his wife again. Either she was a good actress or she genuinely didn't have a clue if Kralle was involved with Matt in shady financial doings. I'd managed to avoid mentioning my visit to Sylvia Wahr to Dan and I ignored the feeling that I was being downright sneaky.

The week back at the college was hectic, the weather a long string of sunny days. Dan and I chatted a few times, mostly swopping stories of how busy we were at work. Evenings I often stayed at my desk until after seven. I'd pick up something for dinner on the way home and be in bed early. Finally, the end of the week arrived. Dan met me outside SUNY on Friday at six sharp.

"It's too nice to be indoors for a meal," he said. "Why don't we get take-out and go to the roof garden at my place, it's got plants, flowers, chairs, the works."

"That sounds great. Where do you live?"

"I'm apartment-sitting in a small coop building next to P.S. 41, the Greenwich Village School on Eleventh Street, off Sixth. One of the guys at the precinct told me about this place. The owner's a professor at NYU, she's off in Italy on sabbatical and the rent's reasonable because she wanted someone reliable here. I'll have to move out when she comes back but she's away for a year, could be longer."

"What a deal."

"So, take-out and maybe a video?"

"Sure, I love roof gardens. We're not allowed on the roof in my building. It's covered in tar that gets sticky when it's hot."

The part of the roof that had been transformed into a garden was larger than I'd expected, a shady green oasis of flowers and bushes. A vine-covered awning stretched over tables and chairs. We spread out the containers of Chinese food and settled down. No one came up while we were there and it was like a private garden. The building was six floors high and in the middle of the block and traffic noise from Sixth and Seventh Avenues floated up faintly, a background reminder of the busy city.

"This is great but not as classy as Gramercy Park," Dan said.

"Better," I said. "If you're in that park, people on the sidewalk ask you to open the gate and let them in. When you say that only people who live in buildings around the park have keys, they get mad. Sometimes they yell."

Dan laughed. "That's embarrassing."

"Yes."

"Okay, that's the first course. There's ice cream in the freezer. Oh, I forgot to pick up a video. Want to look over what there is the apartment and see if anything interests you?"

"What, no etchings?"

"No false pretences. Ice cream without etchings."

Dan reached across the picnic table and took my hand. He kissed my palm lightly.

"You cops sure know how to have a good time," I mocked but I curled my fingers into my palm, holding them against the place where it tingled from his lips.

We gathered up the empty containers and took the elevator down to the third floor where Dan gave me a quick tour. The front door opened onto a long hall that had rooms off it, more convenient than railway apartments like mine where you walk through one room to reach the next. Each room overlooked neighboring gardens. A small kitchen fronted by a dining room was at one end of the hall, at the other end a pleasant living room. In between were two bedrooms and a bathroom.

"Grab a seat while I check on the video stock," Dan said, waving at the couch. He rattled off an eclectic selection, Hitchcock, Monty Python and Woody Allen.

"How about a real oldie? Do you like the Thin Man series, William Powell and Mary Astor?"

"I love them and Asta, their little dog."

We'd both seen the movie before. Just as well because the first time William Powell made loving eye contact with Mary Astor, Dan and I smiled at each other. As easily as we'd smiled, our lips met. Our arms slid around each other and we pulled close. The kisses sent hungry excitement through me. When we came up for air, we stood. Words weren't necessary. Dan led the way down the hall to the first bedroom.

In the interest of scientific reporting, I can verify we didn't make it to the kitchen for ice cream. Why interrupt our delicious distractions for something fattening like ice cream?

Twelve

Who ever said love's a rollercoaster ride had it right. Four days after our blissful weekend, Dan called me at SUNY and what he said knocked me *splat* off Cloud Nine. He was tentative with small talk and eventually came to the point.

"Yoko, I don't know how to say this."

"So say it, Dan, be a man," I prompted.

"My ex-wife came in from Seattle last week," Dan said. "She's visiting her brother in Philadelphia and keeps calling me. Wants me to go down, stay a few days, see if we can make a fresh start."

I mumbled something that sounded like, "I see," though I was thinking, *What the hell?*

Dan hesitated. "I'm taking time off to drive to Philly to face her. I don't think anything's changed between us."

He waited. I didn't know what to say.

"I had to tell you," Dan said. "I don't want to go behind your back. I owe you an explanation."

I couldn't bring myself to wish him good luck but I did manage to tell him to drive safely and sound as though I meant it. By six that night, I'd had it with work. I started to walk home, thinking about Dan's call, remembering what he'd said to me in the late night telephone call the night before. Before he'd decided to visit his ex.

"I can't wait for our next get-together."

He was right, our time at his apartment had been undiluted satisfaction. We'd spent most of it indoors or in the roof garden, only leaving his place once to walk over to my apartment and give the cats fresh bowls of water and food and clean the litter box.

"How about a cup of miso?" I suggested when we'd finished those chores. "We could sit for a bit, keep the cats company."

"Sure," Dan said and I made us two cups of South River's hearty barley miso.

"This is different from soup in Japanese restaurants," Dan said, as he sipped.

"Usually, restaurants serve *suimono*," I explained. "That's a stock made from steeping dried tuna flakes and kelp in water. They strain it then add a dash of sake and some soy sauce. Miso is different. It's based on soy beans and different things are added, even dandelions and leeks. This one has barley, soy beans and sea veggies."

'I could get used to this," he told me and smiled in a way that gave me goose bumps.

I savored the memory of that weekend as I walked home but then I forced myself to face the miserable truth that Dan and I might have had our one and only get-together. The fact that he'd had the guts to tell me what was going on, cared enough to be honest and open was comforting. I had no choice but to wait and deal with his decision, whatever it was, after he'd visited his ex. My stomach gurgled, reminding me that my day had been long and hectic and my lunch skimpy, only two veggie rolls because I hadn't felt very hungry after Dan called.

I was a few blocks from home and considering the merit of rib-sticking, dumpling-thick soup versus chicken pot pie from KK, the Polish restaurant next to my place, which does a fine job with both. Just as I reached the decision to choose my food when I got to the restaurant, two men hurried up, one to my left, one to my right. They gripped my arms tight, crowding me so we'd look like a cozy trio if anyone glanced at us. One deftly flung a large scarf over my head so it covered my face and concealed the large gloved hand he clamped over my mouth. In the seconds before my eyes were covered, I saw that both men wore woolen caps pulled down to their eyebrows and coats with collars pulled up around their ears.

The three of us moved sideways in a bizarre, shuffling dance. I shook my head violently, trying to dislodge the hand over my mouth so I could yell. The guys chatted and laughed loudly to cover the muffled sounds I made. My head-tossing helped the scarf slip a fraction from my eyes and I saw we were headed for a dirty black BMW at the curb. I was maneuvered into the car and we took off with a jerk that snapped my head back.

No one ever tells you how fear floods the body and numbs the spirit. A divorce, 9/11, the sudden death of my parents within months of each other, somehow through those traumas, part of me stayed free to hope. Not now. I'd been abducted, snatched off the street by two men, spirited away in minutes in the early evening, passersby were oblivious to my predicament. *Why?* was a mystery. Exxon executives, the Israeli Olympic Team, these were kidnappings for ransom or political change. Who would think they could get a ransom for me? As for political change, I vote, that's it. That left terrorists, but this was Manhattan, not Baghdad. I was terrified and a really big part of it was that I knew it might be days before my absence was noticed.

Dan was away and for all I knew he was out of my life for good. He'd said he'd call when he got back, but that would be three or four days from now, maybe more. As for my family, Auntie Ai didn't expect me to check in regularly now that I had my own place. Lars and Lanny were visiting friends upstate for a few days. Lars might call, he'd leave a message and not think anything about it if I didn't get back to him promptly. Elliott Forrest, my boss, was on vacation for two weeks. That about covered it. People at the college would have no reason to think there was a problem if I wasn't in my office.

One of the men muttered something and the hand over my mouth was removed while the man to my right adjusted the scarf, pulling it tight so the sliver of light disappeared and I couldn't see. When I protested, the guy wedged on my other side elbowed me in the ribs.

"Shut it," he growled.

I can take a hint. Time for introductions later.

We drove for about twenty minutes, maybe a bit longer. Perhaps we were below Chinatown. Had we'd gone cross-town or headed up to the Bronx? Traffic was light and we moved without delays. I was positive we hadn't left Manhattan. From the sounds I heard and the feel of the road under the car as we drove, I didn't think we'd gone through the Lincoln or Holland tunnels or across the Verrazano or George Washington bridges out of New York. It felt as if we'd stayed on Manhattan's pot-holed streets. Logistics aside, the big question was why would anyone highjack me?

Who were they? What did they want? I started to ask but one of the heavy shoulders pressed hard against mine. Point taken. I "shut it" again and listened to the sounds of traffic, trying to gauge where we were. Finally we stopped. I was hauled out of the car and frog-marched over an uneven sidewalk.

"Goin' up steps." It was the one who'd growled at me in the car.

Keys jangled, and a door was unlocked. We entered a building where the air was still and dank. I was hustled up more stairs, not straight flights like those in my apartment building but a gently curving series of steps. Another wait to the sound of a second door being unlocked then we tramped across bare boards, me stumbling on debris underfoot that I couldn't see.

We came to a stop and I was pushed onto a hard seat and the scarf unwound from my head. Dry-mouthed, I stared at the two men. The woolen hats were really ski masks, now these were pulled down to cover their faces. They didn't want me to recognize them. Good. That meant they weren't planning on killing me, didn't it? One was tall, about six foot, the other was a head shorter. Both were thickset. The tall guy pulled a neatly folded piece of paper out of a pocket. He waved it at the shorter man, who extracted a small tape recorder from his coat pocket and set it on the dusty bench next to me. What the hell? I risked a quick glance around. We were in a cavernous space more like an auditorium than a room. The short man's pudgy fingers hovered indecisively over the controls of the tape recorder. Eventually, he stabbed at a button and nodded at the tall guy.

"Tell us about the equipment Anders developed," the tall guy said, reading carefully from the slip of paper in his hand.

For this I was blindfolded and dragged off? On the other hand, it finally proved what I'd suspected. Someone wanted the prototypes. The *why* was obvious. Take your pick: power, control, cool hard cash. The *who* was the puzzler—*who* was the mastermind? But why bother with me, why not go to where the prototypes were being manufactured? Something was definitely out of wack.

"Dr. Anders? But he's…you know he's dead?"

My question was ignored. Thug One shuffled impatiently. His sidekick glared at me. Uh oh, hostile body language. Talking couldn't hurt.

"I wasn't involved in the actual development of the prototypes, you know, the physical creation of them. All of that was the work of Dr. Anders. Mostly, I was helping him write his paper, really just taking his handwritten notes and putting them on the computer."

I hoped I sounded convincing. I did have a rough idea of the other uses the prototypes could be used for, nothing to do with vision therapy, but I was not about to share that with the two thugs. If the equipment was that valuable, I had to try to stop it falling into the wrong hands.

"I did a lot of research on current equipment to compare the efficiency of the prototypes."

"What equipment?"

"Some is for myopia reduction, you know, when people are nearsighted. There's a lot of different vision therapy equipment for that already but Dr. Anders was taking the science one step further. A lot of steps further."

I stopped my explanation and waited.

Thug One said, "Go on. What about the, um, scalar microscope?"

"Let's see. Dr. Anders was improving on the scalar hand-held microscope, the type of unit that's self-contained. It's like a digital camera. You download the pictures to a computer and can put them on a disk. You can have a micro-lens attachment so it's capable of recording near-infrared light. This unit can be used to see through people's cloudy corneas and even some fabrics or different inks. It's infrared reflectography with conventional IR film. Dr. Anders was increasing the range of what can be examined."

"Keep talking—what about the schedule?"

"When I was at the conference in England, I heard from Bernell, the manufacturer, that the new units are almost built. They were running into delays because there's no one to answer questions now Dr. Anders is dead. Even when they're complete, they have to be tested."

The two stared at me, their eyes more puzzled than angry. I'd bet good money they'd been called delinquents when they were juveniles. Somehow, I had to persuade them that now Fred was dead, the manufacturer knew more than anyone. That really was the truth. Thug One looked at his slip of paper again. Someone knew he needed a crib sheet.

"You're the one who had his notes. Talk about the changes."

That was a sticky point, I really didn't have much of a handle on the changes Fred had thrown into the mix at the last moment. But beyond that, it was obvious that whoever had these two grab me off the street had something to do with the college. The logical choice was Matt Wahr. His wife had obviously told him of my visit. He must have known I'd make the connection from his cousin, Lou Kralle, to him. This was industrial espionage, corporate America or a foreign faction. One of the men fidgeted. God, time to focus. I thought about the struggle I'd had trying to grasp where Fred Anders was headed with his innovations.

"It'll be a while before anyone understands fully," I began cautiously. "Dr. Anders had been working on these projects for some time but I didn't start right when he did, I began much later. A lot of what I did was on comparisons. The changes were very technical, reductions or increases in measurements."

The silence was scary. The nasty look on Thug One's face was even scarier.

"I transferred his handwritten notes to the computer but that doesn't mean I fully understood the work," I repeated hastily, hoping I sounded convincing. It was almost true. "Dr. Anders was a genius, I'm not."

"What's the schedule for finishing the prototypes? Why are there delays?"

"I told you, I don't know. The manufacturer's rep said the units were almost done."

My answer was taken for stonewalling.

Thug One shook his head at my stupidity. He grabbed my left arm and jerked my thumb back. Searing heat like knife blades scraped up my arm into my neck. He halted judiciously short of breakpoint, content with a series of parting twists to my hand that sent Technicolor flashes behind my tightly shut eyelids.

"Hey," Thug Two said. "We were told no rough play."

Thug One laughed spitefully. I bent over my hand, nursing the pain, feeling a physical spurt of anger but also a sense of relief. I'd learned I wasn't supposed to be hurt.

"I'm not trying to avoid answering," I said, surprised at how unwilling I still was to appease them. "The truth is I don't know anything about the schedule. I don't think even Bernell does."

Maybe if I repeated the manufacturer's name enough, that would distract the brutes.

Thug One shifted his feet and my cringe was Pavlovian. Words, give 'em words, I told myself. I dredged up more facts. They'd sound good.

"I compared Dr. Anders' notes with existing equipment like bio-feedback equipment, the Accommotrac for instance."

Two pairs of eyes stared at me blankly. Somebody had the smarts to send them along with some basic questions and a tape recorder.

"Dr. Joseph Trachtman," I added helpfully. "He's a behavioral optometrist in Brooklyn. He used special equipment." Just to fill dead air, I threw in some technicalities. "There was an infrared optometer. Dr. Trachtman reported an increase in unaided visual acuity—you know, someone could see clearly without glasses."

This information had been around for years but the thugs didn't know that.

Thug One looked at his slip of paper. "What about the process as the prototypes were assembled? How long did it take?"

He read the query in a monotone, like a kid called on to read in school and unhappy about it. His accent was not quite Brooklyn, perhaps the lower East Side, that undertone of middle Europe. He was heavy and strong and had enjoyed hurting me. Not a candidate for a Nobel Peace Prize. I couldn't see faces or hair because of the ski masks but it struck me that their build and their voices might help me identify these two later. That thought made me hopeful.

"I don't know. Dr. Anders was the person in touch with the manufacturer about that. I was on my way to see him the day he got back from the manufacturer but he was...."

My voice trailed off as I thought about the day Fred had been found dead. I still missed Fred Anders, hated that he was gone.

"Describe one of the prototypes and how long it took to manufacture."

Yikes, someone had inside information but needed the dots connected. Or was there some problem with the manufacturer? For sure I didn't know anything about that.

"One unit measures the focusing of the eyes. Also, there's a thermal infrared imager that views the blood flow of the face and monitors temperature. And microwave imaging records gait and breathing. But I don't know anything about how long that or any of the units took to manufacture."

The thugs' questions might dance around but the aim clearly was about the manufacturing schedule. The tape recorder whirred on softly and the two thugs looked at me, faces blank, waiting. I dredged up another useless tidbit, trying to look helpful.

"Dr. Anders told me the first stage of development was like the original Model T Ford but the next stage was more 21st century, like when a photo-sensor is connected to a computer. He ran into a snag when the hard drive crashed and he had to upgrade."

"Yeah?"

Tensely, I watched the two men. Thug Two stepped close to me and suddenly pushed me hard so that I sprawled sideways on to the floor.

"Get up. Talk. You better stop lying. When will the prototypes be ready?"

Bingo. I was right, that had to be the prime question. My eyes were level with feet, big feet in big black sneakers, Reeboks. I scrambled up to my knees and started talking.

"I'm not lying," I said quietly. "Everything I've told you is true. I don't know when the prototypes will be ready." Then I added, my voice deliberately helpful, knowing it was useless information and knowing the thugs didn't—only the bastard who'd sent them would know it was useless, "What is done is my computer scan of published research. I'm going over the juvie files now."

"Juvie?"

"Juvenile delinquents."

"Why them?"

"Studies of delinquents in prison have shown they benefited from optometric vision therapy. Part of what I did was to analyze the equipment used on those prisoners."

I wouldn't be surprised if this twosome had juvie files some place. I sucked in air. I was running out of details, useless or otherwise.

A cell phone chirped, startling me and distracting my bullies. Thug One pulled a miniscule unit out of his pocket.

"Yeah?" His tone was downright pleasant.

"Okay." He flipped the cell close. "Come on," he growled.

I started to get up and he casually pushed me back.

"Not you."

The two snickered as I went sprawling in the dust.

Two sets of feet walked beyond my range of vision. Cautiously I raised my head. The tall thug was talking on the cell phone but I couldn't catch what he was saying. They reached the door and left. A key grated as the door was locked. Was this a hideous dream? I squeezed my eyes shut and opened them slowly. I was still on a floor littered with fallen plaster, near a dusty bench in a cavernous, cobwebbed room. And my thumb still hurt. If this was a nightmare, it was a touchie-feelie Disney would envy.

I almost jumped out of my skin when the tape recorder on the bench clicked off. They'd left it behind because they planned to return. I sat on the floor and thought some more about the person intent on finding out about Anders' work. Gus Forkiotis had written a paper about the use of doubles for Saddam Hussein when Hussein was in power. If security analysts were monitoring a foreign leader and trying to understand behavior, they could retrieve the refractive state and eye coordination from a distance and get a handle on how the individual was likely to react. It was all about the way the subject perceived space and time. The prototypes Fred Anders had created were quantum leaps ahead of any current equipment. If they were used in surveillance, an incredible amount of valuable information could be gathered. It was obvious now that my suspicions that the prototypes had been the key to the bizarre happenings of the last few weeks had been on target.

It was hellishly frustrating. Finally, I had confirmation and a cause of what Mary Sakamoto warned about, although how she fit in to the puzzle I still could not fathom, but right now I was in a dangerous situation. Why, I wondered, had the muscle been called away? What would happen when they came back? They hadn't tied me up. They didn't feel threatened. I don't do push-ups and my weight hovers around a hundred and twenty-five pounds but the two who'd bamboozled me into the car had to weigh a good two hundred and fifty pounds each unless they'd cunningly bulked up with bubble wrap under their clothes. No, they wouldn't consider me a threat.

I listened but couldn't hear sounds to signal the men's return. I looked around the huge space, it was a building from another era with its high ceiling. Nearby were rows of massive walnut benches, pushed together in uneven rows. The rest of the room was bare. Several simple light fixtures hung at crazy angles, broken chains dangling. On the height of a second-floor level, a balcony ran on three sides of the space. The dingy white walls were stained by water leaks. Grimed but graceful Palladian windows ran almost the full height of the room, easily thirty feet.

Why did I have a feeling of déjà vu? Then it dawned on me. This place was a duplicate of the Fifteenth Street Quaker Meeting House on Rutherford Place, facing Stuyvesant Square. It couldn't be the Fifteenth Street place. Granted it was a few months since I'd been there to a Sunday meeting for worship but that building couldn't have been abandoned since then. Quakers take time to come to consensus on weighty matters like closing one of their buildings. Besides, I often walked by the Fifteenth Street building and knew it was open. This place had been empty a long, long time.

Small differences were obvious. The Fifteenth Street meeting didn't have walnut benches and the support pillars there had the benches built around them. Here the pillars soaring to the balcony were freestanding. Yet the sense of space and justness of proportion were true to the simplicity that is the beauty of many old Quaker buildings. New Jersey has some venerable Quaker Meeting Houses but my sixth sense insisted I was still in Manhattan. Slowly, I got up, intending to look out of a window. The din of a fire truck speeding by came and went, the siren wail muted by the massive masonry walls. New York was as active as ever. I was the one immobilized temporarily.

Quietly, not wanting to make any noise that might bring the bullies back, I walked to the closest window. Below was a neglected courtyard, bereft of trees, plants or grass. Gray earth had silted over uneven flagstones. A sliver of a narrow street was visible to the left. No parked cars, which was unusual in Manhattan. A Jack Russell on a long leash came into view, followed by a woman hurrying to keep up with her feisty pet. I smacked my hand against the window. The noise didn't travel. Recklessly, I made a fist and pounded. The dog trotted on and its owner disappeared from view.

Frustrated, I leaned my head against the cool of the glass. A taxi drove down the street, followed by several cars, probably a traffic light changing a block away. By craning my neck, I could just make out a small slice of the building on the other side of the street. Its slabs of dark red stone were puzzling familiar. Recognition danced elusively on the edge of understanding. Trashcans were lined at the side of the road. I was turning away when the significance of the number painted on one of the trashcans hit me.

"Thirty-four," I breathed.

Unbelievable. The two men had taken me to the empty Friends Meeting House on Gramercy Park. The building on the other side of the street was 34 Gramercy Park where Lanny lived. I was digesting the amazing fact that I was in familiar territory when I heard steps approaching.

The thugs were returning. More questions. Not willing to play passive victim, I scanned the room frantically to see where I could hide. The end bench on the third row of the mass of benches was angled out past its neighbors. Tiptoeing over, I ducked down and scrabbled my way underneath the seat then tugged at it so the bench slanted in, blocking a straight look at my makeshift hiding space. Huddled under the bench, I waited, feeling vulnerable. The key turned in the lock.

"Where'd she go, what the...?" Expletives poured out in a dazzling flow. Feet scrunched on the floor debris as the men walked close to where they'd left me.

"Check the doors. I'll look over there."

Over there had to be in my direction, close to where they'd left me. Steps came near. I pressed myself to the floor, shrinking down, my breathing shallow, listening as the men talked back and forth, complaining and threatening in equal doses.

"Nope, she ain't here."

Heavy steps echoed as one of the bullies went up to search the balcony and made a discovery that enraged them both. One of the doors on the balcony was unlocked.

"You said you tried all the doors," Thug One said furiously.

I listened in uncomfortable fascination as the two argued, baffled by my disappearance.

"I did." The answer was irritated. "This one's warped real bad, must of stuck. I *thought* it was locked."

The grumbling went on but the news had me thinking that escape was possible. I'd been maneuvered and manipulated and now it sounded as if I had a shot at putting a stop to that.

"How'd she leave the building?" It was Thug One.

"Maybe another door or window ain't locked. There's keys in the office."

More helpful news.

"Yeah? How come we didn't see her?" The bully answered his own question. "She could of hid in one of the rooms on the way down and we passed her coming up."

"What do we tell the big guy?"

A grunt was the answer to that question.

My ears tingled. Big guy? The boss?

The men left noisily. Did they really think I'd escaped? I heard the door being locked, apparently not considered redundant even though a balcony door was unlocked. I counted up to a hundred. No sound of footsteps returning. It took an eternity to inch my stiff body out from under the bench. I waited some more, flexing my arms and legs, gazing up at the moon, watching heavy storm clouds that promised rain sail past the window.

Enough time went by for me to feel I could risk moving. I crept up the balcony stairs, freezing in place whenever floorboards creaked. The side of a small door near the two main doors was curved slightly away from the doorframe and I managed to yank it open after a series of tugs. The sound reverberated loudly, sending my pulse vaulting into the stratosphere. Tensely, I waited but no one came running, no shouts floated up the stairs. The hall up here was empty. Shadows were motionless in the moonlight from the tall windows.

I stepped out onto the landing and looked around. The stairs lay unguarded and inviting. Straining to catch sounds of movement inside the building I heard only outside noises—truck and car engines, horns and sirens that sang of safety if I could reach the street. Cautiously, I went down the stairs, pausing now and then to listen for my captors. I reached street level and was tiptoeing across the lobby when I heard voices outside the huge double doors. Were they coming back? No time to retreat across the lobby and up the stairs without being seen. The key grated in the lock.

I lunged for a door to the side of the front door and ducked inside a small room. It was dark and the narrow window set high up on the wall let in little light. I could just make out a narrow wooden desk against one wall and a chair near it. The desk was questionable security but I was a clear target where I stood. Ducking under the desk, I pulled the chair in front of it and wriggled back against the wall, which was paneled. It was more cover than I'd had under the bench and that hiding place had worked. If the two men gave the room a casual glance from the door, if they didn't come all the way in they might not spot me.

I wedged myself firmly against the wall and was settling down to an anxious wait when I heard a soft click behind me. I stiffened in surprise as the click became a muffled, whirring sound. The wall behind me gave way and I tumbled back into cobwebs and darkness. Before I could move, the paneling started to slide back into position until it hit my legs and stopped. Rolling farther into the dark, I jerked my legs towards me and the paneling slid into place, closing off the outside room.

I lay straining to make sense of what was happening. My heart was thudding like a Con Ed pile driver and my tailbone was protesting—mild enough problems, given that I'd been propelled into relative security away from the two bullies. I couldn't hear any noise on the other side of the paneling. Come to that, I couldn't see anything much of where I was, either.

Carefully I stood. So far, so good. I raised my hand slowly and it grazed rough stone. OK, that had to be a low ceiling, well under six feet high. I started to pat along the wall to the left and felt uneven stone slabs like the ceiling. I counted as I went. Two rough but dry walls later I reached another opening, the size of a narrow door, roughly opposite the paneling I'd fallen through. I retraced my steps to the paneling and started to feel along the wall to the right. Two more walls and I ended up at the other opening again. My hidey-hole was roughly eight feet square.

My vision adjusted and I distinguished a dim glowing line some three feet off the ground opposite me where the other opening was. The line stretched off a short distance then disappeared. Puzzled, I made my way around to where it started and ran my fingers along its faint glimmer. The stone of the wall didn't feel any different. Some sort of phosphorescence had been applied and let off enough of a low glow so that the darkness wasn't total.

I moved forward tentatively, hoping I was going away from problems, not towards them. I could touch both sides of the passageway, which was mildly reassuring. The glowing line didn't end but took me round a corner where the line's dim light stretched off in the distance. Here there were glowing horizontal bands on the floor that turned out to be markers for steps. Cautiously I made my way down the steps, running my hands lightly along the rough walls for security. Who, I wondered, had made access to this tunnel? And why?

Some years back, the neighborhood had been up in arms when a developer wanted to demolish the old Meeting House and erect a thirty-story apartment complex in its place. Lanny had been in the thick of it so I'd heard plenty about the Friends Meeting House on Gramercy Square. For years, the building had sat forlorn and empty. A sign in the front courtyard explained that in its first century, the building had been part of the Underground Railroad. The room behind the paneling in the office— the hidey-hole I'd backed into by blind luck—might have been used to hide people fleeing slavery. I'd been to places in Pennsylvania and seen similar rooms. The nape of my neck tingled. How many beside me had sought refuge in that room? Tunnels were usually not part of the Underground Railroad, although I'd read about the home of Julia and John Putnam in Greenfield, Massachusetts, where a tunnel led from a hidden cellar room to nearby train tracks.

Manhattan has a staggering number of tunnels under the city streets, many are deep ones like those under Grand Central Station that had sheltered the homeless. Someone had broken through from the Meeting House and connected with part of the city's underground warrens. I shuffled along, wondering where the tunnel would end. Now and then, the glowing line would end and re-start a few feet on. My exploring hands found openings and it was obvious from the difference in the air flow that these were entrances to other tunnels. I didn't risk a side trip. Whoever had marked this route had done so for a reason, the logical one being that this route led to an exit.

How long since I'd been snatched off the street a few feet from my apartment? I rarely wear a watch, the clock radio in my kitchen and a wall clock in the office are enough sight of time for me. I wasn't cold. I wasn't even hungry, more like numb. Major plus, I'd given the bullies the slip. The sooner I found the end of this tunnel, the sooner I'd be free. I was considering this when I bumped into a wall. I ran my hands over the surface. It wasn't the rough stone material of the tunnel, it felt like planks; they reached up to the ceiling. Did this wooden wall mean there was an exit to the outside world on the other side? I felt around, from bottom to top, tapping, pressing. I pushed and pressed repeatedly, methodically testing every angle. Nothing happened.

"Jumping Judas priest," I muttered.

I stepped back in frustration and tripped over a soft bundle. Kneeling, I patted the object and decided it was a sleeping bag. It felt dry and it wasn't dusty so it hadn't been lying there long. Did it belong to a homeless person?

Wearily I slid to the ground and sat with my back against the planks. What were my options? If I retraced my route to the Meeting House, the bullies were there. Or were they? Why would they be there if I wasn't? How long was it since I'd given them the slip? Impossible to estimate. By the time I went back, I reasoned, the bullies would have gone. Why would they wait around? I set off, hating to have to retrace my steps but knowing I had no choice.

Thirteen

Ever notice how a return trip is faster than the trip out? Sensory deprivation may have magnified my impression of the distance I'd traveled but it felt as if only a few minutes passed before I was back in the Underground Railroad's hidden room at the Meeting House. Anxious to avoid crashing into the paneling that opened into the office, I watched the phosphorescent line carefully as I scooted along. When the line ended, I knew I was back where I'd started. Question was, where were the bullies? No way did I want to exit and find those two waiting. Pressing my ear hard against the wall, I strained to hear voices on the other side of the paneling. I swear I could hear my blood circulating. I listened for a long time but couldn't hear any sounds. Fine, time to make a break for it.

I felt the paneling, trying to remember how it had yielded. The first time I'd pressed against its mechanism by sheer chance. How to duplicate that? My fingers located a short groove at the top of the paneling. I put one hand in it and pushed and pressed along its length. This didn't bring results. I eased off on the pressure, tried the light touch. Zip, nada, zero. Next I tapped on the groove and immediately the wall swung slowly in. About time. I'm not claustrophobic but damned if I wanted to linger in the eerie isolation of the tunnel much longer.

The chair and desk were where I'd left them angled across the entrance to the hidden room. Better to duck down and crawl under the desk rather than push it aside and risk making noise. First, I crouched, listening. Street noises filtered in but the Meeting House was quiet and still. I squeezed my way out from under the desk and lifted the chair out of the way, putting it down with exaggerated care. I waited. Not a sound.

The door to the hall was open a few inches. Quietly I crossed the office and peered out. The lobby was empty. A bunch of keys on a hook by the door reminded me the bullies had said one of those keys opened the front door. I grabbed the keys and risked another look at the lobby. Still empty out there. Selecting the biggest key on the ring as the logical one for the massive front door, I was about to step out of the office when I heard a door open. The sound was nearby. Was it the bullies? Had they been looking for me all this time and were just now coming out of one of the rooms off the curving staircases?

I couldn't have been more wrong.

Opposite me, a man was fitting a key into the door at the foot of the staircase. His back faced me but I knew instantly it was Matt Wahr. A small gun stuck out of his trouser pocket. Like the rabbit spotting a snake, I froze. My suspicions about Wahr had been on target. He wasn't a decent, law-abiding man, an image he'd projected brilliantly for years at the college. I'd actually felt guilty doubting him. Was it hard for him to stop thieving when he was on a slithery slope down?

Wahr had to be the "big guy" the bullies mentioned. Whatever was going on was dangerous. Mary Sakamoto got that right, although how and where she belonged in the equation was still puzzling. Turning off the questions, I focused on the immediate problem. The bullies had covered their faces but Wahr hadn't covered his because he didn't know I'd see him here. But I had. Sure it was his back but it was a full and unobstructed view and I'd recognized him. Retreat, and a speedy one, was my only option.

My aversion to the tunnel disappeared in a flash. Now it beckoned as a safe place. Wahr locked the door he'd been standing outside, the key grating loudly in the quiet. Not risking another look, I tiptoed back across the office. Ducking under the desk I fumbled for the hidden entrance to the tunnel, pushing in a panic. The panel stayed solidly in place. I pushed again and again until I remembered to tap and it gave way in smooth silence.

I was squeezing through the opening when I heard, loud and clear, a damn cell phone ring. Startled, I moved too fast and kicked over the chair behind me. It hit the bare floorboards with a horrendous crash. Wahr called out but the words were lost as I scrambled through the panel, grateful when I heard it slide shut behind me. What would Wahr think when he saw the fallen chair? If he'd put the sleeping bag at the end of the tunnel, he knew about the tunnel. Would he come in after me? No prize for the answer to that question. The image of the gun jammed in his back pocket galvanized me. I bolted down the tunnel in a clammy chill, following the phosphorescent line and reaching the end of the tunnel in no time flat.

Panting, I leaned against the wall and sucked in deep breaths then, desperate to find an exit, ran my fingers over the planks. Ah, a vertical line. Carefully, I traced a horizontal line connecting to it and finally realized it was the outline of a small door. How to get it open? My exploring fingers couldn't find any grooves like those on the entry to the hidden room at the Meeting House so I tugged and pushed at the top edge of the doorframe. Nothing. I worked my way down the outside edge of the frame, pressing firmly, and finally heard a faint *snick,* the sound a small magnet makes when it releases or pulls something shut. The door sprang back a little. Pushing it farther open, I stepped through the opening into a crowded storeroom. The place was silent and dim. When my eyes adjusted, I could make out stacks of boxes that almost filled the storeroom. I threaded my way across to the door, jittery and super-cautious. Still no sounds of life. I sniffed. Food smells and something else, the yeasty aroma of beer. A Sam Adams would go down well right now.

Warily, I looked out. Plain cement stairs, no covering, to the right. A narrow, low-ceilinged hallway, its floor the same bare cement as the stairs, stretched in front of me. This was a basement. Up the stairs had to be the quickest way out to the safety of the outside world. My breathing quickened at the thought. I crept out into the hall and started up the stairs. Where was I? For sure this wasn't the basement of 34 Gramercy Park or the National Arts Club. How far had I gone in the tunnel? Under the park? Across to the other side, to the Gramercy Park Hotel? Wherever I was, it was a place that cooked food and had beer so it wasn't one of the large apartment buildings fronting on Gramercy Park.

Halfway up the stairs, I heard a faint sound from the storeroom that stopped me dead in my tracks. It was the soft *snick* the door from the tunnel made when it opened. Someone had come out of the tunnel. I looked back. It was Matt Wahr. He stood in the doorway staring up at me, a worried look on his face. This wasn't the urbane Matt who'd worked at SUNY, this was an anxious man. Someone stepped out from behind him. It was Allan.

"I spy the eye sleuth!" he said and laughed, a grating chuckle that wasn't remotely funny. "Those two morons who brought you to the Meeting House thought you'd escaped but I had a feeling you were hiding somewhere nearby. Clever of you to find the tunnel. Or was it dumb luck? Come back here. I want to talk to you."

The tone was harsh, peremptory. Gone was the ingratiating geek from the office next to mine.

Call me Contrary Mary—I ran in the opposite direction. I burst onto a landing. It looked like another basement with its bare walls and a naked light bulb in the ceiling. The tunnel must have come out in a sub-basement. I heard running on the stairs. The hall here was the same low-ceilinged, drab gray as the floor below but it offered a choice of ways to go: right or left. I didn't stop to think, just took off. It's more natural to turn right. That's if you're right-handed. Left-hander that I am, I took the unnatural route and spurted left.

I hared along the narrow corridor. Either the drumming of my heart was drowning out the sound of chase behind me or I was in luck and they'd taken the other turn, the way right-handers would. Another bend in the corridor and I skidded to a stop in surprise. I was back where I'd started. Allan leaned against a wall, waiting. Matt stood next to him, still looking worried. I stood panting, sweaty from the fear-driven flight.

"Time we had a talk," Allan said. "Get down the stairs."

He pointed to the sub-basement. My heart sank but I knew better than to argue. He probably had a gun in his hip pocket like Matt. I crossed to the stairs, hesitating at the top. Allan came up behind me and tapped my shoulder, nudging me forward.

"Keep going."

The two followed close on my heels. A battery-operated lantern was on the floor in the storeroom and the windowless room filled with low light when Matt switched it on. A duffel bag and two wooden chairs were in the far corner.

"Take a seat," Allan said.

"So this is where you've been, Matt," I said, panting still from my mad dash.

"One of the places."

"I'm parched. Do you have water?"

True, my mouth was Sahara-dry but I was determined to dig for answers even though they might hand out lies. Allan was irritated but pulled out a bottle from the duffel bag and tossed it to me. I drank greedily then burped noisily. The hell with manners.

"You asked Matt's wife about Lou," Allan said and I shivered at the hard edge in his voice.

Yeah, and you want to know about Fred Anders' work. You set the bullies on me. You and Matt have done more than cook the books.

"Yes, I asked about Lou," I replied. "When I visited Matt's wife, I saw the huge painting in the living room signed 'Lou, Jr.' and recognized it from the student exhibition on at the club when my godmother was attacked. Lou Junior is Matt's nephew."

"*Was*. He *was* my nephew. He's dead and now his dad is dead."

Wahr looked at me, sorrow in his face. "Young Lou was jailed, drunk driving," he said. "He had an accident, two pedestrians were killed. He got into drugs when he was in jail. Do you know how easy it is to get drugs in jail? He overdosed. He's dead."

I shuddered in disbelief. At last the reason for Lou Kralle's vendetta. Allan watched coldly. He was a far greater threat than Matt's violent cousin, Lou. Allan and Matt were playing for big stakes. I was in the way and now I'd seen them, I was expendable. I fiddled with the bottle of water, took another sip, agonized at what I'd been told. I decided to go for broke.

"You're selling Fred Anders' work to another country for military use?"

"More than one country wants the technology," Allan said.

His face was an ugly, calculating study. Why had no one seen it before? Is it that we see naked corruption rarely or do we shield ourselves from the pain?

I have to keep talking, buy time, hope I can find a way out of this nightmare.

"How does Mary Sakamoto fit in? Why was she shot?"

The gambit didn't work. This was real life.

Allan shook his head angrily. "Enough, get moving."

Sour bile rose in my throat. I clapped my hand to my mouth, took a few deep breaths and managed not to puke.

"Bathroom?" I gulped.

"Upstairs," Allan said grudgingly. "I'll be right behind you. Bullets move quicker than you, no point running."

I walked up the stairs, the two close on my heels. My nausea eased.

"Where are we?" I asked as I went into the restroom.

Allan grunted in disgust at my sad attempt to pry information out of him.

"Move," he said.

I let the door swing in his face and as I was hurrying to a stall, I spotted a basket by the first washbasin. It was full of those books of matches restaurants use to advertise their business. I grabbed one and dropped it in my pocket just as Allan kicked the door open and followed me, standing in the doorway, holding it open. I frowned at him, clapped my hand to my mouth and rushed into a stall and bent over the toilet, slamming the door shut behind me. I made convincing retching noises as I pulled out the matchbook from my pocket and saw that it had the name of the place on it.

We were in Pete's Tavern, round the corner from the Meeting House. Pete's was the historic landmark where O. Henry wrote the classic *Gift of the Magi* at his favorite booth by the front door. I desperately needed thinking time. I'd been to Pete's Tavern a few times and knew the general layout. If I could make it up to the main floor… then what? The front door would be locked. A window, now that was a definite possibility. If I could get a window open, I could…. I took deep breaths to calm myself and flushing the toilet, slowly left the stall.

"Get back to the Meeting House," I heard Allan say to Matt. "If those morons are still hanging around, tell them to get lost, leave the area. They'll get paid."

Matt Wahr shuffled his feet indecisively.

"What are you going to do?" he asked. "We agreed no more bloodshed."

"You'd agree to anything." Allan's voice was contemptuous.

Wahr looked at me and quickly looked away.

"This got out of control," he said.

"Wrong," Allan interrupted, "I'm in control and always have been. Go."

Matt Wahr left without another word.

"You don't know anything about the schedule for the prototypes, right?" Allan said.

Obviously he'd spoken with the two thugs.

"No, Bernell...."

"Bernell's not the manufacturer I'm interested in," Allan said.

Ah, another piece of the puzzle. Allan was having duplicate units made. I didn't have to act to put on a subdued look but if Allan thought I was cowed, he was wrong. I wasn't going to give up that easily. Allan might want to kill me but he'd need the right place, probably back in the tunnel. Allan eyed me, the familiar look of smug satisfaction back on his face even though this time, he had a gun, not that his ego needed any bolstering.

"What now?" I asked, my voice low.

I had a wild idea. It might work if I could take Allan off guard. He moved to the door, waving me ahead of him. Slowly, I walked past him into the hall. Pivoting swiftly and planting my feet firmly on the floor, I grabbed Allan's head in both hands and pushed. As he staggered back against the door, I rubbed my thumbs across his eyes.

If I could dislodge his contact lenses, I'd gain time. Allan jerked his head back, as I'd anticipated. That was good for me and bad for him. It would almost certainly get at least one if not both of the contacts off his corneas, perhaps out of his eyes. Either way, once his contacts were askew, he'd be relatively blind, hampered by the swift, unexpected change in his vision.

Right before I left for England, when I'd given Allan the vision exam he wanted, I'd changed his prescription from the monovision contacts he wore to multifocals. When the new contacts I'd prescribed were delivered, I checked and found the lab had made a mistake filling the prescription so I sent the contacts back. The replacements had come in a day ago and I hadn't had time to check them. Allan was still wearing the old, monovison contacts. Or had been until I dislodged them. Allan yelped and his hands flew up to his face. I didn't wait to find out how far off his corneas the contacts had been dislodged.

I tore along the hall and took the stairs two at a time up to the main floor of Pete's Tavern. Running to the closest window, I wrestled with the lock. An ear-splitting alarm blared when I shoved the window open. Fine by me. Clambering through the window, I jumped down onto the deserted sidewalk. The noise of the alarm hadn't brought anyone to the windows of the places up and down the street. Car alarms don't turn heads any more, why would this alarm be different? I spurted down the street, heading for Third Avenue, risking a look back at Pete's. The alarm clanged on. Of Allan there was no sign. A cab cruised by and the driver looked over to see if I was interested. My hand shot up and I flailed frantically, even though I was the only person on the street. The cab stopped and I scrambled in gratefully.

"Put the meter on and pull up a little closer to Pete's Tavern. Lock the doors. D'you have a phone? I've got to call the police."

The cabbie gave me a hard look to see if I was serious. I must have passed the wacko test because he grabbed the mouthpiece of his two-way unit.

"Nine-one-one?" he asked.

"No, the Thirteenth Precinct."

I gave the cabbie the direct number to Dan's office. Dan was out of town but maybe his partner, Zoran Zeissing, was on duty, although I hadn't seen him since the police had come to the college after the shooting of Mary Sakamoto.

"Ask for Detective Zeissing," I told the cabbie as he punched in the numbers.

Zeissing must have answered the phone because the driver passed me the mouthpiece.

"This is Yoko Kamimura," I said. "Allan Barnes from the college is in Pete's Tavern and he has a gun. He's a murderer. I'm in a cab down the street, watching to see if he comes out of the tavern. A tunnel connects Pete's to the old Meeting House, that empty building on Gramercy Park South. Send a car to the Meeting House, in case Barnes goes back down the tunnel and tries to escape that way. Matt Wahr and two thugs may still be at the Meeting House."

Zoran Zeissing was silent for a nanosecond.

"Your location?"

"East Eighteenth Street, a block off Gramercy Park, uptown side of the street."

I heard the detective calling to the dispatcher to radio squad cars in the vicinity to get to Pete's Tavern and the Meeting House. That done, he came back to me.

"I am on my way, Dr. Kamimura."

Incredible that the detective had recalled I was an optometrist, then I remembered that this was a man with a superb memory.

"This for real or a movie?" the cabbie asked.

"It's for real," I told him and sat on the edge of the seat, staring at Pete's Tavern, ready to duck down out of sight if Allan emerged.

Two squad cars pulled up outside Pete's, lights flashing but no sirens. Allan was on his knees inside when the police found him, he was still searching for the lens I'd dislodged. You lose more than depth perception with the wrong prescription. Some times, you may even lose whatever grasp you have on a balanced perspective. Greed, power, money, you name it, he'd gone over the edge. Whether Allan Barnes ever had a balanced perspective is debatable. In his case, monovision might have given him an inflated confidence that he could outwit the world and garner a fortune. What did he care that it was blood money.

When Allan was in custody, I was finally able to relax. At last the accidents and attacks were behind us. Matt Wahr turned himself in later that night. His involvement had been reluctant. He'd been blackmailed by Allan, who knew about Lou Kralle's wild threat to revenge his son's death. Allan had played with Wahr's head, skilfully fostering a sense of injustice, offering easy money to a man close to retirement. Soon Wahr was in so deep he had no choice but to follow where Allan led.

I was at my desk a week or so later when Dan called and at the sound of his voice, I steeled myself for what he had to say. Was this the end of our relationship?

"Yoko, I'm back," he said, voice quiet. "I'm sorry I was away for so long but nothing's changed between my ex and me. We still rub each other's nerves raw. It didn't take either of us long to see that but after I got back, I needed time to think it over."

"Oh," I said. Pregnant pause.

"I spent time with her but all we did was bicker or plain snarl at each other. On the drive back from Pennsylvania, I couldn't stop thinking about you, hoping I hadn't blown it. Then I heard Wahr and Barnes were in custody and what happened to you." He hesitated for a heartbeat. "Can I see you, maybe have dinner tonight? I'll be done around five. Could we meet somewhere? The Elephant & Castle?"

I hesitated, still upset at how much time had passed without Dan calling me. Yet he had trusted me with the truth when he'd said he was going to see his ex. I'd trust him now. Besides, with Allan Barnes and Matt Wahr in custody, the danger was definitely over. I could celebrate. It was time to christen the electric shabu-shabu pan my mother gave me two years ago. Shabu-shabu is a special meal, perfect for a celebration. I issued the invitation and Dan promptly accepted. That evening, I was ready to leave work by five but first I called Pete Soltys, the owner at KK. Whatever was on KK's menu could be bought raw or cooked, you only had to ask.

"Pete, it's Yoko. Could you let me have a pound of thinly sliced beef, best cut, tonight?"

"Is a sweetheart coming to dinner?"

"You guessed right."

"What time are you stopping by?"

"In about twenty minutes, is that okay?"

"Do you want borscht with that?" Pete asked, knowing I loved KK's beet soup.

"Not tonight, thanks," I told him, "I'm making shabu-shabu." ✉

"What?"

"It's the Japanese version of fondue, no cheese, just beef, veggies and noodles. Everything cooks in a special pot filled with water and when you finish eating the food, you've got a great broth."

On the way home I bought fresh veggies at the Korean grocery a block from my apartment then stopped at Pete's for the meat.

"So who's the lucky man?" Pete asked, holding the bag out but not releasing it. I'd have to answer if I wanted the beef.

"Dan," I confessed. "You know, the detective."

"Ah," Pete sighed. "Romance is in the air. Let us know how you enjoy this," and he put the bag in my hands.

The three interested listeners on the stools at the counter nodded in agreement. Walking out of KK, I met Dan. No hesitation in the way he opened his arms wide. We hugged long and hard and when we broke, I peeked back through KK's front window. Yep, we'd had an audience. Pete and the folks at the counter waved enthusiastically.

Upstairs, as soon as the door to my apartment was shut, we hugged again and kissed, a long, slow exciting kiss, and it was as good as I remembered. Maybe better. Just to be sure, we kissed a few times more, quality control and all that. This time, the cats were the interested audience. They watched curiously but didn't meow one objection, as comfortable with Dan's presence as I was.

"You're the talk of the station," Dan said. "Zoran said your voice was cucumber cool when you called in. You didn't even say you'd been abducted. Just reported how we could catch a murderer or two." He kissed me again, a delicate caress on my cheek. "You're a strong woman, Yoko. I thought you might appreciate a tonic so here's a bottle of champagne. Two glasses if you please, the bubbly's still cold," and Dan pulled a bottle from the canvas bag slung over his shoulder.

"By the way, if you're interested, I've got the inside story of what Barnes and Wahr admitted when they were questioned."

At last the pieces of the puzzle were slotting into place. I moved around the kitchen, setting the table, sipping champagne, enjoying Dan's presence. Listening, asking the occasional question.

"Barnes caused Mary Sakamoto's death. Indirectly, it's true, but he set the wheels in motion," Dan said. "It looks as if the connection with you is that Mary Sakamoto overheard Barnes talking to his partners in crime about harassing you to find out about the schedule for Dr. Anders' work. Allan said he was going after you any which way. He said he'd hire some goons and give them carte blanche and pay them well each time they reported on success. When he could, he lifted information piecemeal from your computer because he was trying to get the equipment made so he could market it, undercover, of course."

"Was Mary Sakamoto involved?" I asked.

"No. She was working at the New York home of the Albany politician, the guy who leaked Wahr's name to the fraud squad for having cooked the books, part of Barnes' plan to blackmail Wahr," Dan explained. "Wahr described you to the goon who shot Sakamoto."

"Why was Mary Sakamoto at the politician's house?"

"Fitting an expensive wedding dress for the politician's daughter in the room next to where Wahr and the politician were meeting. The bride-to-be had her dad come in a few times to see the dress and the door was left open. Sakamoto must have heard the men talk. You were described as the only Japanese woman at the college. Obviously, Sakamoto decided to warn you."

"She knew of possible danger to me but didn't realize how dangerous it might be for her."

Shaken at the ugly truth, I was silent. Mary Sakamoto had been a woman of integrity, a woman who died because she was courageous enough to try to help a stranger.

"The daughter who didn't want to talk to us is a nurse. Works with children hospitalized at St. Vincent's."

"The hospital where my mom taught the nurses," I said.

"I didn't know that." Dan's eyes widened as he grasped the significance of this.

"*That's* the connection," I said. "Mary Sakamoto's daughter must have told her about her teacher, Naoko Kamimura. My mom. It's one of those coincidences where life's stranger than fiction."

Tears filled my eyes for the brave woman who had warned me and for the daughter whose mother had been killed. Dan came to where I stood by the fridge, a bag of red peppers in my hand, and we hugged, a comforting, soothing embrace.

"Now your shirt's wet," I sniffled and fished in my pocket for Kleenex. "Getting hungry, Dan?"

"Yes."

"Okay, I'll start the meal." I took the new shabu-shabu pan off the shelf by the fridge and half-filled it with water. Putting it in the center of the table, I plugged it in and started on the veggies, putting fresh spinach to soak in a bowl of cold water, slicing onion and red peppers.

"Wahr tried to wriggle out of any responsibility," Dan said, picking up the rest of the story. "Insisted he didn't know what the goons would get up to. But he knew Barnes sent money every time the guys reported back."

Finishing with the veggies, I arranged them on two plates and put them on the table next to a dish of soba noodles. The water in the pot was simmering already. As I got the beef out of the fridge, I asked about something that had never stopped bothering me.

"Do you know what caused Fred Anders's death? Was it really a heart attack?"

"Yes," Dan said. "Barnes had the goons visit SUNY late one night and threaten Anders, tell him his family would be harassed if he didn't cooperate. That threatening visit may have triggered the heart attack."

Outrage swept over me at the havoc wreaked. What a relief Allan and Matt were behind bars. Dan filled our glasses.

"Want to hear the rest of the story?"

I nodded. "I've been puzzling over all this for too long."

"That hit-and-run out in Connecticut, when you were visiting the optometrist who took you to the police academy, that was Lou Kralle, the lunatic who attacked you in England."

"I knew that attack had something to do with Dr. Forkiotis being an expert witness," I said. "Kralle's desire for revenge started at Lou Junior's trial."

"Exactly."

"That's the link with Lanny, too?"

"Yes. Lou went to the club to see his son's art when it was in the students' exhibition. On his way out, he passed Mrs. Oldenburgh and heard her talking on her cell phone with Forkiotis about giving a lecture on drunk driving. He followed her upstairs, spur of the moment, told her Forkiotis was wrong. She defended the doctor and Lou lost it, went ballistic."

We sat in silence for a moment and I considered what Dan had told me. Lou Kralle had been on a terrible vendetta to avenge his son's death, revenge fueling that rage.

"The death in England of Matt Wahr's cousin, Lou Kralle, disrupted Barnes' link with the manufacturer of illegal copies of the prototypes," Dan said. "Not one to be thwarted, Barnes developed a new contact but suddenly was told more money was needed because of manufacturing problems. Suspicious, he decided to see if he could find out more about the prototypes from you, hoping the bullies could extract enough information from you to safeguard his investment."

Could my abduction have been avoided if I'd asked Ian Campbell, the super at 34 Gramercy Park, why Wahr was visiting him there? Hard to say. My assumption that Wahr wanted to hide out in one of the building's apartments was half right—assumptions do that, half trick you. Wahr was indeed seeking a hiding place and under the guise of looking over property for SUNY to relocate, asked around in the area about empty buildings. He learned Ian Campbell had a key to the empty Meeting House opposite 34. Wahr arranged to see the place and made a copy of the key. The empty building was a brilliant hiding place, it even had more than one exit. It was common knowledge the building had been part of the Underground Railway and somehow he'd found the location of the secret room.

How Barnes and Wahr discovered the tunnel that led to Pete's remained a mystery but you know geeks and financial types, adept at deciphering the fine print, whether it's annual statements or blueprints. Anyone with enough determination and time can check on New York's underground labyrinth. The more I learned about Allan Barnes, the pattern of deception, dissimulation and disinformation was astounding. Hard to believe the mild techie who stopped in my office too often, ostensibly to shoot the breeze and hit on me, was a ruthless, cold-blooded man with a criminal streak as wide as the Hudson River.

The police had the names of the thugs paid to harass us but so far, they hadn't been caught. Barnes, Wahr and several politicians were embroiled in the white-collar crime of industrial espionage. They'd planned to auction the prototypes on the world market. I don't know what countries were bidding for the prototypes. That was classified information and it never leaked out. It was probably something the diplomats would use in future negotiations.

"The captain had me examine the tunnel from Pete's Tavern to where it connects with the old Meeting House," Dan said, interrupting my reverie. "I walked through that building. It's deteriorated, must have been empty a long time."

"It was built in the late eighteen-fifties," I said as I emptied the plate of soba noodles into the shabu-shabu pot's bubbling water. "The Quakers used it for about a century but then transferred activities to the Meeting House at Stuyvesant Square. Neighborhood activists finally got it designated a New York Landmark. They wanted it to be a performing arts center but that didn't happen. Then the building went to the United Federation of Teachers, but they ended up not using it."

"People pass by and don't even see it," Dan said. "Perfect for a crook's hideaway."

I made a decision.

"Dan, time for me to 'fess up. I went to Brooklyn to visit Sylvia Wahr."

"I know. She told us, we checked in with her regularly. You might make a decent sleuth yet."

"Let's shelve that discussion for later," I told Dan. "Time for shabu-shabu," and I placed the plate of beef slices on the table between us. We sat down to eat.

"What do I do?" Dan asked, looking at the steaming pot.

"Put whatever veggies you want in the water, then the beef. Fish out what you want when you're ready to eat."

"You first," Dan said. "Hey, how do you know which is yours?"

"The age-old query, what's mine?" I said as I took slices of crimini mushrooms, red pepper, onion and cabbage and dropped them in the water then picked up a slice of the paper-thin beef. I'd have to congratulate Pete, the beef was exactly right. I waited a few seconds and pulled out the beef.

"That's cooked the way I like it," I said and fished out noodles and veggies.

Dan didn't waste any time. Adept with chopsticks, he had his veggies in quickly and a slice of beef in and out of the bubbling water as rapidly I had.

"Mmm," he said through a mouthful. "Really good. So this is the Japanese equivalent of fondue. What's the name again?"

"Shabu-shabu because it sounds like the noise made by a washing machine. It's *oishii,* delicious."

"*Oishii,*" Dan said. "Is this what the Japanese have on special holidays like New Year's?"

"Holidays like New Year's are celebrated with days of feasts. My family didn't bring in the new year exactly the way it's done in Japan but one day I'll tell you all about the marvelous meals."

"Promise?"

"Promise."

We ate in silence, content to save conversation for later. Eventually we reached the stage where our chopsticks found nothing when we fished around in the water, which was now a delicious broth. I spooned some into my bowl and Dan filled his bowl.

"That was wonderful," he said, when he was done. "Me, myself and I, we all think you're wonderful, too."

"I've got a CD with Billie Holiday singing that song," I said.

"Know all the words?" Dan asked.

"I know you just combined the first and third lines of the song," I said.

And I didn't add that the second line of the song was, "Are all in love with you."

What was Dan going to say? His cell phone rang. Talk about a rotten time to be interrupted. Dan must have felt the same way. He rolled his eyes.

"If I could ignore that I would." He took the call, listened for a moment then said quietly, "I'm five minutes away. Be right there." Standing, he made a wry face. "I'll call you when I can but it may not be until the morning."

I walked him to the door and we hugged. His goodbye kiss was light.

"More to come," he said softly. "I hate to go."

"We'll catch up later."

He hurried down the stairs, turning once to wave.

That night I lay in bed and though about what I'd learned. It was never made public, not at the trial or later, but the value of Dr. Anders' work to terrorists would have been immense. The ways to use the prototypes beyond the therapy they'd been designed for were staggering. The software of one, let's call it Unit A, could gather a lot of valuable information from a covert scanning of an individual's vision. If mind control was the ultimate goal, surveillance begun with Unit A would set the groundwork brilliantly. It was a perfect tool to analyze potential behavior and know how to manipulate someone.

The grapevine whispered that the Aum Shinrikyo cult led the bidders for Unit A. They'd been responsible for the attack on the Tokyo subway in 1995 that flooded the place with lethal sarin gas. The cult was rumored to have a billion dollar kitty and a dangerously large number of members who were scientists. It was believed that one of their main projects was developing ways to make the brain more susceptible to suggestions through microwave technology or high magnetic fields.

Unit A could also detect drug use with distance surveillance. The possibilities were staggering. Barnes saw the prototypes as future unconventional Weapons of Mass Destruction. What a perversion of equipment designed for benign use. How to guard against fanatics, whether homegrown Timothy McVeighs or someone from another country?

The trial ended. Allan Barnes and Matt Wahr were sentenced and went to prison.

Lanny and Lars left on a short trip to Sweden, the first such venture for Lanny since she was released from the hospital. Lars planned the travel carefully. He knew that sleep deprivation and extended travel schedules could bring on fatigue and emotional swings in TBI victims, even those considered fully recovered. The few e-mails they sent me were filled with good news. Their relationship was deepening and holding. Survivors of traumatic brain injury *are* different, for their personalities are affected and altered. Often divorce is added to the trauma. A widow, Lanny had escaped divorce and her new friendship with Lars hadn't been affected. Altered perhaps, but it was resilient and would grow stronger.

My dad always said you learn from experience. Turned out, that's what Mark Sanders, the suave Chief of Detectives at the Thirteenth Precinct believed. He called with the strangest invitation I'd ever had. I was taken aback. To tell the truth, I was horrified.

"Dr. Kamimura," he began, "We hope you'll consider joining the 13th as a civilian consultant."

My gut reaction, confined to my thoughts, was "No." Followed by, "No way."

"I'm not a detective," I objected immediately.

"Civilian consultants never are."

"Why…?"

"Why are we asking you?" Sanders didn't wait for me to speak but briskly listed what he obviously thought were important reasons for the invitation.

"Your optometric training means you have a certain expertise in understanding behavior. In fact, your studies of psychology and pharmacology are excellent preparation for police work. You're licensed by the state to prescribe pharmaceuticals for the eyes and this means you know the effects of many drugs—including narcotics. All of this gives you valuable insight, no pun intended." Sanders chuckled at his own wit.

I couldn't argue with the captain. I'm a behavioral optometrist, one of the specialties in optometry. Everything he said about my training was accurate but I still was against the idea. Sanders wasn't done.

"Your quick thinking and appropriate action—even when threatened by someone you knew was a murderer—resolved an important case, one that could have had serious ramifications. That's significant in these days of heightened security. Last but not least, you worked well with my two top detectives, Dan Riley and Zoran Zeissing."

"But I didn't do any real detecting," I protested, thinking of the whirlwind of murder and mayhem that engulfed me from Day One. I winced as I recalled the few efforts I'd made to find connections between the almost nonstop sequence of bizarre happenings. I'd kept putting off any attempt at serious sleuthing, partly because of the pressure of work, partly because I'd been thwarted over something like finding someone's address when they don't have a land line and weren't in the telephone directory.

"Detective Zeissing might not agree that you didn't do any detecting," Sanders said. "He recommended you be hired as a civilian consultant because of the way you reasoned your way out of trouble and also for the initiative you showed in visiting Mrs. Wahr."

Now I really was surprised. Hmm, Zoran Zeissing was a brainiac. If he thought I had some ability, I might mull over the invitation.

"I don't know," I said cautiously. "I need time to think about it."

That got me off the hook for the time being. Every now and then I revisited the question. Was it my civic duty to help? I knew Gus Forkiotis would tell me it was. He'd worked with the Connecticut Police Academy for decades, and other practitioners had followed his lead, sharing their time and expertise. But what could I do to help New York's police if I did become a civilian consultant? Did I really want to get close to murder and mayhem again? If I said *Yes* to being a civilian consultant, perhaps I'd work with Detective Dan. Was that a good thing? How much fun would togetherness be if you were chasing perverts?

For the immediate time being, I focused on what I knew. I'd learned I cared enough about Dan to believe what he said about the situation between him and his ex being over. Besides, playing it safe is dangerous. We'd navigated our first major roadblock. Others would undoubtedly come but I had faith that in the future we could negotiate like adults. I trusted Dan. Not bad for someone divorced from a charming liar of an alcoholic gambler.

News about the way I'd thwarted Barnes spread through optometric circles like wild fire. Bob Bertolli called to compliment me and I learned that good-natured man was way more bloodthirsty than me.

"Quick thinking, the way you stopped the bad guy," Bob congratulated me. "Mind you, I'd never have tried to dislodge his contacts. I'd have delivered a thumb strike. That damages the tender area surrounded by the mandible. I'd have liked to see his eyes glaze over. Why stop there? I'd have wanted the pain to send him unconscious. That's actually possible."

"Wow," I cringed at the gruesome image. "You're kidding, right?"

"Hey, it's lifesaving technique for quarrelsome swimmers," Bob said. "My second choice would be to hook my pinky through the lacrimal bone in one orbit. Okay, that's really bad, I wouldn't go that far. Seriously, have you thought about taking karate classes?"

Good advice. I might even follow it. For sure I'll think about it. I'll add it to the list, second to the question of becoming a civilian consultant to New York's 13th Precinct. In the interval between thought, decision and action, it's onward and upward. Just like old times. The times when danger was indulging in too many pizzas. Hadn't been old times for so long.

Postscript - Elements of Truth

Behavioral Optometry, a specialty in the field of optometry, is available in more than forty countries. It has helped countless individuals whose eyesight was excellent but whose vision was not. Among them, Luci Baines Johnson, the daughter of President Johnson, and a roll call of professional and amateur sports teams that includes the New York Yankees, Chicago Black Hawks, San Francisco 49ers and U.S. Olympic medalists.

Eye Sleuth has real behavioral optometrists as well as fictional practitioners. The real ones include Drs. Elliott Forrest, Gus Forkiotis (a nationally recognized expert witness who lectured on vision at the Connecticut State Police Academy for decades), Bob Bertolli (also a lecturer at the Connecticut State Police Academy for decades), Beth Ballinger, Beth Bazin, Sam Berne, Steve Gallop, Paul Harris, Bob Sanet, Simon Grbevski (Australia) and Owen Leigh (England). The Executive Director of the OEP Foundation (www.oepf.org), Bob Williams, is very real and ever tireless in behalf of behavioral optometry. The College of Optometry at SUNY is one of the twenty colleges in the U.S. that offers training in this specialty.

Happily, the magnificent stained glass dome at the National Arts Club is unscathed. The former Friends Meeting House on Gramercy Park South, empty for many years, was indeed part of the Underground Railroad. The building is now the Brotherhood Synagogue.

The number of victims of traumatic brain injury (TBI) caused by auto, sports and industrial accidents grows with tragic speed, two million annually in the U.S. alone. Some survivors are able, with the right support, to return to active lives. Their families, health care professionals and caregivers help in many different ways. The Brain Injury Association of America's website provides good information: (http://www.biausa.org/).

NORA, the Neuro-Optometric Rehabilitation Association, is an international multidisciplinary organization established in 1989 to provide and advocate for vision rehabilitation and the habilitation of neurologically challenged individuals (www.nora.cc/).

Recipes

Lanny's Swedish Meatballs

1 lb ground beef
1/2 cup diced onion
3/4 cup bread crumbs (spelt or whole wheat work as well as white bread)
1/2 cup milk (soy or rice or almond liquid can be used)
1 egg
1 TBS parsley, if dried; if fresh, chop fine & use lavishly
1 TBS soy sauce or spicy sauce of choice
1/2 tsp salt
1/2 tsp pepper
1 lb of mushrooms, chopped & sautéed lightly in butter
1/4 cup olive oil
1/4 cup flour (whole wheat or spelt works)
1 tsp paprika
2 cups boiling water
3/4 cup sour cream

Preheat oven to 350°F (175°C).
Lightly grease a 9x13-inch baking dish.
Combine ground beef, chopped onion, milk, egg and bread crumbs.
Season with parsley, soy or spicy sauce, 1/2 tsp salt, 1/2 tsp pepper.
Mix well.
Shape into small balls and place on baking dish.
Bake for 30 minutes, turning meatballs so they brown evenly.
To make sauce: In a saucepan, combine oil, flour, paprika, 1 tsp salt, 1 tsp pepper. Add sautéed mushrooms and cook over medium heat until bubbling, then gradually blend in hot water and sour cream until smooth. When meatballs have cooked 30 minutes, pour sauce over the top, and return to the oven for 20 minutes. Stir a few times.
Green beans or a salad go well with this. You can also have noodles.
Yoko likes Tinkyada brown rice noodles, which are wheat & gluten-free.
Lanny and Lars like egg noodles.

Yoko's Beef Shabu-Shabu

3-inch dried kombu (kelp)
1 lb Chinese cabbage, chopped
1/4 lb scallions, sliced thin
1 block tofu, cut into bite-size pieces
1 enoki mushroom, cut in half
1/4 lb carrot, cut into thin round slices
1 lb fresh spinach (wash well by soaking in a bowl of water)
1 lb sirloin beef, sliced very thin.

Fill a deep electric pan or a medium skillet two-thirds full with water. Soak kombu in the water, preferably for 30 minutes. Arrange the ingredients on a large plate. Set the electric pan, ingredients and serving bowls with dipping sauce at the table. Heat the water and remove the kombu just before the water comes to a boil. Put a slice of beef in the boiling soup and swish it gently back and forth in the boiling soup until the meat changes color to desired degree of doneness. Dip meat in a sauce of your choice (see suggestion below) and enjoy. Add the vegetables piece by piece to the boiling water, which is gradually becoming soup, and simmer them for a few minutes until they are done the way you want them. Enjoy the veggies dipped in the sauce as well.

Yoko buys a bottle of sesame dipping sauce but you can use any sauce you like or make your own. Here's one traditional recipe:

1/3 cup white sesame seeds
3 TBSP mirin, a sweet, yellowish condiment (12% alcohol)
1-1/2 TBSP sugar
2 TBSP rice vinegar
3-1/2 TBSP soy sauce
1/2 tsp grated garlic
1/2 - 2/3 cup dashi soup (dashi is tuna soup stock, but you could use any stock you like)

To make sauce - Grind sesame seeds well. Add mirin gradually over the sesame seeds and mix. Add sugar, rice vinegar and soy sauce to the sauce. Add grated garlic and mix well. Pour in dashi stock gradually, stirring well.

About the Author

Hazel Dawkins, an editor-writer who started out in London's newspaper world, has worked in Paris and New York and now is based in Greenfield, Massachusetts.

Her factual books on behavioral optometry, a specialty in optometry that is available in forty countries, are published by (and available from) the OEP Foundation in California, the professional organization for optometrists (http://www.oepf.org/).

Eye Sleuth is a cozy of a mystery that introduces Dr Yoko Kamimura, a behavioral optometrist in New York. In it, Yoko is the unwilling center of mayhem and murder. The second Yoko mystery, *Eye Wit*, is a grittier read (think Miss Marple on steroids) created in amiable collaboration with Dennis Berry of Oregon.

All of her books are available at: http://www.murderprose.com.

Made in the USA
Charleston, SC
05 January 2012